THE
DEATH
BOX

J.A. Kerley spent years as an advertising agency writer and producer before his wife demanded he quit work and write a novel, which he thought a fine idea. The result was *The Hundredth Man*, the first in the Carson Ryder series. An avid angler, canoeist and hiker, Kerley has traveled extensively throughout the South, especially coastal regions such as Mobile, Alabama, the setting for many of his novels, and the Florida Keys. He has a cabin in the Kentucky mountains, which appeared as a setting in *Buried Alive*. He lives in Newport, Kentucky, where he enjoys sitting on the levee and watching the barges rumble up and down the Ohio River.

Also by J.A. Kerley

J.A. Kerley

THE DEATH BOX

HARPER

Harper
An imprint of HarperCollins*Publishers*
77–85 Fulham Palace Road, London W6 8JB

www.harpercollins.co.uk

A paperback original

1

First published in Great Britain by *Harper*,
an imprint of HarperCollins*Publishers* 2013

Copyright © Jack Kerley 2013

Jack Kerley asserts the moral right to
be identified as the author of this work

A catalogue record for this book
is available from the British Library

ISBN 978-0-00-749365-4

Set in Sabon LT Std by Palimpsest Book Production Ltd, Falkirk, Stirlingshire

Printed in Great Britain by
Clays Limited, St Ives plc

To James Lewinski,
Who showed me Prufrock

Thanks to the fine crew at the Aaron M. Priest Literary Agency, and an equally splendid group at HarperCollins, UK, most notably Sarah Hodgson and Anne O'Brien. An ex-adman, I also recognize the too-often-unsung heroes in the Marketing department. Great job, all.

1

The stench of rotting flesh filled the box like black fog. Death surrounded Amili Zelaya, the floor a patchwork of clothing bearing the decomposing bodies of seventeen human beings. Amili was alive, barely, staring into the shadowed dark of a shipping container the size of a semi-trailer. Besides the reek of death, there was bone-deep heat and graveyard silence save for waves breaking against a hull far below.

You're lucky, the smiling man in Honduras had said before closing the door, *ten days and you'll be in Los Estados Unitos, the United States, think of that.* Amili had thought of it, grinning at Lucia Belen in the last flash of sunlight before the box slammed shut. They'd crouched in the dark thinking their luck was boundless: They were going to America.

"Lucia," Amili rasped. "Please don't leave me now."

Lucia's hand lay motionless in Amili's fingers. Then, for the span of a second, the fingers twitched. "Fight for life, Lucia," Amili whispered, her parched tongue so swollen it barely moved. Lucia was from Amili's village. They'd grown up together – born in the same week eighteen years ago – ragged but happy. Only when fragments of the outside world intruded did they realize the desperate poverty strangling everyone in the village.

"Fight for life," Amili repeated, drifting into unconsciousness. Sometime later Amili's mind registered the deep notes of ship horns. The roar and rattle of machinery. Something had changed.

"The ship has stopped, Lucia," Amili rasped, holes from popped rivets allowing light to outline the inside of the module, one of thousands on the deck of the container ship bound for Miami, Florida. The illegal human cargo had been repeatedly warned to stay quiet through the journey.

If you reveal yourselves you will be thrown in a gringo prison, raped, beaten . . . men, women, children, it makes no difference. Never make a sound, understand?

Eventually they'd feel the ship stop and the box would be offloaded and driven to a hidden location where they'd receive papers, work assignments, places to live. They had only to perform six months of house-keeping, yard work or light factory labor to relieve the debt of their travel. After that, they owned their lives. A dream beyond belief.

"It must be Miami, Lucia," Amili said. "Stay with me."

But their drinking water had leaked away early in the voyage, a split opening in the side of the huge plastic drum, water washing across the floor of the container, pouring out through the seams. No one worried much about the loss, fearing only that escaping liquid would attract attention and they'd be put in chains to await prison. The ship had been traveling through fierce storms, rainwater dripping into the module from above like a dozen mountain springs. Water was everywhere.

This had been many days back. Before the ship had lumbered into searing summer heat. The rusty water in the bottom of the module was swiftly consumed. For days they ached for water, the inside of the container like an oven. Teresa Maldone prayed until her voice burned away. Pablo Entero drank from the urine pail. Maria Poblana banged on the walls of the box until wrestled to the floor.

She was the first to die.

Amili Zelaya had initially claimed a sitting area by a small hole in the container, hoping to peek out and watch for America. An older and larger woman named Postan Rendoza had bullied Amili away, cursing and slapping her to a far corner by the toilet bucket.

But the module was slightly lower in Amili's square meter of squatting room. Rainwater had pooled in the depressed corner, dampening the underside of Amili's ragged yellow dress.

When the heat came, Amili's secret oasis held water even as others tongued the metal floor for the remaining

3

rain. When no one was looking Amili slipped the hem of her dress to her mouth and squeezed life over her tongue, brown, rusty water sullied by sloshings from the toilet bucket, but enough to keep her insides from shriveling.

Postan Rendoza's bullying had spared Amili's life. And the life of Lucia, with whom Amili had shared her hidden water.

Rendoza had been the eighth to die.

Three days ago, the hidden cache had disappeared. By then, four were left alive, and by yesterday it was only Amili and Lucia. Amili felt guilt that she had watched the others perish from lack of water. But she had made her decision early, when she saw past tomorrow and tomorrow that water would be a life-and-death problem. Had she shared there would be no one alive in the steaming container: there was barely enough for one, much less two.

It was a hard decision and terrible to keep through screams and moans and prayers, but decisions were Amili's job: Every morning before leaving for the coffee plantation Amili's mother would gather five wide-eyed and barefoot children into the main room of their mud-brick home, point at Amili and say, "Amili is the oldest and the one who makes the good decisions."

A good decision, Amili knew, was for tomorrow, not today. When the foreign dentistas came, it was Amili who cajoled her terrified siblings into getting their teeth fixed and learning how to care for them, so their mouths did not become empty holes. When the drunken, lizard-eyed Federale gave thirteen-year-old Pablo money to walk into the woods, Amili had followed to see the Federale showing Pablo his man thing. Though the man had official power it had been Amili's decision to throw a big stone at him, the blood pouring from his face as he chased Amili down and beat her until she could not stand.

But he'd been revealed in the village and could never return.

Good decisions, Amili learned, came from the head and not the heart. The heart dealt with the moment. A decision had to be made for tomorrow and the tomorrow after that, all the way to the horizon. It could seem harsh, but decisions made from a soft heart often went wrong. One always had to look at what decisions did for the tomorrows.

Her hardest decision had come one month ago, when Miguel Tolandoro drove into the village in a truck as bright as silver, scattering dust and chickens. His belly was big and heavy and when he held it in his hands and shook it, he told of how much food there was in America. "*Everywhere you look*," he told the astonished faces, "*there is food*." Tolandoro's smiling mouth told shining tales about how one brave person could lift a family from the dirt. He had spoken directly to Amili, holding her hands and looking into her eyes.

"*You have been learning English, Amili Zelaya. You speak it well. Why?*"

"*I suppose I am good in school, Señor Tolandoro.*"

5

"I've also heard of your prowess with the mathematics and studies in accounting. Perhaps you yearn for another future, no?"

"I have thought that . . . maybe in a few years. When my family can—"

"Do it today, Amili. Start the flow of munificence to your family. Or do they not need money?"

Amili was frightened of the US, of its distance and strange customs. But her head saw the tomorrows and tomorrows and knew the only escape from barren lives came with money. Amili swallowed hard and told the smiling man she would make the trip.

"I work six months to pay off the travel?"

"You'll still have much to send home, sweet Amili."

"What if I am unhappy there?"

"Say the word and you'll come back to your village."

"How many times does that happen?"

"I've never seen anyone return."

Amili startled to a tremendous banging. After a distant scream of machines and the rattle of cables the container began to lift. The metal box seemed to sway in the wind and then drop. Another fierce slam from below as the module jolted violently to a standstill. Amili realized the container had been moved to a truck.

"Hang on, Lucia. Soon we'll be safe and we can—" Amili held her tongue as she heard dockworkers speaking English outside.

"Is this the one, Joleo?"

"*Lock it down fast. We've got two minutes before Customs comes by this section.*"

Amili felt motion and heard the grinding of gears. She drifted into unconsciousness again, awakened by a shiver in the container. The movement had stopped.

"Lucia?"

Amili patted for her friend's hand, squeezed it. The squeeze returned, almost imperceptible. "Hang on, Lucia. Soon we'll have the *agua*. And our freedom."

Amili heard gringo voices from outside.

"*I hate this part, opening the shit-stinking containers. They ought to make the monkeys not eat for a couple days before they get packed up.*"

"*Come on, Ivy. How about you work instead of complaining?*"

"*I smell it from fifty feet away. Get ready to herd them to the Quonset hut.*"

Light poured into the box, so bright it stole Amili's vision. She squeezed her eyes shut.

"*Okay, monkeys, welcome to the fuckin' U S of – Jesus . . . The smell . . . I think I'm gonna puke. Come here, Joleo . . . something's bad wrong.*"

"*I smelled that in Iraq. It's death. Orzibel's on his way. He'll know what to do.*"

Amili tried to move her head from the floor but it weighed a thousand kilos. She put her effort into moving her hand, lifting . . .

"*I saw one move. Back in the corner. Go get it.*"

"It stinks to hell in there, Joleo. And I ain't gonna walk over all those—"

"Pull your shirt over your nose. Get it, dammit."

Amili felt hands pull her to her feet and tried to turn back to Lucia. "Wait," she mumbled. "*Mi amiga Lucia está vivo.*"

"What's she saying?"

"Who cares? Haul her out before Orzibel gets here."

"Orzibel's crazy. He'll gut us."

"Christ, Ivy, it ain't our fault. We just grab 'em off the dock."

Amili felt herself thrown atop a shoulder. She grabbed at the body below, trying to make the man see that Lucia was still breathing. The effort was too much and the corners of the box began to spin like a top and Amili collapsed toward an enveloping darkness. Just before her senses spun away, ten final words registered in Amili's fading mind.

"Oh shit, Joleo, my feet just sunk into a body."

2

One year later

It seemed like my world had flipped over. Standing on the deck of my previous home on Alabama's Dauphin Island, the dawn sun rose from the left. My new digs on Florida's Upper Matecumbe Key faced north, the sun rising from the opposite direction. It would take some getting used to.

On Dauphin Island the morning sun lit a rippled green sea broken only by faint outlines of gas rigs on the horizon. Here I looked out on a small half-moon cove ringed with white sand, the turquoise water punctuated by sandy hummocks and small, flat islands coated with greenery. Like most water surrounding the Keys, it was shallow. I could walk out a hundred yards before it reached my belly.

Which seemed a pleasant way to greet the morning. I set my coffee cup on the deck rail and took the steps to the ground, walking two dozen feet of slatted boardwalk to the shoreline. There were no other houses near and if there had been I wouldn't have seen them, the land around my rented home a subtropical explosion of wide-frond palms strung with vines, gnarly trees dense with leaves and all interspersed with towering stands of bamboo. It resembled a miniature Eden, complete with lime trees, lemons, mangoes and Barbados cherries. After a rain, the moist and scented air seemed like an intoxicant.

At water's edge I kicked off my moccasins and stepped into the Gulf, bathtub-warm in August. The sand felt delicious against my soles, conforming to my steps, familiar and assuring. I seemed to smell cigar smoke and scanned the dawn-brightening shoreline, spying only two cakewalking herons pecking for baitfish. Neither was puffing a cigar. I put my hands in the pockets of my cargo shorts and splashed through knee-deep water toward the reeded point marking one horn of the crescent cove, revisiting the conversation that had led me so swiftly and surprisingly to Florida.

"Hello, Carson? This is Roy McDermott. Last time we talked, I mentioned changes in the Florida Center for Law Enforcement. We're creating a team of consulting specialists."

"Good for you, Roy."

"Why I'm calling, Carson . . . We want you on the team."

10

"I don't have a specialty, Roy. I'm just a standard-issue detective."

"Really? How about that PSIT team you started . . . specializing in psychopaths and sociopaths and general melt-downs? And all them freaky goddamn cases you guys solved?"

I smelled cigar smoke again. Looking to my right I saw a black man walking toward the shore with a stogie in his lips, five-seven or thereabouts, slender, his face ovoid, with a strong, straight nose beneath heavy eyebrows. His mouth was wide, garnished with a pencil mustache, and suggested how Tupac Shakur would have looked in his mid-sixties, though I doubt Shakur would have gone for a pink guayabera shirt and lime-green shorts. A crisp straw fedora with bright red band floated on the man's head and languid eyes studied me as if I were a novel form of waterfowl.

"You the one just moved in that yonder house?" he asked.

"Guilty as charged."

"The realtor tell you two people got killed in there? That the place was owned by a drug dealer, a Nicaraguan with metal teeth?"

The law allowed the confiscation of property employed in criminal enterprises and the place had indeed been the site of two killings, rivals to the drug dealer who had owned the house. The dealer went to prison and the house almost went on the market, but the FCLE was advised to hold it in anticipation of rising home values.

And it wouldn't hurt for time to lapse between the killings and the showings. When I told Roy I was thinking of looking at places in or near the Keys, he'd said, *"Gotta great place you can crib while you're looking, bud. Just don't get too used to it."*

I nodded at my impromptu morning companion. "I heard about the murders. Didn't hear about the teeth."

"Like goddamn fangs. Heard one had a diamond set in it, but I never got close enough to check. You buyin' the place from the guv'mint? Nasty history, but the house ain't bad – kinda small for the neighborhood – but a good, big chunk of land. As wild as it was when Poncy Deleon showed up."

The house itself – on ten-foot pilings to protect against storm surges – wasn't overwhelming: single story, three bedrooms. But it had broad skylights and a vaulted ceiling in the main room, so it was bright and open. Outside features included a hot tub and decks on two sides. Mr Cigar was right about the land: four untamed acres, like the house was in a tropical park. Plus the property abutted a wildlife sanctuary, a couple hundred swampy acres of flora gone amok. I figured the dealer had picked the place for the wild buffer zone, privacy for all sorts of bad things.

"Afraid I'm just renting," I said. "It's too pricy for me."

A raised eyebrow. "Kinda work you do, mister?"

"In two weeks I start work for the Florida Center for Law Enforcement. I came from Mobile, where I was a cop, a homicide detective."

A moment of reflection behind the cigar. "So I guess we both made a living from dead bodies."

"Pardon me?"

"I used to own funeral parlors in Atlanta, started with one, ended up with six. Retired here last year when my wife passed away."

"I'm sorry."

"Why? I like it here."

"I mean about your wife. Was she ill?"

"Healthy as a damn horse. But she was twenny-five years younger'n me an' only died cuz one a her boyfriends shot her."

I didn't know what to say to that so I walked his way, splashing up to shore with my hand outstretched. "Guess we'll be neighbors, then. At least for a while. Name's Carson Ryder."

His palm was mortician-soft but his grip was hard. "Dubois B. Burnside." He pronounced it *Du-boys*.

"The B for Burghardt?" I asked, a shot in the dark. William Edward Burghardt DuBois was an American civil-rights leader, author, educator and about a dozen other things who lived from the late 1800s to the sixties. The intellectual influence of W.E.B. DuBois was, and still is, felt widely.

"That would be right," he said, giving me a closer look.

"You live close by, Mr Burnside?"

He nodded at a line of black mangroves. "Other side of the trees. Daybreak used to find me heading to the

13

mortuary to get working. Now I head out here and watch the birds." He took another draw, letting blue smoke dribble from pursed lips. "I like this better."

"Dubois!" bayed a woman's voice from a distance, sending a half-dozen crows fleeing from a nearby tree. "Du-bois! Where you at? Duuuuuuuu-bois!"

My neighbor winced, pulled low the brim of the hat and started to turn away. "Stop by for a drink some night, Mister Ryder. We can talk about dead bodies. I may even have one you can look at."

I splashed away, the sun sending shadows of my temporary home out into the water to guide me ashore. I slipped wet feet into my moccasins and jogged the boardwalk to the porch, moving faster when I heard my cell phone chirping from the deck. The call was from Roy McDermott, my new boss.

"Looks like we got a regular Sunshine State welcome for you, Carson. I'm looking at the weirdest damn thing I ever saw. Scariest, too. I know you don't officially get on the clock for a couple weeks, but I'm pretty sure this can't wait."

"What is it you're looking at, Roy?"

"No one truly knows. Procurement gave you a decent car, I expect?"

"I signed some papers. Haven't seen a car."

A sigh. "I'm gonna kick some bureaucratic ass. Whatever you're driving, how about you pretend it's the Batmobile and kick on the afterburners. Come help me make sense of what I'm seeing."

14

I hurled myself through the shower and pulled on a pair of khakis and a blue oxford shirt, stepping into desert boots and tossing on a blue blazer. My accessorizing was minimal, the Smith & Wesson Airweight in a clip-on holster. On my way out I grabbed a couple Clif Bars for sustenance and headed down the stairs.

The elevated house was its own carport, with room for a dozen vehicles underneath, and my ancient gray pickup looked lonely on all that concrete. I'd bought it years ago, second-hand, the previous owner a science-fiction fan who'd had Darth Vader air-brushed on the hood. After a bit too much bourbon one night, I'd taken a roller and a can of marine-grade paint and painted everything a sedate, if patchy, gray.

The grounds hadn't been groomed since the dope dealer had ownership, overgrown brush and palmetto fronds grazing the doors as I snaked down the long crushed-shell drive to the electronic gate, eight feet of white steel grate between brick stanchions shaded by towering palms. I panicked until remembering I could open the gate with my phone and dialed the number provided by the realtor.

Phoning a gate, I thought. *Welcome to the Third Millennium.*

I aimed toward the mainland, an hour away, cruised through Key Largo and across the big bridge. My destination was nearby, a bit shy of Homestead. Roy had said to turn right at a sign saying FUTURE SITE OF PLANTATION

POINT, A NEW ADVENTURE IN SHOPPING and head a
quarter mile down a gravel road.

"You can't miss the place," he'd added. "It's the only
circus tent in miles."

3

It wasn't a circus tent in the distance, but it was side-show size, bright white against scrubby land scarred by heavy equipment, three Cat 'dozers and a grader sitting idle beside a house-sized pile of uprooted trees. Plastic-ribboned stakes marked future roads and foundations as the early stages of a construction project.

A Florida Highway Patrol cruiser was slanted across the road, a slab-shouldered trooper leaning on the trunk with arms crossed and black aviators tracking my approach. He snapped from the car like elastic, a hand up in the universal symbol for Halt, and I rolled down my window with driver's license in hand. "I'm Carson Ryder, here at the request of Captain Roy McDermott."

The eyes measured the gap between a top dog in the

FCLE and a guy driving a battered pickup. He checked a clipboard and hid his surprise at finding my name.

"Cap'n McDermott's in the tent, Mr Ryder. Please park behind it."

It felt strange that my only identification was a driver's license. I'd had my MPD gold for a decade, flashed it hundreds of times. I'd twice handed it away when suspended, twice had it returned. I'd once been holding it in my left hand while my right hand shot a man dead; his gamble, his loss. It felt strange and foreign to not produce my Mobile shield.

You made the right decision, my head said. My heart still wasn't sure.

I angled five hundred feet down a slender dirt road scraped through the brush, stopping behind the tent, one of those rental jobs used for weddings and whatnot, maybe sixty feet long and forty wide. I was happy to see a portable AC unit pumping air inside. On the far side, beside a house-sized mound of freshly dug earth, were a half-dozen official-looking vehicles including a large black step van which I figured belonged to the Medical Examiner or Forensics department.

Beside the van three men and a woman were clustered in conversation. Cops. Don't ask how I knew, but I always did. A dozen feet away a younger guy was sitting atop a car hood looking bored. I wasn't sure about him.

The entrance was a plastic door with a handmade sign yelling ADMITTANCE BY CLEARED PERSONNEL ONLY!!! the ONLY underscored twice. Though I hadn't been

18

cleared – whatever that meant – I'd been called, so I pressed through the door.

It was cool inside and smelled of damp sand. Centering the space was a pit about twenty feet by twenty. Above the pit, at the far end of the tent at ground level, were several folding tables. A woman in a lab coat was labeling bags atop two of the tables. Another table held a small microscope and centrifuge. I'd seen this before, an on-site forensics processing center.

I returned my attention to the pit, which resembled the excavation for an in-ground swimming pool, wooden rails keeping the sandy soil from caving. Centering the hole was an eight-foot-tall column with two lab-jacketed workers ticking on its surface with hammers. I estimated the column's diameter at five feet and watched as a white-smocked lab worker dropped a chipped-off shard into an evidence bag. When the worker stepped away, a photographer jumped in. The scene reminded me of a movie where scientists examine a mysterious object from the heavens. Shortly thereafter, of course, the object begins to glow and hum and everyone gets zapped by death beams.

"You there!" a voice yelled. "You're not supposed to be in here."

I snapped from my alien fantasy to see a lab-jacketed woman striding toward me, her black hair tucked beneath a blue ball cap and her eyes a human version of death beams. "Where's your ID?" she demanded, pointing at a naked space on my chest where I assumed

19

an identification should reside. "You can't be here without an—"

"Yo, Morningstar!" a voice cut in. "Don't kill him, he's on our side."

I looked up and saw Roy McDermott step from the far side of the column. The woman's thumb jerked at me.

"Him? This?"

"He's the new guy I told you about."

The woman I now knew as Morningstar turned big brown death rays on Roy. "I'm in charge of scene, Roy. I want everyone to have a site ID."

Roy patted dust from his hands as he approached, a luminous grin on his huge round face and the ever-present cowlick rising from the crown of semi-tamed haybright hair. He called to mind an insane Jack O'Lantern.

"I'll have someone make him a temporary tag, Vivian. You folks bring any crayons?"

Morningstar's eyes narrowed. "Condescension fits you, Roy. It's juvenile."

Roy climbed the steps from the pit and affected apologetic sincerity. "I forgot his clearance, Vivian. I'm sorry. All we have time for now is introductions. Carson, this is Vivian Morningstar, our local pathologist and—"

"I'm the Chief Forensic Examiner for the Southern Region, Roy."

"Carson, this is the Examining Chief Region of the – shit, whatever. And this, Vivian, is Carson Ryder. We're still figuring out his title."

20

Morningstar and I brushed fingertips in an approximation of a handshake, though it was more like the gesture of two boxers. Roy took my arm and swung me toward the pit. We stepped down on hastily constructed stairs, the wood creaking beneath us.

"Now to get serious," Roy said. "Damndest thing I've seen in twenty years in the biz."

Three techs stepped aside as we walked to the object. Seemingly made of concrete, it resembled a carved column from a temple in ancient Egypt, its surface jagged and pitted with hollows, as though the sculptor had been called away before completion.

"More light," Roy said.

The techs had been working with focused illumination. One of them widened the lighting, bringing the entire object into hard-edged relief.

A woman began screaming.

I didn't hear the scream, I saw it. Pressing from the concrete was a woman's face, eyes wide and mouth open in an expression of ultimate horror. She was swimming toward me, face breaking the surface of the concrete, one gray and lithic hand above, the other below, as if frozen in the act of stroking. The scenic was so graphic and lifelike that I gasped and felt my knees loosen.

Roy stepped toward me and I held my hand up, *I'm fine*, it lied. I caught my breath and saw ripples of concrete-encrusted fabric, within its folds a rock-hard foot. I moved to the side and saw another gray face peering from the concrete, the eyes replaced with sand

and cement, bone peeking through shredded skin that appeared to have petrified on the cheeks. One temple was missing.

My hand rose unbidden to the shattered face.

"Don't think of touching it," Morningstar said.

My hand went to my pocket as I circled the frieze of despair: two more heads staring from the stone, surrounding them a jumble of broken body parts, hands, knees, shoulders. Broken bones stood out like studs.

My hands ached to touch the column, as if that might help me to understand whatever had happened. But I thrust them deeper into my pockets and finished my circle, ending up at the screaming woman, her dead face still alive in her terror.

"It was found yesterday," Roy explained. "A worker was grading land when his blade banged a chunk of concrete. The foreman saw a mandible sticking out and called us. We had the excavation started within two hours."

Most municipal departments would have needed a day to pull the pieces together, maybe longer. But that was the power of a state organization. The FCLE arrived, flashed badges, and went to work.

"What formed the column?" I asked.

Morningstar tapped the object. "The concrete was poured into an old rock-walled cistern. Stones initially surrounded the object, but the techs spent last night dislodging them."

"Any idea when it was put here?"

"Could be a few months, could be two years. I'll get closer as we analyze more samples."

"You're gonna find different times," called a basso voice from above. "Older bodies, newer ones. The bottom bodies may go back years, decades even."

I looked up at a guy on ground level, mid-forties or so, dark complexion, black suit, gray shirt. His sole concession to festivity was a colour-speckled tie that seemed from one of Jackson Pollock's brighter days. The man's gleaming black hair was swept back behind his ears. He wore dark sunglasses on a prize-winning proboscis, more like a beak. With the clothes, nose, and down-looking pose he called to mind a looming buzzard.

"What you been up to, Vincent?" Roy asked.

The guy brandished the briefcase. "Copying property records at the Dade County assessor's office. Someone had to know the cistern was here, right?"

Roy nodded approvingly. "Come down into the hole, Vince. Got someone you should meet."

I shook hands with Vincent Delmara, a senior investigator with the Miami-Dade County Police Department. Though the FCLE might swoop in and start bee-buzzing a crime scene, shutting out the locals invited turf wars which, in the long run, had no winners.

"You're thinking these bodies were built up over time, not just dumped all at once?" Roy asked Delmara.

"We got us a serial killer," Delmara exulted. "He's been using the hole as a dumping ground over years. We're gonna solve a shitload of disappearances."

I understood Delmara's enthusiasm. Miami-Dade, like any large metro area, had a backlog of missing persons. If this was a serial killer and the bodies were identified, a lot of cases could be cleared and families granted closure.

"I'm thinking he used an ax," Delmara said. "He dumps the corpse in the cistern and pours in concrete to cover. They were supposed to stay hidden for ever, except development got in the way."

"What do you think accounts for the brownish cast to the concrete?" I asked. "And the rusty streaks, like here?"

"Mud mixing with the cement. Dirt."

Roy produced an unlit cigar to placate his fingers. "The only problem I got is picturing a guy mixing a tub of 'crete every time he dumps a body. It gets riskier with repetition."

"Maybe he gets off on the risk," Delmara said. "Mixes his concrete as an appetizer, dumps the body for his entree, jacks off into the hole for dessert." Delmara circled his fingers and mimed the concept.

"For Christ's sake," Morningstar said.

"How many crime scenes you been at where jism's squirted all over the place, Doctor Morningstar?" Delmara grinned. "More than a few, I'll bet."

I closed my eyes and pictured the area as if it were a time-lapse documentary, day turning into night and back to day, clouds stampeding across blue sky, white clouds turning black, sun becoming rain becoming sun again.

"Maybe the concrete was poured in dry to save time

24

and risk," I suggested. "Rain would soak the cement powder, time would harden it."

"Genius," Roy said, clapping a big paw on my shoulder. "No fuss, no muss, no mixing. Plus cement contains lime, which helps decomposition." He looked at Delmara. "What you think, Vince?"

"Tasty."

"You think we got us a serial killer, Carson?" Roy asked.

I turned to the column to study a splintered ulna, a severed tibia, a caved-in section of rib cage. Many seemed the kind of injuries I'd noted in car crashes. Whereas Delmara was seeing an ax used on the bodies, I was picturing a sledgehammer. Or both, the violence was that horrific. Something felt a shade off, though I couldn't put my finger on it; having no better idea, I nodded.

"It's the way to go for now."

"Hell yes," Delmara said, punching the air. "We're gonna close some cases."

Morningstar stepped forward. "Excuse me, boys. But if you're done being brilliant, I'd like to get back to work."

Delmara made notes. Roy and I retreated up the steps as Morningstar motioned her team back into place. The chipping of chisels began anew.

We stopped at the entrance. Roy lowered his voice. "Look, Carson, I want you to start work early and be the lead on this case."

"No way," I said.

"I need you, Carson."

"Your people are gonna be drooling for this case, Roy. It's a biggie."

"How many bodies did John Wayne Gacy stack up under his house before he got nailed?" Roy said. "Twenty? Thirty? How about Juan Corona? We might have a grade-one psycho out there, Carson. Your specialty, right . . . the edge-walking freaks?"

"I've not even met your people, Roy. If I start by giving orders I'll start by stepping on toes. Bad first step."

"You were here ten minutes and figured out the concrete angle."

"A conjecture."

"It's the kind of thinking I need. And don't worry – I'll deal with any delicate tootsies." He slapped his hands – *conversation over* – and headed outside. I followed, thinking that if his people let a newbie waltz in as lead investigator on a case this big, they must be the most ego-free cops the world had ever produced.

4

The semi-truck rumbled down the sandy lane in the South Florida coastal backcountry, a battered red tractor pulling the kind of gray intermodal container loaded on ships, traversing oceans before being offloaded to a truck or train to continue its journey. Tens of thousands of the nondescript containers traveled the world daily and it had been calculated that at any given moment over three per cent of the world's GDP lay within the containers of Maersk, the world's largest intermodal shipper.

But those were official loads. This particular shipment was a ghost, its true contents never recorded in any official documents. With the complicity of bribed clerks and customs agents, this simple gray box had boarded a ship in Honduras, sailed to the Port of Miami and been offloaded to the red tractor, with only the kind of glancing notice that came from eyes averted at the precise moment the container ghosted past.

"Looks quiet to me, Joleo."

The passenger in the cab porched his hand over a scarred and sunburned brow, his dull green eyes scanning a stand of trees in the distance. Between the treeline and the truck was a corroded Quonset hut, a hundred feet of corrugated aluminum resembling a dirty gray tube half sunk in the sand. The passenger's name was Calvert Hatton, but he went by Ivy, tattooed strands of the poison variety of the weed entwining his arms from wrist to shoulder.

"Our part's almost over," the driver said, pulling to a halt. He was tall and ropey and his name was Joe Leo Hurst, but over the years it had condensed to Joleo. "Go move 'em to the hut, Ivy."

Ivy jumped from the cab and walked to the rear with bolt cutters in work-gloved hands as Joleo climbed atop the hood to scan the area.

"I still hate opening that damn door," Ivy grumbled. "After that shipment last year . . ."

"We've done a bunch more since then. You remember one shipment that went bad?"

"I get nightmares," Ivy whined.

Ivy wore a blue uniform shirt that strained over a grits-and-gravy belly and his thinning hair was greased back over his ears. He reached the bolt cutter's jaws to the shining lock on the container and snapped the shackle. He climbed the tailgate to undo the latch on the doors, jumping down as they creaked open.

"The goddamn stench," Ivy complained, pinching his nostrils as he peered into the module. "OK, monkeys, welcome to the Estados Unitas or whatever. Come on, get off your asses and move."

A rail-thin Hispanic man in tattered clothes lowered himself from the container on shaky legs. He was followed by twenty-two more human beings in various stages of disarray, mostly young, mostly women. They blinked in the hard sunlight, fear written deep in every face.

"They all OK?" Joleo asked, now beside the cab and smoking.

"All up and moving."

The Hispanics stood in a small circle at the rear of the truck, rubbing arms and legs, returning circulation to limbs that had moved little in a week. Ivy was lighting a cigarette when his head turned to the incoming road.

"Cars!" he yelled. "Orzibel's coming."

Joleo squinted in the direction of the vehicles and saw a black Escalade in the distance, behind it a brown panel van.

"Relax, Ivy. He's just gonna grab some of the load."

"That fucker scares me. He gets crazy with that knife."

"Right, you get nightmares."

Joleo was trying to joke, but his eyes were on the Escalade and his mouth wasn't smiling, watching the car and van drive round the final bend and bear down on them. The black-windowed Escalade stopped hard at the rear of the truck, the van on its bumper. The Hispanics, senses attuned to danger, backed away, the circle re-forming beside the truck.

The driver's side door opened on the Escalade and a man exited, as large as a professional wrestler and packed into a blue velvet running suit bulging with rock-muscled arms and thighs. He seemed without a neck, a round head jammed atop a velvet-upholstered barrel. The head was bald and glistened in the sun and its features were oddly small and compact, as if its maker's hand had grasped a normal face and gathered everything to the center. And perhaps the same maker had tapped the eyes with his fingers, drawing out all life and leaving small black dots as cold as the eyes of dice. The dead eyes studied Ivy and Joleo as if seeing them for the first time.

"Yo, Chaku," Joleo said. "S'up, man?"

If the driver heard, he didn't seem to notice. The package of muscle nodded at the passenger side of the Escalade and another man exited the vehicle, or rather flowed from within, like a cobra uncurling from a basket.

His toes touched the sand first, sliver-bright tips of hand-tooled cowboy boots made of alligator hide. He wore dark sunglasses and walked slowly. His black silk suit seemed tailored to every motion in the slender frame. His snow-white shirt was ruffled and strung with a bolo tie, a cloisonné yin-yang of black enamel flowing into white.

The man was in his early thirties with a long face centered by an aquiline nose and a mouth crafted for broad smiles. His hair was black, short on the sides and pomaded into prickly spikes at the crown, a casual, straight-from-the-shower look only a good stylist could imitate.

A brown hand with long and delicate fingers plucked the sunglasses from the face to display eyes so blue they seemed lit from behind. The eyes looked across the parched landscape admiringly, as if the man had conceived the plans for the intersection of earth and sky and was inspecting the results. After several moments, he walked to the Hispanics, a smile rising to his lips.

"*Hola*, friends," the man said, clapping the exquisite hands, the smile outshining the sun. "*Bienvenidos a los Estados Unidos. Bienvenido a gran riqueza.*"

Welcome to the United States. Welcome to your fortunes.

Eyes rose to the man. Heads craned on weary necks.

"I represent your benefactor," the man said in Spanish. "We are happy you made the journey. If you work hard you can make vast amounts of beautiful American dollars."

His words sparked a nodding of heads and the beginnings of smiles. This was why they had left their homes and villages. The man gestured to the Quonset hut. "Most of you will go to the building and wait. Soon you will continue to Tampa, Pensacola, Orlando, Jacksonville. Some will be returning with me to Miami. Wherever you go, money awaits. All you have to do is honor your contract, and . . ." the hands spread in munificence, "the divine cash will shower into your palms."

The smiles were full now, the heads a chorus of bobs. Someone yelled "*Viva el Jefé.*"

Long live the Chief.

The smiling man entered the group, basking in smiles and *Viva*s and hands patting his back as though a saint walked among them. He studied each face in turn, paying particular interest to the dark-haired women. One kept shooting glances through bashful, doe-like eyes. He took her small hand, holding it tight as she instinctively tried to pull it away.

"What is it, little beauty?" he said, patting the hand. "Why were you staring so?"

A blush crept to her neck. "I first thought . . . when you stepped from the beautiful car . . . we were in the Hollywood."

"What makes you say that, little one?"

The blush swept her face as her eyes dropped to the ground. "You are so handsome," she whispered. "Surely you are in the cinema."

"You are far too kind. What is your name?"

"Leala . . . Leala Rosales."

"I need four women and one man for Miami, Leala Rosales. Would you like me to show you the most beautiful city in the world, my city?"

"I . . . I . . . don't know if . . ."

"You have stepped into a new world, Leala. Now you must trust yourself to jump."

"I will . . . Yes, I will go with you, señor. Can my friend Yolanda come as well?" She pointed to a nearby girl.

32

"Perhaps the next time, Leala. There is only so much room in the car."

"It looks very big."

"Appearances can be deceiving. Hurry to the car, Leala. I will meet you there in a moment."

The girl ran to the Escalade. The man's white teeth flashed. "Did you want a fresh boy, Chaku?" he said in English. "Come look at the selection."

The first sign of life in the driver's eyes. He tapped the skinny shoulder of a male youth no older than fourteen, and pointed to the van. The boy understood nothing but that he was to move toward the vehicle, so he moved.

The handsome man walked among the Hispanics, directing three more women to the van, pointing the others toward the Quonset hut. The driver and passenger jumped from the van, two bandana-headed Hispanics with tattoos on arms and necks. They hurried the four selections into the rear of the vehicle. As the new occupants climbed inside, the driver opened a side door and retrieved two magnetic signs saying A-1 WINDOW TREATMENTS and applied them to the sides of the van.

The handsome man turned to the hulking driver. "Let me talk to these gentlemen in private, Chaku." The comment was followed by a small and cryptic flick of the blue eyes. The driver retreated to the Escalade as the man gestured Ivy and Joleo to the side of the trailer. In the distance the Hispanics walked toward the gray hut. They were smiling and laughing.

The handsome man's eyes flicked between the men. "Did it go smoothly?"

"Yes, sir," Joleo said. "Like always."

"Are you receiving your compensation correctly?" He turned his eyes to Ivy.

"Yes, sir," Ivy said, trying to keep his gaze from falling to his shoes. "A day after every delivery. Th-thank you, Mr Orzibel."

Orlando Orzibel flashed his supernova smile. "Good work deserves no less. And good work means quiet work, right?"

Both heads bobbed. Orzibel nodded in satisfaction and turned away. He stopped and turned back. The smile had disappeared. "So how is it I heard of lips speaking my name in a filthy little bar last month? A rathole called Three Aces?"

Ivy seemed to waver on his knees. His mouth fell open to show darkened teeth. "I . . . I . . . it was a mistake, Mr Orzibel. It'll never happen again. And all I said, was—"

An arm from nowhere wrapped around Ivy's neck, lifting him off the ground. The huge driver had somehow left the Escalade and crept across the crunchy sand and beneath the trailer without making a sound.

"And your lips not only used my name," Orzibel said, "they implied my business."

"A mistake . . ." Ivy gasped, pulling at the arm around his neck as his face reddened. "It'll never hap . . . gain. Please—"

34

Orzibel nodded and the hulk named Chaku opened his arms and Ivy fell to the ground. Orzibel lowered to a squat. A knife had appeared in his hand, a dark-bladed commando knife with few purposes but destruction.

"Please, Mr Orzibel . . ." Ivy begged, tears falling down his cheeks. "Remember how I helped you with the cement last year . . . made your problem go away? How I worked all night for you . . ."

The knife whispered through the air and Ivy's lower lip dropped in the dirt below his face. His eyes were disbelieving as his fingers touched the open teeth, coming away shining with blood.

Orzibel picked up the lip with the point of the knife and held it before Ivy's horrified eyes. "Eat it," he hissed. "Eat it or die."

"No, pleagggh . . ." Ivy wailed.

"Eat," Orzibel commanded. "Eat the lip that spoke my name."

"I ca-ca-cand," Ivy bubbled, blood spattering with his words.

"You have three seconds," Orzibel said. "One . . ."

Ivy's shaking hands plucked the flesh from the knife, tried to bring it to his mouth, dropped it in the sand. "I c-c-cand," he moaned, his words mushy through blood and the mucus pouring from his nose.

"Two."

Ivy retrieved his lip and brought it to his open teeth. He began to bite gingerly at the strip of meat, but a torrent of vomit exploded from his throat and washed the lip from his fingers.

"Three!" The knife whispered again and Ivy grabbed at his throat, his forearms glistening with the blood pouring from his slit neck. After scant seconds his eyes rolled back and he fell backward. Orzibel bent over the twitching body and wiped the knife on its shirt.

"You have the plastic in the trunk, Chaku?"

"Always."

"When he drains, wrap him tight and put him in the trunk. Tonight we'll drop him down the hole in the world. Be sure to purchase ample concrete."

5

Ernesto "Chaku" Morales took the shining Escalade on little-known dirt roads skirting the Everglades, driving beside mangrove-studded drainage canals as the sun burned toward zenith in a cloudless sky. The air reeked of heat and stagnation. Lizards darted across the path as listless vultures hunched in low branches.

Chaku thought about his new boy. The old one had grown vacant in the eyes; the drugs, Chaku knew, both blessing and curse. At first the boys liked flying to dizzying heights where the village lessons turned to vapor. But later they started to hide in the drugs, becoming sullen and useless.

A new boy would be fun, Chaku knew as he spun the wheel, turning right, then left, ignoring the sounds in the rear of the Escalade. There was much to teach them, although the learning always started hard. Like with the fresh girl in back, Leala Rosales. Once they'd stopped so Mr Orzibel could have Chaku thrust the girl's sobbing face beneath black water in a drainage canal. That always got a new arrival's attention and made lessons easier.

It was a simple lesson Mr Orzibel had started the girl with today, basically a lesson in English.

She was learning the meaning of the word *Blowjob*.

Roy said he'd meet me in Miami and climbed into his vehicle. I aimed in the same direction, taking Highway 1 and angling through South Miami and Coral Gables toward the heart of the city.

Miami was basically foreign to me, known on a pass-through basis when a vacation found me drifting over from Mobile, my pickup bed clattering with fishing gear. It seemed less a defined city than a metroplex sprawling from Coral Springs to Coral Gables and including Fort Lauderdale, Hollywood, Pompano Beach, Hialeah, and two dozen more separate communities squeezed between the fragile Everglades and pounding Atlantic. Drive a mile one way and find homes that could satisfy Coleridge's version of Kubla Khan, a mile the other and you seemed in the slums of Rio.

The main headquarters of the FCLE was in Tallahassee, in the panhandle. Though it didn't make logistical sense – Florida crime centered in large cities in the peninsula: Miami, Tampa/St Petersburg, Orlando, Jacksonville and so forth – Tallahassee was the state's capital and thus the political center. Like every government agency, FCLE had to keep its ears and voice close to where the funds were allocated.

But the bulk of the employees in Tallahassee worked on legal and clerical staffs to adjudicate crimes in the capital's collection of courts. The investigators were spread across the state. The main South Florida office was in Miami. The department leased office space in the towering Clark center, Miami-Dade's governmental seat, and I figured Roy was somehow responsible for getting FCLE into such a plum address in the heart of the city.

Roy's official title was Director of Special Investigations, but the title was misleading, as Roy had never carved a wide swath in the investigative world. He was a showman, a dazzler, a back-slapping reassurance salesman who could zigzag a conversation so fast you wondered where you'd left your head. I'd heard Roy McDermott could waltz into a budget-cutting meeting in Tallahassee, work the room for a few minutes (he knew every face and name, down to spouses, kids, and the family dog), give an impassioned speech too convoluted to follow, and leave with his portion of funds not only unscathed, but increased.

To pull this off required results, and the endless to-the-ground ear of Roy McDermott tracked careers the way pro horse-track gamblers shadowed thoroughbreds. He had a gift for finding savvy and intuitive cops stymied by red tape or dimwit supervisors and bringing them to the FCLE, filling his department with talented people who credited Roy with saving them from bit-player oblivion. To pay him back, they busted ass and solved crimes.

I found a parking lot and paid a usurious sum for a patch of steaming asphalt, the attendant staring at my pickup as I backed into a spot.

"That 'ting gonna start up again when you shut it off?"

I walked to the nearest intersection and felt totally discombobulated. The streets were a pastiche of signs in English and Spanish, the gleaming, multi-tiered skyline foreign to my eyes, the honking lines of traffic larger than any in Mobile. A half-dozen pedestrians passed me by, none speaking English. Palms were everywhere, stubby palms, thick-trunked palms of medium height, slender and graceful palms reaching high into blue.

What have you done? something in my head asked. *Why are you here?*

The breeze shifted and I smelled salt air and realized the ocean was near. Water had always been my truest address and the voice in my head stilled as I took a deep breath, clutched my briefcase, and strode to the looming building two blocks and one change of life distant.

"Grab a chair, bud," Roy said, waving me into a spacious corner office on the twenty-third floor of a building rabbit-warrened with government offices.

I sat in a wing-back model and studied the back wall. Instead of the usual grip'n'grin photos with political halfwits, Roy's wall held about twenty framed photos of him hauling in tarpon and marlin and a shark that looked as long as my truck. I smiled at one shot, Roy and me a few years back on Sanibel, each cradling a yard-long snook and grinning like schoolboys.

"First, here's your official job confirmation," Roy said, handing me a page of paper. "Before you leave we'll get your photo taken for a temp ID. It may not glow in the dark, but even Viv Morningstar will let you live if you show it."

"When comes permanent ID?" I asked.

"When we decide who you are. You're the first of the new specialists we've hired who's a cop. Are you cop first, consultant second? Or vice versa? Details, details."

"Does it matter?"

"Yes indeedy-do, my man. In a state-sized bureaucracy every description has its own weight and meaning. F'rinstance, are you a consultant, which gives you the scope to go outside the office and initiate actions on your own? Are you an agent, which means full police powers but stricter adherence to chain of command? Are you solely a specialist, which means you can only be involved for certain crimes? There's a bureaucratic niche for everything and a word to describe it."

"Where's Yossarian?" I asked.

"What?"

I waved it away. Roy leaned back and laced his fingers behind his head. "I'm looking for the job description that gives you the most clout without having to sit through

41

every useless goddamn meeting. We're still feeling our way along here."

"But I *am* able to command an investigation?"

A wide grin. "You already are, in fact. Or will be after you meet the group. I told them that you're the lead investigator on this thing, the freak angle and all."

"How'd they respond? My taking the case?"

Roy seemed to not hear, busy checking his watch. "Whoops, the crew's been cooling their heels in the meeting room. Let's put you on the runway and see how pretty you strut."

I followed Roy to a windowless conference room, fluorescent lights recessed into a white acoustic tile ceiling. A large whiteboard claimed the far end of the room and beside it an urn of coffee centered a rolling cart. I saw four people at the conference table, three men and a woman. They were tight and fit and looked like they knew their way around a gym floor. I tried a smile but got nothing back but eight eyes studying me like a rat crossing sanctified ground.

"My top people, Carson," Roy boasted. "There are fifteen other investigators and you'll meet them all soon enough, but this is the A-plus Team: Major Crimes. When it's too much or too big for the munies to handle, even the big-city departments, it comes to our division of the FCLE, right, my cupcakes?"

No one so much as nodded. A squealing sound pulled my attention to the guy heading the table, pressing fifty and looking like a retired heavyweight boxer, six-four or five, two-fifty or thereabouts, heavy features under a slab brow and steel-gray crew cut. Thick fingers were busy pinching pieces from the lip of a Styrofoam cup. He'd pinch, add the piece to a growing pile beside the cup, pinch again. Each pinch made the cup squeal.

"This is Charlie Degan," Roy said. "It was Chuckles here who almost single-handedly took down the Ortega mob back in 2004."

I smiled and nodded. "I remember when the Ortega enterprises went belly-up. Helluva job, Detective Degan."

He nodded without commitment as the fingernails chomped at the cup. I doubted anyone else could have called the monster Chuckles, but it sounded as natural as rain from Roy McDermott.

Roy moved down the dour queue to the sole woman in the room, early forties, her olive face holding huge dark eyes framed by hair as brightly strident as a new trumpet. Her teeth were toothpaste-commercial white and could be glimpsed in flashes as she chewed pink gum.

"This is Celia Valdez," Roy said. "Ceel was the FCLE agent of the year last year."

My offer of congratulations was cut off by a snap of gum. Roy moved to the next guy, fortyish and olive-complected with flint-edged cheekbones and slender, cruel lips below a pencil-thin mustache. His chestnut hair was just long enough to display a curl and he wore a gray silk suit with a pink shirt and turquoise tie. I wouldn't

43

have been surprised if Roy'd found the guy at a Samba competition.

"That brings us to Lonnie Canseco. Say hi to Carson, Lon."

Canseco rolled eyes. I hoped it was how he showed joy.

"Lonnie came here from Pensacola, where he did first-rate work in Homicide. But the advancement breaks weren't coming his way. So I grabbed the collar of his Bill Blass suit and yanked him to my crime crew."

Canseco yawned. Roy smiled and progressed to the last face at the table, a slender black guy. He was in his mid-thirties with a mobile, puckish face and short hair, wearing a loose brown blazer over blue slacks, his white shirt open at the neck.

"And this fella on the end is Leon Tatum. Lee was a county mountie who got fired for asking questions about the local landfill. He spent the next four months digging into records and asking questions. What you get for that, Lee?"

"Fired."

"But Lee moved to Tallahassee to root through records up there. Turns out the fill was being used for dumping hazardous chemicals and had been for years, a huge moneymaker for some corrupt politicos."

"Four or five years back?" I said. "I recall the FBI perp-walking a Florida politico who'd been involved in a chemical-dumping scheme. That was yours?"

Tatum shrugged, no big deal. Roy shook his head.

44

"Unfortunately, our brothers at the federal level managed to grab the lion's share of the credit and we all know how that goes."

"Fuckers," Degan grunted, torturing the cup. "Dirty, rotten, underhanded, ass-sucking federal snotlickers."

"Two weeks later Lee was here." Roy beamed. "Jeez, has it been five years, Lee?"

Tatum puckered and blew McDermott a kiss. "Every day one of sweetness and light, Roy."

Roy looked out over his crew with paternal joy. "And that's the crime crew, our crème de la crima of investigative specialists and my sweet beauties. Plus there's our art expert, gang consultant, computer whiz, financial guy. You'll meet them as you need their specific services."

A cleared throat. Everyone turned to the guy in the corner, chair tilted back against the wall. When I scanned him my eyes didn't register *Cop*, they said, *Skate Punk*. I ballparked him at twenty-five or so, with the whippy build of a skateboarder though the upper body had spent time with the weights. He wore a floppy tee advertising a bar in Lauderdale under a black leather vest, tight and beltless Levis pulled from the bottom of the laundry basket, white socks and blue suede Vans with rubber soles.

"Sorry," Roy said. "This here's Ziggy Gershwin, Carson. He's currently with us for, uh, training. Charlie's his mentoring officer."

I looked at Degan, still tormenting the cup. Pinch. Squeak. He didn't look thrilled. Roy slapped my back, gave me the *Say Something* look and I pushed a bright and false smile to my face and started to stand. Before I could open my mouth, Canseco pushed from the table.

"Can we go now, Cap?" he said. "I got work to do."

The rest of the crew made the motions of escape. No one so much as glanced at me. Roy held up both hands. "Hold on . . . As I mentioned to y'all yesterday, Carson's gonna lead on the cistern case. That means you folks have to be his resources."

Someone moaned. It wasn't Valdez since she was already complaining. ". . . guess my big question, Cap, how come Ryder's getting this action? We know the rules, we know the territory, we've got the chops. A cistern stuffed with corpses should be ours."

Roy crossed his arms and leaned the wall. "You know what I been telling you, sweet peas. Mr Ryder knows how crazies operate. He's the best."

"It's fucking Florida, Roy," Degan growled. "Every fourth person is a psycho. We've all tracked 'em and taken them down. We don't need a freakin' profiler."

"There's more than profiling," I said. "You've got to—"

"Figure out are they organized or disorganized," Canseco interrupted, "sexual or nonsexual. Sadistic? Vengeful? We all know how to read psychos and every shrink tries to turn it into a bigger deal than it is."

"Fucking A," Valdez popped. "Fucking A-plus."

Roy rubbed his big palms together. "How often do you hear me say my mind's made up, chillun?"

''Bout once every two years, boss," Tatum said.

"Then you got nothing to worry about for the next twenty-three months. Class dismissed."

The group filed out like scolded schoolchildren. Only Gershwin acknowledged my existence, pausing to extend his fist as he stepped past. I knocked my knuckles against his.

"Nice meeting you, Alabama," he grinned. "Welcome to the Sunshine State."

6

"Leala Rosales? That's your name?"

"Y-y-yes, señorita."

"Stop your bawling. You look like you have something to say. What is it?"

"Th-the man, the man who b-brought me here . . . h-he did things to me in the car. Fi-filthy, sinful things and—"

A crack like a whip.

"Do you know what that slap was for little Leala? LOOK AT ME WHEN I TALK TO YOU! It was for being a snitch. NEVER tell me such things. And what the gentleman did was not filthy . . . it's how you make money. And you better start making money, little Leala. You have a debt to be paid off."

"P-please, señorita. I want . . . to go back. To g-go home."

"In that case you must pay what you owe plus the return costs. Do you have thirty thousand dollars?"

"I HAVE NOTHING! I w-was told that . . ."

"You must work, Leala. It's as simple as that. And there is one very important thing you must know: It is about the police. They are *muy peligrosa*, dangerous. They hate illegals and will throw you in prison for ever. Look into my eyes, Leala, so that you will see the truth. Do you see it?"

"Y-yes."

"The man who told you of our service. Back in Honduras. Does he not know exactly where you are from?"

A tentative nod. "*Si*. He has been to my home."

"Then here is God's truth, Leala: If you are ever stupid enough to talk to the police, you will never see your mama again. You will return to a headstone."

"No . . . please . . ."

"So now you know what you must do. Pay your debt."

"I c-c-can cook, I can clean. I-I was told I might be a housekeeper."

"Are you a virgin?"

"I-I did not hear. What did you say?"

"You seem as stupid as you are beautiful. I'll say it slowly so maybe you can understand: Are you a virgin, Leala Rosales? Have you managed to keep the peasants and priests from your pussy?"

"The man in the car, he . . ."

"He fucked your mouth. Hopefully you learned

something useful. Come here and lift your dress. My finger will tell me."

"P-please señorita, I beg you. No."

"No is not a word you can use any more, Leala Rosales."

The footsteps of the investigative staff disappeared down the hall. Roy broke the silence. "That went well, I think."

"Went well? I was smelling a lynching."

"You're over-reacting, bud. My guys are intuitive detectives, edgy and a bit self-centered. Like most natural-born dicks they're basically high-strung children."

I shot Roy the eye. He said, "Present company excepted, of course."

"It was like they had a personal grudge against me, Roy. I understand being pissy about me having the case, but it seemed bigger than that."

Roy beamed at me like I'd just called every winner at Hialeah an hour before the starting bell. "You are beautiful, Carson. Reading people, situations. You absolutely nailed it."

"Nailed what?"

"Initially I planned to add a junior investigator to the staff, got Tallahassee to budget the extra bucks, with enough left over to bump my guys up a well-deserved grade in pay, two actually."

"And?"

"Then I thought, why a junior investigator? I'll put the money into a seasoned pro. The idea felt so good I thought, *Go even further, Roy*. So I decided to not only hire a senior investigator but one who was a specialist in crazos as well, more bang for the buck. Bingo, here you are."

I replayed Roy's scenario in my head, following the money. I was making double my salary in Mobile. I sighed. "Degan, Valdez, Canseco, Tatum . . . not one of them got a raise, did they, Roy? What would a two-grade jump average, about seven grand?"

"Closer to ten, actually. No big deal, there's another state budget session in the winter. I'll get the guys their jumps then."

Not being a high-strung child I avoided banging my head against the wall. "So not only do I grab a plum case from your crew, I've pulled ten grand from their wallets."

Roy's brow wrinkled in puzzlement. "I told you some of this, right? Before you got here?"

"No, you didn't."

"Sorry, things get tangled in my head at times. Probably because I'm still figuring it all out."

"The crew hates me," I said, perilously close to a moan. "They won't rest until I go down in flames."

Roy's hand fell over my shoulder. "You're a pro and they're pros. Maybe it'll be a teensy bit tough at first, but I know you, buddy. You're gonna fly like an eagle."

I slumped in Roy's footsteps as he led me to where my office would be when in Miami, right now just a fifteen-by-fifteen box with a cheap metal desk and chair and a phone on the floor. The *why-am-I-here?* thoughts started afresh.

"You can work from wherever suits you, Carson. Here or at your place or from a ship at sea. If a police chief from Deltana says he's got a perp killing hookers and chopping off their toes, you can advise what to look for. Or go to Deltana and handle the case directly. Your decision."

"You give your people a lot of autonomy."

"I'm a lazy bastard. When my crew handles stuff without me even knowing it, I'm thrilled. Basically, all I want to see are files stamped *Case Closed*."

"Speaking of crew, what's the word on that other guy? The kid who looks like a skate punk?"

Roy frowned, a rare event. "Ziggy Gershwin. Christ, did you ever hear a goofier name? Gershwin's kind of a special case."

A trio of clerical types passed by the open door, two women and a guy. They shot micro-glances inside: *Look at the new guy.*

"Special?" I said. "How is Gershwin so special?"

"A couple months back a trio of Albanian psychopaths grabbed a ten-year-old kid from West Palm, wanted five mil in ransom. The family called the authorities. BOLOs went out on a green van noted at the scene, everything real hush-hush. Gershwin was a newbie county cop working in Glades County, rural, west of Okeechobee. Two days after the grab – by then the family had received a pinky finger—"

"Jesus."

"Gershwin is roaming the backcountry and sees a green panel van parked outside a rental house . . ."

"He gets curious."

Roy nodded. "He pulls down the road and sneaks back. Blinds are tight, nothing moving, just a single-story ranch with an outbuilding separated by a hundred feet of open grass. He creeps to a side window, peeks inside and sees the Albanians in the living room and the kid taped tight on the couch. Gershwin also sees a freakin' armamentarium: Uzis and AKs, handguns, grenades and even a goddamn mounted RPG. It looked like an NRA convention in there."

"He calls it and sits tight?"

"SWAT positions behind a canebrake on the far side of the house, everyone scared a full-on assault meant a dead kid."

I felt my heart thumping. Roy pulled a cigar and began twirling it.

"In the meantime, one of the Albanians is getting progressively freakier. He's suddenly got a knife out, grabbing the kid's hair and pulling his face up. Gershwin realizes the guy is gonna slice the kid's nose off."

Roy studied the cigar as if wondering whether he could get away with smoking in the building.

"Christ, Roy, don't leave me hanging. What'd Gershwin do?"

"Radioed the commander that the Albanians were dragging the kid out the back door."

"Gershwin *lied*?"

"Said he needed a fast distraction. Naturally, the SWAT team charges toward the rear. The Albanians hear the commotion, forget the kid and run for the artillery."

My palms had started sweating. "Damn. And?"

"Gershwin smashes the window and tosses two grenades, a flash-bang and a stunner, comes in after them. He nails one in the chest and the others dive out a side door screaming, 'No shoot, no shoot.'"

I replayed Gershwin's action in my head. Saw the looming knife. The need for a split-second decision. "You know the odds against that kid coming back alive, Roy? Gershwin did a helluva job."

Roy sighed. "What troubles folks is how he did it. If the Albanians had launched an RPG a dozen cops could have been massacred. Gershwin didn't have the pay grade to make that decision, Carson."

"Maybe Gershwin didn't have time to argue seniority."

Roy started to argue, paused. "Thing is, Gershwin is here and we gotta deal with him for a few days."

I gave him a puzzled frown.

"History lesson, Carson: The abducted kid's grandfather hit Miami with ten pesos in his skivvies and within a year owned a grocery store selling Latin specialties. Now they're coast to coast. The kid's family has power in Tallahassee and told some major politicos that Gershwin deserved his assignment of choice."

I nodded. "Gershwin picked the FCLE, obviously."

"I get a lot of favors from Tallahassee, Carson. Sometimes I have to do one."

"What's gonna happen with Gershwin?"

"I'll let Degan seem to train the kid for a couple weeks, then get Gershwin a desk in Vehicle Theft." Roy winked. "You can't hotdog much there."

7

I left Roy to his Machiavellian hijinks and headed out to the forensics dig, since I now owned the case. The site was as busy as a beehive in spring, chisels tapping, soil being sifted through mesh, photos flashing as bits of fabric or bone were removed from the grisly sculpture, new horrors revealed beneath the old. Morningstar was beside the column, arms folded as she watched a pair of techs extricate shards of clothing from a torso still half-buried in the matrix. I stood aside as they fastidiously bagged the evidence and passed me on the steps.

Morningstar shot me a look when I hit bottom.

"Rumor has it this monster is gonna be your first case, Ryder."

"Not my choice, Doctor."

"Roy's concept of baptism would be to fling the kid

into a pond. You still on board with Delmara's serial-killer theory?"

I circled the mass of concretized humanity, still unable to absorb the full horror. "If so, he's as angry as a psycho can get. Incredible rage."

"We have four complete bodies free. Every spine is shattered, most limbs broken, usually compound. A jumbled mess."

A tech called out a question from above and Morningstar muttered, "Do I have to do all the thinking?" and started up the steps. "Look, but don't touch, Ryder," she said over her shoulder. "It may be your baby, but I'm in charge of birthing it."

It was just me remaining in the pit and I leaned against the buttressed wall and stared as if waiting for a voice to call from the tumble of bodies, a voice to say, *Here is the story of our death, please let it not be in vain.*

But the stone lay as silent as the ruins of Ozymandias, and after a few minutes I climbed to the upper level and quietly left the tent. Until Morningstar's team found something to point me in a direction, I was a compass in a world without North.

Orlando Orzibel was bored. Most of the clients were paying their fees and he'd not had to go out on a threat run, always a nice time-killer: one hand held the knife, the other an open palm, fingers waving for money. If the money didn't materialize, arrangements were made. If the arrangements weren't honored, the knife went to work.

He checked his phone, no word from Chaku, who should be dumping the hillbilly biker, Ivy, in an hour or so, five minutes to throw the fat scuzzer down the hole, pour a couple bags of dry 'crete, book away. That fucking hole had been a gift from the universe.

Orzibel sighed and grabbed his remote, playing a porn DVD on the five-foot screen in the corner. He watched for several minutes, his hand drifting to his crotch as a burly bodybuilder with lightning-zagged tattoos pounded away at a diminutive Asian. The woman screamed and pretended to resist, but it was obvious she was a professional, probably wondering what kind of pizza she'd order after she drank the guy's jizz.

Fuck fuck. Orzibel flicked off the video and tugged at his genitals. How long since he'd gone to the basement? There were four girls tucked away down there, plus Chaku's new toy. All were fresh procures, raw, not yet ready for assignment, though getting close.

The process could always be sped up.

With the pounding bass of electronic dance music pulsing through the walls, Orlando Orzibel descended to the shadowy basement of the nightclub, a warren of concrete-walled rooms. The nightclub had been built by Mob money during Prohibition, the main floor a speakeasy, the basement used for prostitution and other illicit activities. The water-seeping wall was still strung with dozens of ancient and fraying wires mounted on ceramic insulators; the wires originally connected to banks of telephones forming a subterranean bookie operation, the largest in all Miami.

Orzibel wrinkled his nose at the smell of mold and unlocked the heavy gate at the base of the steps. Built of cyclone fence welded within a reinforced steel frame, the gate had taken three powerful men plus Chaku Morales to hang it on its industrial-grade hinges. Orzibel pushed open the first door he came to, seeing two girls asleep on a mattress, a ragged cover over their bodies. What were their names? Did it fucking matter? They were heading to Jacksonville tomorrow. He bypassed the next portal, the room holding Chaku's fresh bride, not Orzibel's business. He pushed open the following door, saw one of the new acquisitions – Yolanda? Her eyes grew huge and terrified. He'd had a session with her yesterday.

"Later, *puta*," Orzibel said, pulling the door tight. He reached the next door. Who was in here? Ahh . . . little Leala, the pretty one. Orzibel replayed the trip back from the delivery, felt her struggle under his hands. He touched himself.

Yes!

Orzibel pushed open the door to a cramped room, the walls gray and stained with leakage, pipes and ducts crowding the ceiling. Two king-size mattresses were on a frayed green carpet and an open toilet was in the corner. A small and battered television sat on a stool in the corner, the program – a soap opera on Univision – blurry and tinted a bilious green.

On a mattress and swiftly pushing back into the corner was the girl. She was a beauty and Orzibel felt a wild grin propelled to his face. "Ah, how's our little Leala today?" Orzibel crooned. The girl cowered in the corner, pulling a blanket over her ragged yellow dress.

"G-go away, señor."

"What did you say to me?"

"Please, señor. No."

Though she was terrified, there was something in her eyes. *Dios* . . . could it actually be defiance? He snapped the blanket away and threw it to the floor. "You do not make the rules here, Leala," he said, unbuckling his belt. "Let me see . . . where did we leave off?"

"I do not w-want to—"

'YOU DO NOT TELL ME WHAT YOU WANT. I TELL YOU WHAT TO DO!" Orzibel dove onto the bed and grabbed the girl's arms. "Open that pretty mouth, Leala."

"No!"

What was it with this one? His hand slashed and Leala's head spun. "One call and I can have your mama's eyes carved from her head. Do you know what that feels like, Leala?"

Crying. Orzibel's frenzied hands pulled his pants and silk boxers lower as he perched on his knees, his fingers grasping the girl's hair as he pulled her close. "Work on this the way I taught you. With tenderness."

Her head moved closer and her lips parted. But her face seized in agony and her hands rose as if guided by a separate force, pushing him away. Leala's legs kicked at Orzibel as she backpedaled across the mattress.

"Filthy little bitch," he hissed, yanking his pants to his ankles. He seized her hair and wrestled her to him, climbing over her, clamping her arms to the mattress and spreading her with his knees. A hand tore away her underwear.

"OPEN IT UP!"

"NO NO NO . . ."

He spit in his palm and rubbed it over his penis, then grabbed Leala's shoulders and fell across her, his tongue licking her face as his buttocks rose and fell. The act took under a minute and he emptied into her with a shuddering gasp. He startled to a sound at the open door but when he turned saw no one. He withdrew and Leala sprawled as if dead, her slender legs wide and a circle of blood at the apex.

"You are a woman, now, Leala," Orzibel proclaimed as he stood unsteadily. "You can do a woman's work."

8

The horrific column at the forefront of my mind, I drove home to Matecumbe Key, unable to understand the level of violence frozen into the concrete. I had a couple of pieces of fried chicken in the fridge and took them to the deck. The sun was riding a pillow of purple clouds to the horizon and a golden light suffused the air. A wobbling strand of pelicans skimmed across the cove barely a foot above the waves.

"Hey neighbor," a voice called, suspending my unsettled thoughts. I saw Dubois Burnside at the point of the cove. "You doing anything important?" he called through cupped hands.

"Not sure I ever have," I returned.

"How about you come by the house?" he said, overlarge gestures miming the pouring of a drink.

I shot a thumbs up. "There in fifteen."

I threw on a fresh shirt and snatched up a bottle of liquor I'd received at a going-away party last month, dropping it into a brown bag. Burnside's home was past a football-field-long buffer of vegetation and surrounded by a cream-colored wall with an ornamental gate at the entrance, a pair of mirroring flamingos perched on single legs. I hit the buzzer and heard the gate unlatch.

I walked down the drive to his home, a combo of styles, Moorish Art Deco, I suppose, the Moorish displayed in two stories of textured stucco tinted yellow and topped with terracotta tiling, the Deco reflected in flamingo-themed grating over wide and manteled windows. The drive ended in a portico shading a blue 500-series Mercedes and a spiffy red Beamer convertible. The plate on the Merc said FUNRL 1, the Beamer's said ZAZZI.

The front door was iron-belted mahogany recessed within an arched vestibule, more Moor. Marble slabs framing the portal sported bas reliefs that echoed the Deco flamingos. The door opened as my hand reached for the iron handle. Instead of Dubois Burnside, I beheld a handsome black woman in a floor-length red gown with a décolleté my eyes did not follow to its conclusion because that would have been impolite. I judged the lady in her early forties, and she was not much shorter than my six feet.

"You must be Mister Ryder. I'm Delita Matthews."

She extended her hand on a long and slender arm dressed in silver hoops. "Dubois will be with us in a minute. I told him to change into some decent clothes and not wear them saggy old pants. Every time I catch up to them pants I toss 'em in the trash."

"And every time I fish them out, baby," Burnside said as he strolled into the room in threadbare cargo shorts beneath an extravagantly embroidered Mexican wedding shirt. His feet flapped in ancient huaraches.

Delita aimed a long red fingernail at me like I was Exhibit A in a courtroom. "We got company."

"He ain't company, he's our neighbor."

The woman shot Burnside a raw glare but when she spun to me the eyes were Kahlua and cream. "You must be thirsty, Mr Ryder. May I get you a drink?"

"Actually," I said, pulling the bottle, "I brought this along. It's supposed to be pretty fair and I thought—"

"Hot damn," Burnside said, plucking the bottle from my hand and squinting at the label. "This is thirty-year-old brandy." He held the bottle up to Delita Matthews. "*Company* brings hoity-toity wine, girl, *neighbors* bring fine brandy. Grab us a couple tumblers."

"We have brandy snifters, Dubois."

"I wanna drink it, not slosh it around."

But snifters it was and I poured hefty tots for Burnside and myself, Miz Matthews demurring. "I'm meeting friends at the Saddle Club in a few minutes," she said. "There's an orchestra and dancing, but Dubois refuses to go."

"I boogie," Burnside proclaimed. "I don't cha-cha."

Miz Matthews sashayed across the floor to the door,

opened it and started out. A second later she leaned back in. "You using them coasters ain't you, Dubois?"

"Baby, you got 'em covering the table from end to end," Burnside called over his shoulder. "A man can't set down his glass without landing on a coaster."

The door closed and Burnside took a sip of brandy. "I don't know what this thing is I got for bossy-ass women, but I got it. Had four wives and ever' one had a face like an angel and a thumb built for mashing me down."

The psychologist in me wanted to ask about his mother, the diplomat in me demurred. We shot the breeze for twenty minutes, Burnside providing the low-down on local bars and eateries. Talk inevitably drifted to occupations. "In my line of work I've seen some badly mangled bodies, Dubois," I offered. "I'm always amazed when I see what a good mortician can do."

Burnside set his snifter on the table – between two coasters – and leaned forward. "Remember that scene in *The Godfather*, Sonny's been shredded by machine guns and Marlon Brando tells the mortician to make Sonny presentable at the funeral? I been there, Carson."

"You knew Marlon Brando?"

"Ha! I mean I've had to do reconstructions where the body was more putty and paint than person. A couple decades back two workers were on a catwalk at a paint company, standing above a huge mixing vat with these big steel propellers choppin' through the paint. The catwalk tore from the wall and these two poor guys got

65

dumped into the vat. Before the machine shut down the bodies got all busted up and mixed in together."

"Jesus," I said, aghast.

"You wouldn't believe the time I had getting the deceased cleaned and arranged in whole bodies again. It was like doing a jigsaw puzzle with meat."

Pictures started to arrange in my mind. I saw bodies whirling in paint. Arms, legs, faces became a kaleidoscopic jumble as I set my glass down on one of a dozen coasters.

"I gotta go, Dubois. I need to make a call. Give Delita my regards."

"You all right, Carson?" Burnside frowned. "You look like you're seeing a ghost."

I blew out the door and dropped into a sprint with a gibbous moon lighting my way. I had to call Roy and have him set up a meeting first thing in the morning.

Dance music pulsing from below, Orlando Orzibel sipped a mineral water and considered his escapade with Leala Rosales. He'd lost control, a bad thing. But the little bitch had it coming, talking to him like that. Before leaving he'd told the weeping girl to wash herself, rinse the sheet, and keep silent on the matter if she valued her mother's life. The little whore would not talk.

The cell phone buzzed from the glass table beside Orzibel. He snatched it up, checked the number, grinned and put the phone to his ear. "You must be finished with the business in the trunk, Chaks . . . Got that Ivy planted, right?"

After a few seconds the grin inverted, his voice a tense whisper. "A tent? A fucking tent? Bulldozers? I figured that hole would stay hidden until Christ himself showed up."

Orzibel hung up and threw the phone to the couch. He went to his desk and retrieved a second phone, a burner, to be used and discarded. He dialed a number from memory.

"It's Orlando, Jefé. It seems we have a problem."

9

Roy had set the meeting at eight a.m. Instead of the three promised members of the investigative crew there was only Valdez. Luckily, Delmara, Morningstar and Gershwin made the table look less empty.

"Where's Tatum and Canseco?" I asked Roy. "Degan?"

"Turns out they had other commitments."

I gave him a look. He said, "They're busy boys."

"I got a crime scene needs me," Morningstar said, long and elegant fingers ticking colorless nails on the tabletop. Gershwin yawned in his tipped-back chair. Delmara sat a pen and pad in front of him and scratched his beak.

"Dr Morningstar," I said, laying out my case to the small audience, "would you outline the scope of the injuries you've been able to identify?"

"Like I've said, I'm seeing the kind of injuries I associate with high-impact vehicle accidents." Her hands went to a file of photos on the table. "I have the exact details here if you—"

"Have you found any seams in the matrix, Doctor? Yesterday I theorized dry cement poured into the cistern atop added bodies. After further thought, I suspect the next layer would not perfectly adhere to the preceding concrete. It would leave discernible seams."

She shook her head. "The concrete matrix appears to be contiguous. Where are you going with this?"

"I'm pretty sure I know how the bodies got there."

"How?"

"In a cement-mixer truck."

Eyes-wide stares from everyone. Roy said, "Explain that one, Carson."

I spun my index fingers around one another. "Ever see the inside of a mixer drum? It's an inside-out auger. The rotating vanes force concrete deeper to keep it mixed. At the jobsite the rotation is reversed and the screw action lifts the concrete up and out of the drum."

"Jesus," Morningstar said, reaching into her file and pulling out eight-by-ten photos of the column, staring at the jumble of arms and legs and faces and concrete. "It explains the brownish cast to the concrete," she said quietly. "It's blood."

"Sure explains the damaged bodies," Roy said.

I nodded. "It's a blender on wheels."

Morningstar rose, clamped shut her briefcase. "There's a lot to do before I can verify anything like your mixer theory, but I have to say it's decent, Ryder."

I nodded my thanks and she was gone. Roy turned to Valdez and Delmara.

"Guys?"

"I gotta think about it," Delmara said. He was trying to look upbeat, but I'd punctured part of his serial-killer explanation. Roy angled to Valdez.

"Ceel?" Roy said to Valdez.

"Just what is it you're looking for, Ryder?" she said, aiming her big eyes into mine. They weren't saying *Congratulations on a spiffy idea.*

"Looking for, Detective Valdez?"

"The Carson Ryder morning show here. You want something, right?"

"We have to start looking into concrete mixing companies, Detective. We need someone who can ask the right questions and tell when the answers are shaky. A pro." I used the inclusive *we*, hoping to spark camaraderie. There was a coterie of FCLE investigators at Roy's disposal – and, I supposed, mine as well – but I wanted the experience of the department's top people, hoping a few hours of working together might diminish the wall between us.

Valdez reached to the floor for her briefcase and popped it open, coming up with a two-inch-thick folder. She dropped it on the table, *whump.*

"These are *my* current cases. Where does *we* fit in?"

I resisted the urge to look to Roy for assistance and didn't hear any, the silence of the Buddha.

"Or," I said, "I could grab some folks from the pool investigators downstairs."

"That sounds like a good idea," Valdez said, standing.

Delmara followed suit, tucking his notepad into his suit jacket and forcing a half-smile to his face. "Nice idea on the mixer, Detective," he said, following Valdez out the door.

Roy grabbed my shoulder. "Great theory, Carson! Morningstar was gushing over the idea."

"Gushing?"

"If Vivian isn't pissing on an idea, it's gushing. You're winning her over, bud."

"Yeah? What about the others?"

We heard a cleared throat and turned to see Gershwin, chair tipped back, dressed in black jeans and a T-shirt advertising a surf shop. Both Roy and I had forgotten about the kid. "If y'all don't need me for anything," he said, "the folks in maintenance would like me to mop the bathroom with my tongue."

Roy tucked away his notes and nodded absently. "Good for you, kid. Keep it up."

Gershwin shook his head and was gone.

10

Roy and I elevatored down to the investigators' floor, a horizontal hive of cubicles like I'd vacated in Mobile. Harry and I had our jammed-together desks closest to the elevator and my eyes turned there when the door opened, seeing not a lineman-sized black man dressed in a clashing color palette, but a white guy in his mid fifties with a wind-tunnel blowback of gray hair and Elvis Costello glasses. It wasn't Harry but a Florida version of Martin Scorsese, and for a moment the world felt unsteady.

Where am I?

"Here you go, Carson," Roy said, snapping me back to the present. "Grab who you need."

I studied the cubicles, most empty. The ones holding people held busy people: some guys on phones furiously scribbling notes as they talked, two women and a man bent over a desk and arranging photos, a pair of guys arguing in another cube.

"Everyone looks busy, Roy."

He laughed. "What . . . you think I keep my lovelies sitting in a corner and jiggling their nuts while they wait for an assignment? Who looks good, Carson? Pick an assistant or two. Shit . . . wait . . . let me introduce you to everyone."

I heard myself giving my *Happy to Be on the Team* speech a dozen more times while trying to remember a roster of names.

"How about Gershwin?" I said, seeing the kid reading in a far corner. "He doesn't look busy."

Roy looked uneasy, like I might actually be serious. "That would make Gershwin a member of the crew, Carson, maybe not a great idea right now. The others might get a bit miffed that—"

"Who gave me the You're-in-Charge speech, Roy?"

Roy puffed out a resigned breath. I walked across to Gershwin, still licking his thumb and turning pages. "What you reading?" I asked.

He held up the Yellow Pages for Miami-Dade. "I'm scoping out the concrete section. I didn't know anything about this crap before."

"You got anything going on right now?" I said. "I might be able to use you."

He tossed the book and leaned back in the chair with his hands behind his head and kicked his heels up on the desk. His smile was as wide as it was false. "What, Alabama . . . you need coffee? A shoe shine? Someone to run your laundry to the cleaners?"

"You seem to have an attitude problem, Gershwin."

"I came here to work and instead I get treated like I spit in the face of everyone in the FCLE. You know what F-C-L-E spells, right? Fickle. McDermott treats me like I'm transparent, and everyone else looks the other way when I walk in a room."

I pushed his feet off the desk. He wasn't expecting it and it brought him to sitting erect. I sat where his feet had been and looked him in the baby browns. "If you're unhappy all you need to do is complain to the family of that kid you saved and have them pull strings on your behalf. Again."

The chin jutted. "I never asked them to push for me."

"Your refusal technique must be flawed. A powerful family offered you an unearned step up and you took it."

I'd scored a hit. The kid started to argue, had nothing. He nodded at me. "Truth is, I was tired of handling DUIs, brain-dead methheads and crackers screwing their dogs and daughters. I wanted action and when the kid's family said to pick my spot, I said Miami."

"And here you are. What do you expect to happen?"

"What else? McDermott's gonna dump me at some backwater desk until I get tired of pushing paper and retreat to the sticks."

"And that's what you plan to do . . . quit?"

"That's McDermott's plan. Mine is to, to . . ." He pulled up short and frowned.

"What?"

"I dunno," he said, honestly perplexed. "I don't have a clue."

I pushed the Yellow Pages his way. "Here's an idea: start checking concrete companies for employees with criminal records. Or does that lack the action you're looking for?"

11

The dark-haired woman finished tapping on the MacBook Air and switched it off. She sat behind a mahogany desk, antique and polished to a soft gloss. The sole light flowed from a Tiffany-shaded desk lamp and the woman's olive skin seemed to glow in the light. She wore a sedate navy ensemble, her dark hair curled in a businesslike chignon.

"I'll be finished in a moment, Orlando," she said.

There were no personal trappings in the room, no pictures of family or mugs with funny sayings. The desk held only an in and out basket, the latter holding a neat stack of various invoices. The office – painted in a sedate, mossy green with two windows draped in burgundy – was almost as large as Orzibel's.

The woman turned to the credenza behind her desk. The doors opened to a built-in floor safe the size of a mini-fridge, welded to the frame of the building and immovable. The safe was designed to resist nearly any assault short of cannon fire. She locked the computer in the safe and reclosed the credenza.

"When is the man arriving?" she said, looking across the room.

"The client is downstairs with a bottle of Dom Pérignon," Orzibel said, waiting in a wing-back chair with hands tented beneath his chin. He was in soft black leather: jacket, vest and pants. His boots were tipped with silver and ticked in time to the bass notes filtering through the floor.

"Dom? On the house?"

Orzibel laughed. "What he spends with us, I don't care if he drinks a case of it."

"Is the product ready?"

"Tericita, and Alicia. And Yolanda from the fresh shipment. I will present them when the client is ready, a parade. The man likes little parades before his party."

"All dressed the same, right? For his choosing?"

"*Si*. It must be the pink dresses and pink canvas shoes. White panties. And red scarves for the hair. I keep a supply of several sizes in my office for when the client wants a party."

"Mr Chalk hurt one last time, Orlando. Badly."

"He paid well for his sport." Orzibel's long fingers made the money-whisk. "Are you suddenly concerned about their welfare?"

"I'm concerned about arousing attention. The man is not of normal mind."

77

Orzibel waved her words away. "I have taken extra precautions by reserving a rear cabana suite at the Oceana, where sounds cannot travel through the trees. Chaku will stay nearby during the man's festivities, though he will not interfere unless sounds carry."

"We must be able to trust the owner of the Oceana, Orlando. Totally."

"The owner has a side business selling various substances. He knows we know this. And I promised him an evening with one of our best products. Free."

The woman gave Orzibel a look of irritation and turned to retrieve the MacBook from the safe, setting it on her lap. "You must always tell me when you make side arrangements, Orlando. I must note it or the records will be off."

"Instead of praise for my careful planning I get a lecture on my memory? Would it be painful to your mouth to say something nice?"

"I have a duty to keep the accounting, Orlando."

"Yes indeed," Orzibel said, voice wet with sarcasm. "How dare anyone forget the numbers for your precious accounts."

The woman's eyes turned cold. "I keep precise numbers not for me, Orlando Orzibel, but for the one above. El Jefé. Mock me and you mock him."

"I mock no one," Orzibel said, sitting straighter and looking as if the room had grown tight. "I will go and start the parade."

The woman nodded, then seemed to find an afterthought

worthy of a frown. "One more thing, Orlando: What of the new one named Leala? Why haven't you chosen her for the parade?"

A pause. "A *peon*, that Leala. The client deserves better. I'm sending her to Madame Cho. Cho will get stupid little Leala started in her career."

"It's not stupidity, Orlando. It's ignorance . . . the naïveté of a peasant. There's a difference."

A mischievous light came to Orzibel's eyes. "Were you ever that ignorant, *cariña*? That naïve?"

"How else did I get here?"

Orzibel uncurled from the couch and crossed the room, leaning against the desk with his arms crossed. "Ah, but you showed a special light, *amiga*. And you used it well, didn't you?"

The woman returned the computer to the safe and turned to see Orzibel's leer.

"Don't look at me like that, Orlando. It's not to be."

"You are not his, *princésa*. El Jefé has others. Surely you are not blind to it: you see everything."

"I am his when he needs me. And he needs me to run this enterprise."

A flash of anger. "I run this enterprise."

The woman hid a smile. "Ah, forgive me, Orlando. I meant the part of the enterprise that keeps track of things. So that he can—"

"So he can count the money we make," Orzibel said.

"Be careful, Orlando. Dangerous words lead to dangerous places."

Orzibel froze, eyes darting side to side as if fearful of hidden listeners. "I was not speaking against *him*," he said quickly. "I have nothing but respect for his enterprises. He should be praised for having so much money to count."

"Which bring us back to Leala, Orlando. Her innocence, her naïveté. That's what our special client pays big money for, no? Why did you not include her in the parade?"

"Did you not hear?" Orzibel snapped. "I decided to send Leala to Cho."

"But Leala is a virgin, is she not? Worth more money?"

"Why are you questioning me? You make decisions about the numbers. I make decisions about the product."

The woman leaned back in the cushioned chair and regarded Orzibel as if he were a caged animal at a zoo. "Things get a bit hot yesterday, Orlando?" she said after a moment's reflection. "Just couldn't control yourself? Again?"

"I have no idea what you're talking about."

"I inspected Leala myself, Orlando. Two days ago she was a virgin. What would my finger find today?"

"Fuck you," Orzibel hissed. But at the edges of his eyes, fear.

The woman's eyes remained level and unblinking. "What would you do if the Jefé discovered he has lost money because you lost control, Orlando? Could you ever return to pimping runaways collected from parks and bus stations?"

Orzibel's hands clenched into fists, his eyes blazing. He seemed to waver between worlds. Then, as if depleted of oxygen, his head slumped forward. He started to speak, but threw his hands up in surrender.

"I-I had a moment of weakness. It was all a mistake and I humbly beg you to, to . . ."

The woman began laughing. "Begging demeans you, Orlando. Plus it's not sincere."

"I am confessing my sins! The girl's flesh was too beautiful for my will. Something dark came over me and I—"

"Please, Orlando, you're turning my stomach. But be assured I will keep my tongue on the matter and you will stay safe from wrath. Go with the girls you have selected. But make sure Chaku stays close during the man's pleasures. Mr Chalk is truly sick."

"Sick is money," Orzibel muttered, turning for the door. He paused in the entrance. "*Gracias* for your silence in the matter of my weak moment. I am in your debt, Amili Zelaya."

"Here you go, Carson." Roy handed me a small box and a file folder bulging with official documents. "You're officially official. I got you a brand-new shootin' iron, too, a Glock 17. And your shield."

I took the badge and almost moved it to my pocket, but it felt so good I closed my fingers around the metal. "What's my designation, Roy? You ever figure that one out?"

He handed me my ID card. I stared. "'Consulting Investigative Agent, Senior Status'? What's it mean?"

Roy grinned like he'd just invented the rainbow. "I'm not quite sure, since you're the only one. You're an investigative agent like the crew, but you're also a full-time consultant like the art and finance guys. It gives you the broadest range of freedom I could buy."

"How about 'Senior Status'?"

"That's kinda like four-star general in the pecking order. It means people will want to be nice to you."

"The crew?"

"Well, most people."

"What's this second box?"

"Gershwin's party favors. You got 'em for him, you can give 'em to him."

I saw a bunch of papers and a holstered nine, the holster stained and the weapon nicked and losing its finish. "OK," Roy said, "So maybe it's not a new piece. Tell the kid to keep it in the holster and we'll do fine."

I studied Gershwin's new ID card. "Provisional Investigator?"

"I let him in the door, but he's not getting the big key. This'll let him do whatever odd jobs you need."

I thanked Roy and turned for Gershwin's private Siberia. On the way I dropped the badge in my pocket and patted its weight. It felt good.

"Provisional?" Gershwin asked when I got back, staring between me and his new ID.

"Don't start with me," I said. "I'm a four-star general."

He slid the card in his wallet. "That mean I have to salute you, Alabama?"

"No. It means you call me Detective Ryder. You have to keep your ass on the concrete firms, our only lead. There's a lot to do in digging up employees with records."

Gershwin reached for the Yellow Pages and opened to a sticky tab. "There's over twenty concrete companies in the area, more if you include surrounding counties. If each company has twenty employees to be checked out, that adds up to—"

"I knows how math works, kid."

A smirk and waggled finger. "Ah, Deee-tective Ryder, but what if there's a short cut that names ex-cons working around concrete trucks?"

"Sure. And what if there's a pot of gold at the end of the rainbow?"

He handed the book to me. "What do you see?"

"Ads for concrete companies."

"Look closer. A lot of them have little logos: Better Business Bureau, Business Alliance of Florida, American Association of Concrete Haulers, that sort of thing."

I nodded. "True. What I don't see is a listing of the criminal backgrounds of the employees, which is what we've got to get working on."

"Check out the Redi-flow company, lower right."

A half-page ad featuring a drawing of a truck dispensing concrete into a foundation as workers looked on. The ad had the usual listing of professional-organization logos plus an outline of a fish holding the letters CPP. "It's all the same except for the fish logo," I said. "You know what it means?"

"It stands for the Christian Prison Project, religious businesspeople who mainstream ex-cons back into civilian life, get them starter jobs. I figured that's what Redi-flow does, and if so, they have ex-cons on the payroll, right?"

I'd thought the kid was joking, but he'd combined brains and observation and come up with gold.

"So we're going to the Parole Board next, Gershwin?"

He waved a sheaf of pages. "Nope. They just faxed me a list of company hires. The business is owned by a dude named George Kazankis. Turns out Kazankis has hired twenty-six ex-cons in twelve years in business."

I felt my pulse quickening. "Light-timers or hardcore?"

"Anyone's fodder for Kazankis's personal ministry. He's also got a good record for keeping them straight: most have managed to stay out of the joint."

I shot a thumbs up. "Sounds like we pay a visit to Mr Kazankis. But first we stop by the motor pool."

12

"Son of a bitch," Gershwin said, staring at yards of gleaming black metal and chrome. "That's yours?"

I looked to the guy who just handed me the keys, a label on his stained blue work shirt embroidered with the name Julio. He nodded. "All yours, Detective Ryder. Captain McDermott said you were senior status. That means the Tahoe."

I climbed inside. After my pickup, the thing felt like I was in the pilot house of a destroyer. The instrumentation appeared to have been pulled from a Cessna. The new-vehicle smell made my head light. I jumped out.

"Got anything smaller, Julio?"

Julio stared at me like I'd asked a waiter to return a prime filet and bring a can of tuna instead. "But this is what all senior personnel drive, Detective."

"Dude," Gershwin said. "I mean Detective Ryder, this is hot wheels deluxe."

"What else you got, Julio?"

"All the others are standard cruisers."

I saw a line of cars and trucks across the lot. "What are those?"

"Seized contraband, vehicles taken from criminals. When someone gets caught the state can take away—"

"I know how it works, bud," I said, not mentioning my house was in the same condition. "Anything available over there?"

"All are, I suppose. They get taken out for surveillance because they don't look like police vehicles."

We followed Gershwin to the line-up, a dozen cars and trucks, some looking new, most in obviously used condition. I was immediately drawn to a beige Land Rover Defender, fully outfitted with heavy black grille guard, full roof racking, and a high-sprung body with more right angles than curves.

"Tell me about the Rover, Julio."

"That?" Gershwin wrinkled his nose. "It's left over from an Indiana Jones movie."

"You don't want the Rover, Detective," Julio argued. "It's sprung like a tank."

"And built like one, too," I said, admiringly. "Where'd it come from?"

"A Lauderdale dope dealer who had it custom-outfitted in South Africa for a month-long safari, but cut the trek short after three days. When he had the monster shipped

86

over here, he liked how it looked a lot better than how it rode, probably why it's only got two thousand miles on it. I also don't think he much liked a manual transmission after the novelty wore off."

"The Tahoe," Gershwin pleaded.

"How long would it take to outfit the Rover with a siren, flashers, and an on-board computer hookup, Julio?" I asked. "Given that y'all don't look too busy around here."

Gershwin moaned.

Thirty minutes later, feeling better than I had all day, I aimed the revamped Rover for Redi-flow. It was southwest of Miami, down toward Homestead. Once off the highway we wove through streets that turned from storefront businesses to small and brightly painted houses clustered on miniscule lots festooned with tropical foliage. The houses soon grew sparse, the land as much sand as dirt, errant terns pecking at prickly pears for insects. I smelled swampland nearby but never saw water.

Within minutes we banged past a lot holding smaller dozers and graders, cranes, trucks, and machinery of indecipherable usage, and a small abandoned building beneath a faded sign showing a crane and proclaiming OLYMPIA EQUIPMENT RENTAL – SINCE 1975.

Gershwin pointed. "Think they'd rent us a crane, sahib? You could shoot at lions from above."

"The Rover is fine. And it's Detective Ryder."

We passed over rail tracks into a complex dominated by piles of gravel and sand, metal towers hovering in the air, one large silo emblazoned with a tall cross, below it the words REDI-FLOW CONCRETE, INC . . . A MIX FOR EVERY NEED. A half-dozen mixing trucks sat on the lot and two were pulled to one of the towers, workers standing beside them. In a far corner of the lot was a jumble of metal boxes and round tanks. I'd seen them at construction sites: portable mixing units conveyed on semis and set up where needed.

We pulled beside a squat building marked 'Office' as a helicopter blew by overhead, low enough to read the word EVERGLADES AIR TOURS on the fuselage.

Kazankis was in his early fifties, tall and square-built and in a blue uniform dusted with cement. He was ruggedly good looking, wavy silver hair pomaded and combed back from his high and sun-brown forehead. His voice was deep and resonant and had Kazankis stood with a Bible in his hand and started preaching about salvation it wouldn't have been much of a shock.

I showed my new ID. "Why we're here, Mr Kazankis, is we're investigating a crime involving an amount of poured concrete that probably took a mixer."

"You came to us because of who we hire?" he said quietly, meaning ex-cons. "I feel it's my calling to help the fallen back to their feet."

"I'm not questioning your calling, sir. I may wish to question some of your employees."

"Our employees are no longer criminals. When first from prison, I employ them here. Some stay, others move to new careers. The record speaks for itself."

"An exemplary record, indeed," I said, credit due. "But you've had failures, Mr Kazankis. It goes with the territory."

"True. I'll be the first to admit cases of recidivism. Not, thankfully, very many. But given that the possibility exists . . . what may I do for you, Detective?"

"First, sir, what can you tell me about this sample?" I opened my briefcase and handed over a bone-free chunk of concrete. Kazankis flicked a thumbnail over its surface.

"Low aggregate. Mainly sand and cement with a dye, one of the umbers. Is this part of the crime you're investigating?"

I nodded. "Have you ever had a loaded truck stolen?"

"A truckload is mixed, then goes directly to the site. A person might steal a truck at night, but it would be empty."

"Maybe I'm looking for concrete diverted to another usage. This would have been around a year ago."

Kazankis frowned. "I'm sorry, Detective, but I can't recall details that far back."

"Would it be possible to get a printout of all employees from that period?" I asked. "It would save us a trip to the Parole Board."

"Certainly." Mr Kazankis sat by a computer, made some taps on the keyboard, and a printer behind the desk began humming. Our next move would be cross-checking employee names against violent crimes. Records in hand, we turned to the door.

Gershwin halted. "One more question, Mr Kazankis.

Do your employees ever take concrete home or anything like that? For use later?"

"Like for next-day delivery? It would harden in the truck."

"I guess I mean their own projects. Like fixing a sidewalk or whatnot."

Kazankis thought a moment, brow furrowed beneath the silvered blowback. "Sure, lots of times an employee will lay a patio or a driveway. We give them the materials at cost. It happens too often to keep track of."

"I understand," I said, again turning to go. "Guess we'll have to keep digging into employees with records. Sorry if we . . ."

When I turned to nod farewell to Kazankis his head was canted and his eyes were turned inward, as if doing calculations in his head. He snapped his fingers.

"Paul Carosso, by gosh! Now I remember."

"Pardon me?" I said.

"It was almost quitting time, Detective. Paul came in, said he'd been working on a new driveway. He'd hired a couple concrete workers for the following week and was gonna get the pour scheduled then. But Paul said if he could get the concrete, they could lay the drive that evening. I said sure, grab a load and return the truck in the morning. But make double-damn-sure that barrel gets washed out."

"I thought you didn't remember such things," I said. "Was something different?"

"It was kind of unusual. Paul's not a detail guy. He

90

could do better at keeping his uniforms clean. He leaves candy and food wrappers in the cab. I have to get on him about washing the barrel completely clean. If the mix hardens you need to break it out, a real pain. When I got there in the morning I asked Burle Smith, the yard foreman, if Paul brought the truck back in decent condition, dreading the answer."

"And your yard guy said?"

"Burle said Paul musta climbed into the drum with a toothbrush, it was that clean."

I looked at Gershwin. Would it be this easy? Kazankis caught the glance. "Are you going to want to talk to Paul?" he asked, an edge of nervousness in his voice.

"Dunno yet," I said. "And I'd appreciate if you didn't mention this conversation to him."

Kazankis promised to keep our confidence. Gershwin and I were angling for the door when he called us back. "Excuse me, gentlemen."

"Yes, sir?"

He started to speak but couldn't. He cleared his throat and tried again. "The color in the sample of concrete you showed me, the rusty brown. It's not dye, is it?"

"No, sir."

His eyes fell. "I pray no one here was involved."

I nodded, not mentioning that I was hoping in the opposite direction. It would mean we had a solid lead.

Paul Carosso lived near Richmond Heights in a tired suburban community within listening distance of highway

821 and I figured after a couple months you grew immune to the twenty-four-hour rumble of diesel engines. Or most people would; me it would drive nuts after about a half hour. The driver's house was a single-story crackerbox bungalow with mildew on the siding and a piece of soffit hanging from the eaves. A palmetto squatted in the front yard, flanked by a banana tree with white rot on the leaves. The scruffy patches of grass were unmowed. The small yard was cyclone-fenced with a sign on the gate saying PRIVATE PROPERTY – KEEP OUT. The drive was outside the fencing and led to a single-car garage.

The gate was unlocked so we went to the door and pressed the bell. No reply. Figuring the bell was in the same decrepit shape as the rest of the place, I knocked.

A curtain parted on the front picture window. "I don't want nothing," a voice yelled. "Peddle your shit somewheres else."

"We're not salesmen," I said, holding up the shield. "We'd like to ask you a few questions."

The door swung open. Carosso was older than his pic in the prison discharge file, but it was the same face: round and poorly shaved, heavy-lidded eyes under a receding hairline. He wore a sleeveless white tee with sweat stains under the arms and the kind of uniform pants you get for ten bucks a pair, as formless as pajama bottoms.

"Questions about what?"

"A load of concrete you brought home from Redi-flow last summer."

92

"Concrete? I don't know nothing about—"

"How 'bout you invite us in or step outside?" I said.

He rolled his eyes and stepped to the stoop, Gershwin and I backing up to give him space and to give our noses some distance between Carosso and his body odor.

"I don't bring concrete home. I deliver it to other people."

"Your boss remembers, Mr Carosso. You brought home a load of concrete to install a new driveway." I studied the drive across the fence, a dozen feet away, cracked and studded with weeds, the same drive poured when the house was new, maybe forty years ago. "I don't see any new driveway, Mr Carosso. I don't see repairs."

"The fuckin' workers never showed," he said. "It never got done."

He looked down, thinking, and I stepped closer by a couple inches.

"So where did the mix go?"

"I drove it out by the glades and poured it into a drainage ditch. And no, I don't remember where."

"Try."

When he looked west I moved another inch, brushing back my hair to cover the motion. He said, "It was over that way somewheres."

Carosso was sweating heavily. He turned his head to cough and I stepped into the edge of his personal space. "Mr Kazankis says you're not a detail guy, Mr Carosso. It's hit-and-miss whether you'll get the barrel clean."

"What does that mean about anything?"

Gershwin sensed it was his turn. "Mr Kazankis checked that day. Says the barrel looked like you climbed inside and scrubbed it out with a toothbrush. What made that batch so different you needed to eliminate every trace?"

"I just fuckin' hosed it out like always. Kazankis musta got the trucks mixed up."

I shuffled another inch forward. "Mr Kazankis doesn't strike me as a man who gets much wrong. Except maybe the occasional hire."

Carosso's face spun my way. He hadn't seen me move, but his body felt my nearness and didn't like it. "Whaddaya want with me? I drive a goddamn concrete truck for sixteen lousy bucks an hour. Look at the shithole I live in. Why you picking on me?" His last sentence was a peal of desperation, like a frightened child.

"I need to see that load," I said, knowing he could feel my breath on his face. "It's important."

"I don't know where it is. I don't know nothing. Leave me alone!"

He backed inside and slammed the door. Gershwin gave me a raised eyebrow. "Jumpy as a cat on meth. El schmendriko knows something."

"On that we agree," I said. "Let's go back to the office and chase some paper."

We climbed into the Rover. "It's an oven," Gershwin complained. "We were out five minutes and you could bake cookies in here."

"The insulation is a bit thin," I said as we pulled away. "But sweating clears toxins from the body."

Paul Carosso wiped his brow with his shoulder and pulled a fifth of Jim Beam from a kitchen cabinet, sucking down long, gurgling swigs. He wiped his mouth with the back of his hand and flipped open his cell phone. He dialed, missed the number in nervousness, dialed again.

"It's me," he said, breath tight and voice strained. "The fucking cops just left. Tell me again how this makes sense."

13

Gershwin and I headed to HQ to bang out the paperwork on Carosso. I still saw only one desk and a single chair, the disconsolate phone centering the floor. "I can swami on the carpet," Gershwin offered, folding his legs and squatting beside the phone. He grinned and lifted the handset. "Plus I can be your secretary."

"Screw this," I said. "It's Friday. Let's find somewhere we can work with a beer nearby, I'm thinking beside my elbow. You know anywhere?"

"Most cops here head to Morgan's Grill, eight blocks south. I been there once. Everyone looked at me like I had radioactive lice."

"Pick somewhere you like. No loud music, please."

"Yes, boss," Gershwin winked. "I got just the place for a guy like you."

Gershwin pointing the way, I drove north on Biscayne

for a bit, exiting into an area of older neighborhoods interspersed with strip malls and fast-food joints, everything a tad seedy, like maybe it had once been *the* place to live, but then everyone came back from World War II and wanted bigger houses on wider lots.

"Here we are," Gershwin said, pulling beneath a canopy of arching royal palms and into an asphalt lot bleached gray by the sun. The sign seemed like a relic from Vegas in the forties, crossed palms outlined in pulsing neon and framing the joint's name.

"Tiki Tiki?" I said.

"It's pronounced Ticky Tiki," Gershwin corrected. "But only the regulars know that, and most of them have forgotten it."

We had our choice of parking spaces, the only other vehicles a scarlet Lincoln Continental of venerable age and two six-passenger golf carts under fringed fabric sunshields. The joint was a sprawling single-story stucco and rock structure with a false thatched-straw hairdo. The requisite palms bordered the front alongside a broad, foliage-filled courtyard with stone benches where folks might sit and ponder Polynesian thoughts, a fountain spraying a parsimonious strand of water into an algae-thickened pool where foot-long goldfish swam. A sound system played "Sweet Leilani" into the hot air.

Flaming torches accompanied our walk up a pseudo gangplank into a décor seemingly from a university production of *The Pirates of Penzance*: weathered wood walls, ropes and hawsers strung willy-nilly from the ceiling, false windows like outsize portholes, the openings holding cheesy, over-bright paintings of imagined Polynesian scenes.

I loved the place.

"Zigs!" a voice trumpeted as the door closed behind us. "Is that my sweet boychick?"

A woman nearly as round as tall slammed into Gershwin like a bowling ball and wrapped him in a hug. Her black hair fell to where a waist should have been, and she wore a flowered muumuu that could have tented a den of Cub Scouts. Her earrings were clusters of miniature coconuts and bananas and her fingers wore a blaze of rings.

Gershwin cleared his throat and nodded toward the woman affixed to his rib cage. "This is Consuelo Amardara, Detective Ryder. An aunt."

"*The* aunt," the woman corrected. "He has more *tias* than Bimbo has bread, but I am *the tía . . . tia numero uno*." She reached up and pinched his cheek. "Right, *mi bubbie*?"

Gershwin reddened and turned to scope out the interior. Two elderly men sat at the bar and a half-dozen women of the same generation played mah-jongg at a distant table, each with a brightly colored drink at an elbow. I figured they'd puttered over on the carts, probably from a nearby old-folks home.

Ms Amardara patted Gershwin's belly. "Skinny as a stick! When was the last time you ate, Ignacio? How about I fix you a poquito nosh?"

I was enjoying Gershwin's discomfort, but not as much as I was enjoying Miz Amardara, an amazing hybrid of Latina mamacita and Jewish mother, her speech the intersection of Crown Heights and Spanish Harlem. She turned an appraiser's eye on me.

"And you could use a few pounds, also. Let me fix a plate of sandwiches."

I shot a glance at the drinks at the ladies' table. "Actually, I'd prefer a cocktail, Miz Amardara. What's your best rum drink?"

"Consuelo's Delight: three rums – light, golden, and demerara. Plus coconut milk, lime, papaya, and my special secret ingredient."

"We'll take two."

Gershwin shot a look at his watch. "Aren't we still on duty?"

"We're detectives," I said, moving toward a booth in a shadowy corner. "And I want to see if I can detect the secret ingredient."

Amardara shuffled to the bar and Gershwin followed me, looking dubious. I picked a seat in a back booth dressed with an orchid and candle flickering from the top of a squat, ceramic palm, giving Gershwin a raised eyebrow as he sat across from me.

"Ignacio?" I said. "Your first name?"

He nodded. "My father was Jewish, my mother Cubano. She got to pick the first name."

"And the middle?"

He sighed. "Ignacio Ruben Manolo Gershwin. As a

99

kid I was nicknamed Iggy. I was kinda hyperactive, zigging and zagging all over the place. A teacher started calling me Ziggy and it stuck."

I smiled. "If I'm to judge by your aunt's patois, there's a big Jewish clientele here."

Gershwin grabbed a menu from a nearby serving cart. The first spread displayed pseudo-Polynesian offerings. I flipped to the next spread and gave Gershwin a raised eyebrow.

"Pastrami is Polynesian?"

"A lot of the surrounding community's Jewish, has been forever. The bused-in clientele includes a lot of Jewish tour groups from New York. Auntie spent upwards of twelve hours a day here for over two decades and she's part Jewish by osmosis. I grew up thinking chopped liver was a standard burrito filling."

"She raised you?"

"For several years. It's a long story." His face didn't invite asking for an explanation.

Miz Amardara bustled up and set two tall and frosty glasses before us. I lifted the glass to my lips and pressed them through foam and took a sip. My eyes rolled back in ecstasy at a sweet taste leavened by tangy citrus tartness, a soft kiss heightened by a transient touch of teeth. And drawing all the tastes into harmony was a dry and elusive perfume that melted away the moment it appeared.

"Magnificent," I said, the hush in my voice displaying

reverence. "And as a secret enhancement, the touch of cloves is perfect, Miz Amardara. You are a genius."

"Cloves," she gasped, framing a dropped-open mouth with her fingertips as she backed away. "One sip and the man says cloves."

"Uh-oh, Detective R," Gershwin said, shaking his head, "I think you just made a friend for life."

14

Leala awakened on a mattress on the floor of the room that smelled like sweat. The clock on the floor showed 6.42 a.m. The day said SAT. She was in the basement of the *discoteca*, Leala knew, dark and cave-like with rooms in all directions. Some were locked, others weren't. At the far end of the hall was a door made of thick metal fence with two big locks. You could see through the fence to the bottom of the stairs that came from the *discoteca*. Pipes ran along the walls and ceilings and you could hear music from above.

Is Yolanda back? her awakening mind asked.

Last night the man named Orlando entered and grabbed Yolanda and said she was going to be in a parade. When Yolanda told the man she did not want to go, he laughed and dragged her down the hall to a stinky bathroom.

"Wash yourself," Leala heard the man tell Yolanda. "Then put this stuff on. I've brought a lipstick and make-up . . . you like playing dress-up? Tonight is big time dress-up, little one."

The Orlando man had left the door open and Leala peeked down the hall. After a few minutes she saw Yolanda exit the bathroom, her face painted like a doll and a bright red ribbon tying her hair back. She wore a short pink dress and her feet were in pink canvas zapatas. The shoes were too large and made a clopping sound as the man unlocked the grated door and pushed Yolanda up the stairs.

With no one to talk to, Leala had fallen into quivering dreams. Dreams of voices. Of doors opening and closing. She blinked her eyes and remembered Yolanda was going to a parade.

What did that mean?

Leala tiptoed to Yolanda's confines. There, on the bed, staring at the ceiling, was Yolanda, a yellowed sheet over her body. Leala crept inside and closed the door at her back.

"Yolanda," she whispered, crossing the room. "What happened? What was this parade?"

Yolanda stared past the ceiling pipes and ducts and thumping music, as if she was looking for God above. Her lips were puffy and smeared with lipstick. Pieces of her hair had been pulled out. When Leala eased the sheet down her breath froze in her throat. Yolanda was covered with bite marks, some just tooth shapes, others broken through the skin.

"Oh, poor Yolanda," Leala said. "What has happened to you?"

Yolanda grimaced and stiffened. Leala heard a rustling sound and pulled the sheet further down: her friend was passing water. It was pink and sprayed down scratched legs smeared brown with dried blood. More blood crusted at the apex of her thighs.

"*Madre de Dios*," Leala said. "What caused . . ."

Yolanda closed her eyes and turned away.

"A terrible thing. Worn around the waist like a belt."

"We have to escape this terrible place. We must think of a plan."

"I cannot think now, Leala. I hurt too much."

Leala studied her friend. She looked *roto*, broken. "I will find a way out, Yolanda. Then I will be back for you."

"Remember *la policía*, Leala? They will put you in jail or return you to this place. That is how it works here."

Leala pointed upstairs. "*They* told us that. And everything they told us has been a lie. But I will be careful. And I will be back."

Yolanda's eyes filled with terror. "I will not be here. They said I would soon go elsewhere to do . . . the work."

Leala pulled Yolanda's hand to her breast, bending to kiss her fingers. "I will find you wherever you are, dear *amiga*. Find peace in sleep and I will find us a way out of Hell."

Leala heard footsteps coming down the stairs. She gave Yolanda's fingers a final kiss and retreated to her room as the grated door opened at the far end of the hall. She heard two pairs of shoes approach, pause for a moment at Yolanda's door, then continue. Leala pulled the sheet to her neck and pretended to be asleep. The sheet was stripped away as the one named Orzibel spoke with a mocking laugh.

"I hope you are rested, little slut. Today is the day you start paying your debt."

15

On Saturday I surrounded myself with the case materials, pages and photos on floor, table and countertop. Whenever I felt about to drown in horror I'd retreat to the deck to suck down fresh air and let the sun beat some of the pictures from my brain. It worked until I shut my eyes.

I was trying to absorb every aspect of the case, true; but it was also true that I was hiding within the files and folders and pictures of torment. Ever since my arrival I had been postponing a call to my brother, Jeremy.

The call was not as easy as it sounded. Jeremy's life was six years longer than mine, and more troubled. Our father had been a civil engineer renowned for brilliant responses to engineering problems, but he contained a pathological anger. When his needs were not met – someone late to the table, an errant glance, a report card less than exemplary – he'd fly into black and violent rages. His anger had focused on Jeremy, maybe because my brother physically resembled our father: fair and blue-eyed and with a loose and angular build. They also shared the same complex and brilliant mind, staring at a problem until it fell into components, then self-resurrected as a solution.

Our mother, simple and rural, had no concept of the situation. When the shattering rages befell our home, she would retreat to her sewing room, the machine's high drone eclipsing my brother's anguished screams and calls for help.

I had just turned ten when I suddenly became the choice for the anger, the beatings, the ranting, unintelligible lectures as I huddled in a corner, trying to push myself into the wall itself. And not only had our father selected me as the focus of his rage, his madness was seeping into every crack of our existence. Where weeks had once passed between rages, the horror now rang nightly through the halls. Another change: whereas our father had always threatened punishment, he was now threatening death.

"Get out here, you little bastard. I made you and I can kill you."

Then, one afternoon beneath a blue Alabama sky, everything changed for ever. My brother Jeremy, sixteen years old, slight and sensitive and his face dusted with gentle freckles, lured our father into the woods, bound him to a pine tree and disassembled him with a carving knife.

"I never seen nothin' like it," I recall one ashen cop telling another on our rural front porch, police cars filling the long dirt driveway. "There was blood and meat ever'where. They found a kidney hanging up a tree."

My brother sailed through the investigation. He soon left for college and a few years passed. Then came word that Jeremy had been implicated in the murder of five women, all with vague to startling resemblances to our mother. Given the mitigating circumstance – insanity – Jeremy was sentenced to life in prison.

Jeremy's first break came when his case was noticed by Dr Evangeline Prowse, the head of the Alabama Institution for Aberrational Behavior. Intrigued by his penetrating intellect, she won his transfer to her institution, lodging him in a sort of maximum-security college dorm alongside some of the fiercest and most depraved minds to ever spring from human seed.

Jeremy prospered, eliciting friendships with hulking, insane murderers and drooling serial rapists, making it his hobby to understand their delusions and motivations, and thereby able to stroll inside their minds and make sense of the floor layout. And thus to control them, at least within certain bounds.

Then, a few years back and for reasons that may never be truly known, Dr Prowse arranged Jeremy's surreptitious escape from the Institution, flying with him to New York City. Within days, all hell broke loose, and I found myself in Manhattan, where I discovered my brother's past was more complex than anyone might think. And while not fully innocent of the murders, his participation was not, I felt, deservant of a life in a cage.

Eluding capture, Jeremy had recently reappeared in the guise of Dr August Charpentier, a retired Canadian psychologist now living in a remote mountain setting in eastern Kentucky and spending his days studying local flora, gardening, and charting financial news from around the globe.

Taking my laptop to the deck, I looked out over the cove, the wind still, the water blue and smooth as glass. I drew up my courage and Skyped Jeremy's computer. A pause as the connection established. His face filled my screen, slender and delicate with large and piercing eyes. He remained in his Dr Charpentier disguise, longish hair and neat, professorial beard, both artificially gray. He wore a blue T-shirt, his chest broader than I remembered, muscle, not fat.

I forced a nonchalant smile to my face. "Howdy, big brother. How's the weather up there?"

The blue eyes tightened to slits and the voice that returned was brittle and Southern and hissed through clenched teeth. "Where the hell are you, Carson? You're not on Dauphin Island. Are those palms I see behind you? WHAT IS GOING ON? WHERE ARE YOU?"

Jeremy was near panic. Despite his repeated proclamations of being an independent spirit escaped from the system and living without the "shackles" of needing anyone, my brother seemed pathologically reliant on my structured world. My life had a pattern, the only one my brother knew, and I had broken it.

I sighed. "Calm down, Jeremy. Take a few deep breaths."

"HOW CAN I BREATHE WHEN I HAVE NO IDEA WHERE YOU ARE?"

"I've experienced a few changes, brother. I'm in Florida. I live in Florida."

"CHANGES? WHAT? WHERE?"

"Easy, Jeremy. There's no shift in emphasis, only in location. I'm renting a house on Matecumbe Key."

A pause as my words sank in.

"You're still a cop?"

"Long story short: A person I knew with the Florida Bureau of Law Enforcement called and offered me a job as an investigative specialist in a new section at the FCLE. The politics at the MPD were wearing me down. Plus I called the Chief of Police some names on television, which didn't enhance my prospects for advancement."

"What of your old partner, Harry Nautilus? Did he finally turn on you?"

Jeremy had an odd jealousy of Harry, probably because he was my prime confidant. "Leaving him was the hardest part, but Harry is nearing retirement and in love with a woman named Sally Hargreaves. I expect to see them here any day, fishing rods in hand."

"And the woman you were diddling . . . Holliday?"

"Um, that's kind of . . ."

Up in the air? Put on pause? I'd wanted Wendy to

come with me, she'd wanted to come with me. But she was into her first year as a Mobile cop and leaving wasn't a smart move.

"You ran through another one, right?" my brother snickered. "Some things haven't changed. You still have that ridiculous animal thing?"

"Mr Mix-up is staying in Mobile until I find a permanent place." The new house seemed quiet without my rambunctious, multi-variety canine companion.

"So tell me about where you're living," Jeremy said. "Paint me a picture."

Jeremy was calming down. He knew my new position on the planet and was programming it into his mind. I spent several minutes detailing the land and my immediate neighborhood, ending with a description of Dubois Burnside.

"It sounds like your dream home, Carson. Right down to having a corpse-dresser next door. You're intending to buy the place?"

"Too expensive. Especially since I'm keeping the Dauphin Island house. I rent to tourists for a grand a week in season, eight in the off. The firm handling the rentals thinks I can keep it occupied two-thirds of the year."

A pause as Jeremy absorbed the information and processed it through his fiscal mechanisms. "An income stream, then? Yes . . . that works. But it's not enough to buy your little Eden in the Keys?"

"Not by a long shot."

My brother understood finances, as he had turned to making money as a new endeavor. Three years ago, after a period of intense study of the stock market, he claimed the market had but two true states, blustering drunkard or scared child. Jeremy claimed gobbets of profit from this insight and I believed him, money too trivial for my brother's lies. The stock market was simply a hobby at which his brilliant but unconventional mind excelled.

He leaned close to his camera, his face filling my screen. "I've got more goddamn lucre than I know what to do with, Carson. I can't buy a Maserati, I can't build a distinctive abode, I can't do anything fun without calling attention to myself, which I mustn't do, lest the constabulary take an interest in my existence. I'll give you the money."

"I thank you for your offer, Jeremy. But I prefer to make my own money, just like you do. Secondly, you can't simply give me money. It would have to be reported."

He stared at me for a long moment. "This event has been hard on me, Carson. Not knowing where you were. I realize I should see you more." There was a strange flicker of mirth in his voice.

"What do you mean?" I asked.

He touched his mouse and disappeared.

16

Monday morning I met Gershwin at a Mexican restaurant on the southern edge of Miami, anxious to brainstorm more on the Carosso connection, our only solid lead.

"You figure Carosso did something weird with the concrete load?" Gershwin said, ladling salsa verde over huevos rancheros. "That was why he was so hinky-dinky?"

"He might have actually done as he said, dumped it. Or diverted the concrete to some site where he got paid for the load. He was afraid of being fired for stealing 'crete. He might not have a thing to do with the murders."

"How about we add pressure anyway?"

A Redi-flow dispatcher told us today was Carosso's off day and we were at his door in twenty minutes. "I hope the guy's taken a shower since Friday," Gershwin said. "It was like standing beside a rotting mule."

I banged the door. "Mr Carosso? It's Detectives Ryder and Gershwin. We need to speak to you again." Nothing. I banged twice again, to no avail. I found Gershwin in the side bushes peeking in the window. "Uh-oh. You better check this out."

I saw a body on the floor and kicked the flimsy door open to find Carosso staring at the ceiling as a syrupy red halo encircled his head, the product of a slit throat that looked like a huge and hideously grinning second mouth. The room stank of blood and released body products. Flies had found their way inside; they always do.

Three Miami-Dade units arrived in minutes, the senior officer a fortyish sergeant named Shep Bertleman. He was a string bean, six-two or so, maybe a hundred fifty pounds with a pocketful of nickels. His eyes were large and thoughtful and his nose had been broken a time or two.

We showed identification, mine making me the de facto owner of the scene. Bertleman was respectful but didn't know me well enough to trust my getting things right so he covered the scene as well. I liked him from the git-go.

When we finished he stood beside me, smelling of talcum powder and a fresh haircut. "FCLE, huh? I hear y'all going through changes over there."

"I'm part of it. Hired over from the Mobile department."

"Celia Valdez, she's fine, right?"

"We haven't had a chance to talk much."

"Ceel was hired outta our department. I was pissed

at McDermott for stealing her. Still, the man knows quality."

The FCLE forensics team arrived like a techno army commanded by a petite woman who could have played lead in a stage production of *Peter Pan*, a layered shag 'do framing a pixie face. I nodded as she came my way, foot-pushing a heavy case across the floor.

"You're Ryder, I take it. I'm Deb Clayton. Pleased to meet you and all that. You found the vic?"

"Me and Gershwin over there."

"Looks pretty cut and dried. Or maybe slit and bled out. You take your look?"

"Yep. All yours, Miz Clayton."

"It's Deb. And welcome to the weird and wonderful world of Fickle."

I looked out the window to see a Miami-Dade Medical Examiner van pulling up. The two departments shared the facilities of the MDME, the FCLE having staff pathologists. From here on, the scene was the province of the evidence pros and medical folks.

Gershwin and I headed out to canvass neighbors, finding the closest one was visiting relatives in North Carolina. No one knew much about Carosso and I got the feeling it was one of those neighborhoods where everyone has secrets and won't poke into yours if you don't poke into theirs.

We watched the ambulance take Paul Carosso on his final journey and headed back to the office, happy to find two desks, two desk chairs, two chairs for sitting,

115

one low couch, two file cabinets and a whiteboard. Each desk had a computer terminal linked to a printer and both phones worked. A box of office supplies was in the corner.

We sat and started digging into Carosso's financial records. An hour of calls to various banking voices revealed that two grand had been deposited in Carosso's account a year ago. Though it wasn't much, it was an anomaly, most deposits being paycheck range: three to five hundred every couple weeks.

Gershwin leaned back with purple skate shoes on his desk and his hands jammed in the front pockets of his paint-tight black jeans. "Maybe Carosso got a big payoff and spent it on something, had two grand left."

"I don't think the guy owned anything that cost more than fifty bucks."

My phone rang, Morningstar. "Hello, Doctor," I said in my most charming and inoffensive voice. "What can I do for—"

"I need those fibers tested now, not yesterday . . ."

"Excuse me, Doctor?"

"Wake up, Diego! Get me more one-quart evidence bags . . ."

I realized that Morningstar had dialed, then started issuing orders, forgetting the phone in her hand.

"One goddamn Coke," she bayed. "How hard is that?"

"YO!" I yelled. "DOCTOR MORNINGSTAR!"

A beat, and I heard the phone bump her cheek. "Yeah, Ryder. I hear you. Whatdaya want?"

"You called me."

"Oh yeah. How about you haul your ass to the site?"

"Haul my what where?"

A pause while she reconsidered her tone. "Can you stop by, Detective? We've got some new information you'll find interesting."

We booked to the site and entered the tent – IDs predominant on our chests – and found Morningstar at the upper bank of examination tables. She looked up as we approached.

"I heard you just sent a body to the morgue, Ryder. Connected to this case?"

"Can't say yet. If it is, it adds a new urgency."

"Doctor Wilkens will handle the autopsy since I seem to be living here. And to that end, we have another complete body extraction."

I saw a body on her side on a reinforced table, almost fetal, legs drawn up, one hand floating in the air, the other below, the spine and rib cage compressed by huge force. Her preserved face projected forward, mouth wide below a straight nose, the empty eye sockets like twin screams.

It was the woman who had called to me from the stone, the one trying to swim free. I knew it was an illusion, that her lifeless body had pressed against the wall of the cistern, her face and hand wedging between stones lining the cistern, eluding the concrete and appearing frozen while swimming.

Morningstar turned to me. "The big reason I called

you here? I'm wondering about the serial-killer line Delmara is pushing."

"Why's that?"

"So far we've pulled nine skulls, seven females and two males. Several skulls provided a look at dentition. A lot of decay, but the teeth display the kind of contemporary dentistry done by first-world dentists on charity missions."

"Meaning?"

"I'm getting there. BELT!"

A tech sprinted over and set a brown leather belt in Morningstar's outstretched palm. The belt was crusted with cement, but a section near the corroded buckle had been cleaned.

"You can't see the words with the naked eye, but under a microscope we've made out HECHO EN HONDURAS – made in Honduras. BRACELET!" Morningstar barked and the belt became a silver-colored ID bracelet, the opening heartbreakingly small. She handed me a magnifying glass and pointed to a cleaned area of the bracelet. I squinted at faint letters etched into cheap potmetal.

"T-e-g-u . . ."

"Tegucigalpa," Morningstar said. "A souvenir from the capital of Honduras. And for the frosting on the cake . . ." Morningstar snapped her long fingers and the bracelet became a three-centimeter-square piece of jewelry.

"There's this, a tin medallion stamped with the Nuestra Señora de Supaya, the patroness of Honduras."

"A serial psycho who targets Hispanics?" I said, my

118

mind racing. "Mainly women? That's what you're saying we have here?" I was springing to conclusions: a killer from the same culture moving in areas he knew, using the native language . . . But Morningstar had other experience and shook her head.

"How much human trafficking did you see in Mobile, Detective?"

"Almost zero."

"South Florida is the entry point for a fair amount of human cargo from the Caribbean and the Southern Hemisphere. Europe, even. I think we're seeing a delivery that went wrong."

"This trafficking . . ." I said, suddenly feeling like the last runner in the Boston Marathon. "Where can I find out more?"

17

Morningstar made me an appointment with an expert. The next morning I threaded through lunchtime traffic up to the University of Miami, parking outside the Sociology department. I jogged the steps to the third floor and found an empty reception office. Classes, I figured.

"Hello?" I called down a short hall with several doors. "Professor Johnson?"

A woman rolled out a door in a wheelchair. That was the first thing I noticed, the second was the eye patch. She was of African heritage and looked to be in her mid forties, moon faced. Her hair was long and braided with bright beads and she beckoned me to her office. "You must be Carson Ryder," Victoree Johnson said in a voice infused with Caribbean rhythms.

"We were handling a case initially thought to be a serial killer, but Dr Morningstar—"

"She told me the details. Have a seat."

I sat in a chair, she rolled around to face me. The office was small and jammed with books and bound reports.

"Was that your opinion, Professor?" I asked. "Human trafficking?"

"Hondurans, mostly female and too poor for regular dental work . . . add that to the quantity of bodies and I'd say it's probable these people died together rather than being murdered by a maniac, though whoever traffics in humans is as cold-blooded as any serial killer."

"It looks like sixteen or seventeen people died. This has happened before?"

"In the Southwest it's becoming common. As the borders tighten, the coyotes – human smugglers – turn to more desolate crossings, like the deserts. Remember the old westerns, Detective? The man on horseback in the desert looks down and sees a bleached cattle skull in the sand? Today he's more likely to find a human skull."

I suppressed a shudder. "Is there much trafficking in the US?" I asked, aware of my country's often dishonorable trek from slavery to freedom.

"The US is not Eastern Europe, or Thailand, or Russia," she said. "but if there are places where people, especially women, are used in vice, trafficking is there."

"Trafficking for sex, then."

"Sexual slavery is the mainstay of human trafficking in the US, women brought here as sex machines. They're forced to work until they fall apart, at which point they're replaced with another machine."

"Are they kidnapped from their home countries?" I asked.

"Most are as willing as contestants on *American Idol*, seeing the US as offering money, a glamorous life, beautiful places to live, delicious foods in every direction. They're easy prey for vultures who ply the villages, men who seek out youthful girls and boys with wide dreams. The typical line is that they get here and do some simple work – gardening, cleaning – for a couple months. After that they have no obligation."

"The garden never appears."

"They arrive to be told they owe thousands of dollars and can work it off with sex acts. Refusal brings beatings, rapes, starvation, drugging. The slaves are stripped of will and do as they're told."

"Why not go to the police?"

A sad headshake. "The law where these people come from is often corrupt and biased against the poor: They're terrified of authority. Secondly, these are rural folks, highly religious and attuned to mores regarding purity. Though their debasement comes at the hands of others, they believe the fault is in them. The overwhelming shame is reflected in the suicide rate."

"Given their daily horrors, I still can't understand why more don't just hail a cop cruiser. It's got to be better than—"

Victoree Johnson reached forward and touched my

knee, her eyes filled with quiet sorrow. "There's another form of leverage. The worst form."

I thought a moment and closed my eyes at the simplicity of the hold. "The old stand-by," I sighed. "Threaten the family back in the home country."

Johnson mimed waving a knife. "Do what we say or your mama loses an eye, a sister gets a nose cut off. It's not a threat. Those who traffic in their fellow humans have no bottom."

"How do they get here? It's not as if there's a thousand miles of border to cross, like with Mexico. South Florida's surrounded by water."

"Lately we're hearing rumors of human cargo brought here in containerized shipping modules. They're packed in like sardines."

"Into a port as secure as Miami?" I'd read how Homeland Security had ramped up checkpoints and procedures after being called on lax security a few years back.

"I figure it's bribery. It takes many people to secure a port, but only one or two highly positioned people to know when human cargo is arriving and pay eyes to look the other way."

I nodded. It was the same with drugs. "Why might these people have died?" I asked, returning to the problem of the column. "There's no desert in South Florida."

"They could have come in on an old truck or boat and carbon monoxide leaked. It's not without precedent. They might have been on a small boat that capsized, that's happened with Cuban refugees. Or perhaps they were inadvertently poisoned with bad food, or smuggled in beside bags of poisonous chemicals in a shipping container."

"But if these people are worth so much when they get here – working for sex – why not keep them safer on the journey?"

A sad smile. "You ever see a hog truck out on the road, Detective Ryder? How much protection does it get?"

"There are millions of pigs shipped every year."

"Exactly," Johnson said. "Who cares about one lousy shipment of bacon?"

"Did you make the delivery to Madame Cho?" Amili asked. She sat at her desk with laptop in hand. Orlando Orzibel lounged on the couch and pared his nails with his knife. The late morning sun had brightened the cloudless sky to a brilliant hue and clear light streamed through the window.

"I had Chaku run the product over."

A raised eyebrow. "You did not go personally?"

"I prepare them, others deliver them," Orzibel sniffed. "I am not Federal Express."

"Who did you select?"

Orzibel frowned at the open window and strode over to pull the drapes, then returned to the couch. "Luisa Mendoza and Leala Rosales."

"Were they ready?"

Orzibel waggled his hand, *so-so*. "As they ever are

when they're that fresh. But Cho is stern with training and discipline, so Leala and Luisa will soon be industrious little tug-job factories."

"And Yolanda – how is she?"

"I don't think medical attention is needed."

"How long until she's fully recovered?"

The unconcerned flick of a hand. "Does it matter? All expenses are paid by the client."

"The freak."

"Call him what you wish. I pad the doctor's bill, of course," Orzibel grinned. "We make more money when he hurts them."

"No amount of money covers the risk."

"What risk? Chaku stepped in when things got loud. The client was angry for the moment but thanked him later. He actually tipped Chaku for restraining him in his wilder impulses. Chaku said even he was frightened by the man's . . . passions."

Amili tapped at the laptop and frowned. "The freak is getting more passionate, Orlando. Two sessions last year, four already this year. Last year the girls returned frightened but not injured. This year Mr Chalk has hurt three, two quite badly."

"He has the money to pay for his pleasure." Orzibel paused and turned his gaze to Amili. "Once the client was in a clear mind, he wanted to have a discussion, to feel me out on a subject. He stepped into this particular pond very delicately, and when he knew he could trust me, we went swimming together."

"Get to the point, please."

Orzibel turned. "The client would like to purchase a girl, Amili."

"He does. Several times a year."

"You don't understand, Amili. Mr Chalk does not intend to return the girl. It would be impossible."

18

"How long since you checked table fourteen, Michael?"

Michael Ballentine and Alberto Fuentes spoke quietly and polished glassware behind the copper-clad bar in the Orchid Lounge, the main watering hole in one of the premier hotels in Key West. Far from the din and tumult of Duval Street, the hotel was near the airport, nestled amidst stately king palms and lush, multitiered landscaping that provided a buffer between the hotel and the highway.

Ballentine glanced at his watch. "Eight minutes. I'll head over soon. They're guzzling hard tonight."

"They had a shitty golf round," Fuentes speculated, drawing on two decades of experience. "Or the market dropped."

The Orchid was dark, candles flickering on tables and in booths cushioned with red leather, the candles in crystal chimneys. It was before the dinner hour and a dozen customers populated the lounge, businessmen mostly, talking business and golf.

The door from the lobby opened and the pair turned to a man in an immaculate vanilla suit cut to make the most of a mesomorph build, the lapels slender and the shoulders padded for extra width. His shirt was cobalt blue, the tie a muted scarlet. The man's face was smooth and strikingly round, with a button-dab of nose and high, pudgy cheeks above a red pout of mouth. His mouse-brown hair fell coyly over an eye, pushed back every few seconds, like a tic. Though the man was in his early thirties, he wore the face of an insolent child, a caricature, almost, like a smug ventriloquist's dummy.

The man paused inside the entrance and electric-blue eyes vacuumed the lounge, absorbing every detail, as if crucial to survival. The lips pursed in self-satisfaction and his beurre manié loafers sauntered lazily toward the bar.

"Oh, Christ," Ballentine said. "It's Chalk. I thought he'd gone to one of his homes on the mainland."

"For some reason he's stayed in KW this summer."

"How about you serve him, Alberto," Ballentine said. "He'll leave a twenty-buck tip on a thirty-buck tab."

"No, *amigo*," Fuentes's grin was wide beneath the expansive mustache. "I am in charge, and you need the money more."

Ballentine snapped his vest straight. He took a deep breath, forced a smile to his lips and walked to the guest, now pulling back a stool.

"Good evening, Mister Chalk. Can I get you the usual?"

The man started to sit but paused, head suddenly canting as if hearing a single discordant note in an otherwise perfect symphony. The blue eyes lifted and fixed on Ballentine. *He doesn't look at you*, Ballentine realized. *He looks through you.*

"My usual?" Chalk said as he resumed sitting. His voice was high, almost feminine. "When did I start having a *usual*, Michael?"

"I, uh – don't you generally order a Sazarac, Mr Chalk?"

The guest regarded Ballentine. Seconds ticked by.

"I have ordered Sazaracs before, Michael. That is quite true."

"Then may I prepare you a—"

The man's rising hand cut the barkeep off. "But I have ordered gin and tonic and the occasional margarita, Michael."

"Well, I can sure make you any of—"

"Wait, Michael. I'm curious. How has the Sazarac become my signature drink?"

Ballentine had served people for a year and had been in dozens of meandering, pointless, and often incomprehensible conversations, learning to handle people with skill and diplomacy. But somehow, with this guy, it was like being dropped in a box with the air drained out as the sides closed in.

"I . . . my mistake, sir. I should have asked if I could get you what you had the last time I served you."

"And you recalled that as a Sazarac, Michael? It that my understanding?"

"Yes, sir, I'm sure that's what I recall."

"What if it was a gin and tonic, Michael? Did you consider that?"

Ballentine slapped his forehead. "That's what it was! I don't know how I could have forg—"

The man shook his head sadly. "It wasn't a gin and tonic, Michael. Not a gin and tonic at all."

"The margarita, then?"

"Absolutely not."

Ballentine frowned, perplexed. "What was it, sir?"

The man looked at Ballentine as if he were mentally challenged.

"A Sazarac, of course."

Ballentine retreated into professionalism, bowing slightly and spinning away to the mixing station. "What is it about the guy, Alberto?" he said as he poured ingredients. "It's like he's from another planet."

Fuentes lowered his voice to a whisper. "Mr Chalk has wealth, and when people bow to his dollars he believes they are bowing to him. It gives him the illusion of strength and the more he plays with people the stronger the illusion. Yet for all his dollars, Mr Chalk is a confused child, albeit a nasty one, I think."

"Where did he get all this money?"

"His parents give him vast sums of money to not bother them. They have homes across Europe and he gets the United States as his playground. There is no communication between them but money."

"That's sad. It almost makes me feel for the guy."

Fuentes shook his head and waggled a *no-no* finger. "Mr Chalk is a *monstruo* and you must feel nothing for him, because that's exactly what he feels for you. Be pleasant and professional, give him what he requests and nothing more. And never, ever tell him anything about your personal life."

"Why?"

"He will use it to wound you."

Ballentine shot a glance at the guest, now smiling blankly into the air, if enthralled by a single, glittering thought.

"*Monstruo*, Alberto? What is that?"

"A freak, Michael," Fuentes said. "The man is a freak of nature."

I returned to the site convinced I was seeing a trafficking operation gone awry. Evidently the news preceded me, Roy pacing outside the white tent smoking a cigar. "Doc Morningstar just found a man's sandal in the mix, clearly made in Honduras. Everything's pointing to a single origin for the bodies, which screams human trafficking."

"I've just come from a meeting with a specialist in the area, Roy."

He nodded. "I've heard Victoree Johnson speak before. She's big on public awareness, talks at libraries, social clubs, political get-togethers. Impressive woman who knows the ugliest aspects of the trade, which you'd expect."

"Because she studies it?"

"Victoree was a slave herself. Haitian, sold by her

131

parents when she was eleven. She was bought by a wealthy American couple to do housework. She did other things for hubby and the teenaged son. Oh, and the wife, too. Some family, right?"

"Jesus," I whispered.

"They got tired of Victoree when she turned fourteen and gave her to a pimp who sold her to men who liked 'em with big eyes and little ages. She finally tried to run. But Mr Pimp wanted to teach a lesson to his other girlies so he carved out an eye and sliced off an ear, that's why she wears her hair so long. Victoree stayed with the guy – what happens when being a piece of sexual commerce is all you know. He put her on the street doing mouth jobs at twenty bucks a pop, working from sundown until the last drunk john finally headed home. That was all Victoree Johnson knew for the next three years."

"How did she get free?"

"She woke up one morning in a fourth-floor walkup and found her best friend dead on the floor, an OD. The friend looked so peaceful Victoree decided she wanted to go there. She didn't have enough dope for a hot shot so she figured she'd dive off the fire escape. She had her hooking bag slung over her shoulder, some huge leather thing. Victoree drops two stories onto a freakin' flagpole sticking off the building and snaps her spine. But the strap of the bag catches and holds because Victoree weighs about seventy pounds. She's hanging up there like the ragged flag of everything that could go wrong until someone calls it in."

"That was it? All over?"

"Some cop got her into a program. She was clean in a month and in school in three. Intercessions were made on her behalf and she was naturalized. She's about to get a PhD in Sociology and fights against human trafficking. It's an incredible story. Most sex slaves never live to see forty."

"It's amazing that she did."

A laugh from Roy.

"What?" I asked.

"Victoree Johnson will be forty in eleven more years, Ryder. It's a rough life."

Roy reluctantly stubbed out his cigar against his heel and we entered the tent, the over-cranked air conditioning feeling like a meat locker. "Jesus," Roy said. "One second it's ninety-five, the next it's sixty. Bet you won't miss coming here, Carson."

His words threw me. "Is the operation heading to the morgue? Are they that close to dismantling the column?"

"The case is over, bud. Gone."

"What?"

"We thought the site was a dumping ground for a serial killer's vics. But it's a grave for victims of trafficking. Not our jurisdiction."

Five days into the case and I finally thought we had an angle to pursue. If Carosso's murder was part of the scheme, we might make a connection and start zeroing in on the mastermind. And the case was getting stripped away on a turf technicality? "We're looking at as many as seventeen bodies, Roy," I argued. "And the person behind this is as cold and calculating as any sociopath."

"That may be true. What's also true is the jurisdiction is shifting to Homeland Security. The borders got breached, bud. That's their biz and fifteen minutes after I called, they were here."

We neared the column. I saw two suited men studying the diminished structure, which now resembled a four-foot gray pencil-tip poking from the ground.

"Homeland Security, Roy?"

"As soon as I called to say they had a new case in their bag, they were on their way."

"Will they be as fast to solve it as they were to claim it?" I asked, trying to keep my anger in check.

Roy didn't seem to hear, instead giving me a fast background as we approached the stairway to the pit. "The senior guy is Sherman Rayles, a former US Army major and West Pointer."

"What was Rayles's last military assignment?"

A pause. "He worked at Gitmo."

Guantanamo. Where his assignment could have involved anything from grilling suspected terrorists to managing the purchase of salad forks. Roy saw my uncertainty.

"He's spit'n'polish, Carson. Dedicated to the mission, y'know?"

"But will his mission including solving the case?"

"Well, of course. But maybe he'll come at it from a different angle."

We descended the steps and the two men turned to inspect us. The older man was Rayles, a bit under average height with a face that would look at home on a recruiting poster: rectangular head, aquiline nose, square jaw with a pinch of dimple, salt-and-pepper hair buzzed short on the sides. He stood as straight as if a bolt of lightning had fused his spine into a plumb line drawn from earth to sky, and his chin jutted like it was his primary sensory organ.

"Carson, this is Sherman Rayles, Deputy Director of Homeland Security, South Florida Division. And this is Robert Pinker, his assistant."

I shook hands with the pair. Rayles leaned back with his knuckles beneath his chin and studied me. Chances were that Homeland Security agents – fingers-in-every-pot types – had noted my move from Mobile and vetted me before I arrived. Depending on who they talked to I would be a free-rolling problem solver or a loose cannon. Unfortunately, HS was a bureaucratic hyperhive, and folks admiring of hive structure didn't generally admire mine.

"Carson Ryder," Rayles recited as if reading from a bullet-point presentation. "Eight-year homicide investigator with the Mobile Police Department. Three years as a street cop before that. Youngest patrol officer to ever make detective. You've earned a reputation for apprehending deranged criminals." He paused. "Among other things."

"Best man with psychos in our business, Sherm," Roy

beamed, his hand slamming my back like I was choking. "Nails 'em like nailing boards to a barn."

"Um-hmm," Rayles said, the eyes narrowing.

"Seems like human trafficking gone bad." I nodded toward the diminishing obelisk to give Rayles's eyes something different to study while I returned the once-over. Rayles's black shoes were polished to an icy luster. His charcoal-gray suit, like his crisp white shirt and blue tie, was pressed so board-hard I knew the combination was his work uniform. He would wear a specific and unvarying uniform for gardening, another for golfing. When he wore pajamas he would think of them as his sleep uniform.

"I read the background," Rayles said, the sturdy chin bobbing. "All the ID'd bodies are Honduran and I expect the pattern will hold."

"How deep is Home Sec's interest in trafficking?" I asked. "After no threat to the Homeland is detected."

Rayles cleared his throat. "We're interested in the routes used by the traffickers. This time it's a bunch of peasants trying to slip in, next time it's a team of bin Ladenites with a tank of ricin."

Robert Pinker, Rayles's adjutant – a thirtyish guy with solid neck and shoulders and green eyes that followed his boss's every move – nodded like a good employee, then bent to study the column. I figured Pinker'd heard all this before.

"Really think you'll find a route?" I asked.

"We'll rattle cages in Honduras. After time goes by

people down there will wonder where family members are and break their silence."

I shot a glance at Morningstar. She was leaning back, but her full attention was on Rayles.

"Time goes by?" I said.

"Right now all these bodies –" Rayles nodded to the column – "are no-names. If the traffickers discover we're on the case, they'll change whatever happened here. A lot of times they know we're coming, so by the time we get there, they've moved on. It's frustrating."

Pinker's phone buzzed and he jogged to the pit wall to take the call. I watched as he made quick notes on a pad before slipping the phone back into his jacket and making subtle eye contact with Rayles, who excused himself. The pair went to the edge of the pit to discuss the notes. I realized Pinker carried Rayles's phone for him, the Major obviously too important to answer his own messages.

As Rayles huddled with Pinker, I considered what he'd said about staying ahead of illegal activities. Few enterprises are as Darwinian as a profitable criminal one. If one lineage to profit is impeded, the organization evolves to circumvent the impediment. If a tunnel beneath the border is discovered via sensitive microphones that detect the sound of shovels, the next tunnel is burrowed near a building site, the construction noise masking the shoveling.

But it bothered me that Rayles's first instinct was providing reasons why he might not succeed, and not the ways he would. Back in Mobile, Harry and I started with the idea that we would prevail, and when reality got in the way, we ignored it or beat it into a means more amenable to our ends.

But I was no longer in Mobile. And Harry Nautilus was no longer by my side.

Rayles rejoined us with Pinker a perfect two steps behind. "I guess that's it for you folks," Rayles said, checking his watch. "I'll pass the files over to a team of our people and they can get started."

I handed him my new business card, the first I'd handed out. "Call me anytime, Major Rayles. Day or night."

He looked at me like I'd started speaking Abyssinian. "Whatever for?"

"I can spare time to sit in on meetings. Toss out an idea or—"

His hand rose to cut me off. "You worked this case when it was thought the work of a deranged mind, which put it in your jurisdiction. What I see are illegals who slipped in under the radar, which puts it in mine. I thank you for your concern, Detective Ryder, but I doubt we'll need your help."

19

Madame Cho straightened her silk sheath – bright orange, embroidered with Chinese dragons, one side slit to mid-thigh – and crossed her legs as she sat on the tall stool in the anteroom of the Taste of Heaven Massage Parlor. It was her newest parlor and best location yet, just off Interstate 95, where men could see the tall sign from the highway and exit at the next interchange for some special relaxation. The room was dimly lit, perfumed with jasmine incense, and decorated with sedate paintings of pagodas and framed Chinese calligraphy, all bought on sale at Pier One. The man who supplied the towels once asked what the symbols said.

"How I fucking supposed to know?" Madame Cho had yawned. "You think maybe I'm Confucius or something?"

Cho pulled her calculator and began tallying the previous day's receipts. A national gathering of appliance dealers was in town, men mostly, with money to burn on food and drink and pleasures of the flesh. Madame Cho had several of her girls passing out handbills near the convention center and hotels. She also paid hotel employees to recommend her establishments, and nighttime business had been good.

She heard the swinging doors to the rear of the parlor, looking up to see Leroy Hotchkins, the bouncer. Hotchkins was nearing fifty, an ex-Arena Football player in earnest recovery from crack addiction. He was big and black and when a customer was too drunk or didn't finish in the allotted time and got riled about paying more, his appearance usually chilled the situation.

"Where the hell you think you going?" Cho said.

"To the Seven-Eleven. I wanna Big Gulp and the *Herald*. There's only one customer back there."

"Hurry your sorry ass up. I don't pay you to . . . shit, I've got no idea what I pay you for."

"I'll take off the next Saturday night you got a car-dealer convention in town and you'll find out quick."

Hotchkins left and the door swung slowly back to the frame. "Close goddamn door!" Cho screeched. "I'm not paying to air condition the outside."

Cho muttered and went back to her calculating. A minute later the rear doors swung open and Cho saw a balding, fortyish man, tucking his blue shirt into gray slacks.

"I want my money back, lady. The girl. She won't . . . massage. She just stands there with tears dripping down her cheeks. Jesus."

"I'm very sorry, sir. She's new. I get you another girl right now."

"I don't feel like a massage any more. I want my money back."

"Another girl treat you right. You get massage just like you want. Refresh you all over."

The man's hand was out, fingers scratching the air. "Money, dammit. Now."

Cho paid and the man stomped out the door just as a trio of smiling customers were entering. The look on the departing man's face made the newcomers turn away. Cho picked up a bamboo backscratcher and went to a room in the back, opening the door to see a head-down Leala Rosales beside a massage table.

"What you doing to my business?" Cho demanded.

"Please, I want to go home," Leala said. "This is a terrible place."

"Little bitch!" Cho brought the backscratcher across the girl's arm like a riding crop. "I give you good room, oil, solid table, towels. I pay for everything. All I ask is for you to give the handjob!"

Cho whipped at Leala with the backscratcher. Leala screeched and batted at the whipping backscratcher as welts rose red and angry on her raised arms and hands. Cho began flailing at Leala's face and driving her into a corner.

141

"I'll beat your eyes out. Try to make the money blind!"

Leala cowered, the bamboo stinging across the skin of her face. Cho drove in harder, screaming curses as the stick blurred in the air. Then, from seemingly nowhere, Leala screamed and lunged at Cho, knocking her fully across the room. Cho's scrambling legs tangled and she tumbled to the floor.

Absolute silence. The pair stared at one another for a split-second, Leala as if absorbing new information, Cho in unbridled fury. Cho stumbled to the door, calling down the long hall. Within seconds four other young women were in the room, their eyes expressionless. They were heavily made up and wore plastic Chinese shoes and thin Oriental robes that stopped at mid-thigh.

"Beat her," Cho demanded, pointing at Leala. The four women's eyes were dull and perplexed. They looked at one another.

"Wha' for?" one asked.

"I'm ordering you to beat her," Cho repeated. "I see blood and everyone gets a half-day off next week."

One of the masseuses, a heavier, Asian-inflected girl with dead eyes beneath baby-doll bangs punched Leala in the face.

"Harder!" Cho yelled.

The large girl punched Leala again, knocking her to the floor. Tentatively, the other girls stepped up and started kicking.

"More," Cho yelled. "Kill the bitch!"

Leala tucked into a fetal position as kicks rained in

and Cho whipped at the girl's flailing arms with the backscratcher. Then, as if levitating, Cho was lifted straight into the air.

"That's it," Hotchkins yelled to the girls, a struggling Cho locked in his arms. "It's over. Back to your rooms NOW!"

As if a switch had been flicked, the girls stopped kicking Leala. They padded away like robots as Cho wriggled furiously in Hotchkins's grip. "Let go me, ape-man. I kill little whore!"

"That's just it, madam," Hotchkins said. "You pay me to protect them."

"Not from me, stupid man."

"If you tear her up, how you gonna get your money back?"

Cho stopped fighting. "Put me down, big fool."

Hotchkins set Cho on terra firma. She glared at Leala but seemed afraid to approach her. "YOU! Get your ass out to lobby. You going back to store for refund."

I followed Roy outside, leaving Rayles and Pinker to confer with Morningstar. "So that's it for the investigation?" I asked when the doors closed behind us and we crossed the parking area. The air was hot and purple-bottomed thunderheads boiled in from the west, their rumpled crowns lit white as cotton by the sun. The squall would cross us momentarily.

"You can go back into relaxation mode, Carson. One nice thing is you're all signed up and ready to go."

"There's still some bodies in the concrete, Roy. What if—"

My words were cut off by a lightning blast and the first hard drops from the clouds. We hunched and sprinted to our vehicles. Roy pulled beside me in his big black Yukon, yelling over the pounding rain and beating of his wipers.

"How are things out there on Matecumbe? Everything working out all right?"

"It's a helluva place, Roy. The house and land."

"Any other places nearby catch your eye?"

"Haven't had time to look. Why?"

"The legal types want to put the place on the block soon, part of a large auction of confiscated property. Guess you'll have to find other digs, bud."

"Shit. How soon?"

"A couple weeks. Uh, that's max."

"Any idea what the place will sell for?"

"It's appraised at a million-six. I told you not to get too attached."

I smiled and nodded, but felt like I'd been kicked in the sternum. "See you later, Roy. Thanks for the heads-up."

I drove out to Matecumbe in a funk. I had gotten attached to the view. The open living area. Having my own private jungle. Plus I enjoyed having Burnside as a neighbor.

I arrived without recalling the drive, fixed a Myers's and tonic and slunk to the deck. The chlorophyll-laced

144

air from the surrounding tropical forest smelled rich and fecund and primordial. I looked over my green and private cove as an elegant white schooner crossed the far blue waters. The thought of moving elsewhere was depressing, but there was nothing to do but bite the bullet and go.

A half-hour and a second rum passed. My funk deepened as the sun bent to the west and the breeze freshened, adding a salt scent to the colors of Paradise already filling my head.

My message alert went off and I checked the screen. SKYPE ME.

Jeremy, probably making sure I hadn't moved to yet another state. I sighed, went upstairs to the computer, and made the connection. My brother wore a T-shirt emblazoned with the logo of a food co-op in Lexington, his neck thicker than I recalled. He sat in an expensive ergonomic chair in his second-story office, the window wide behind him and offering a verdant glimpse of the eastern Kentucky forest, pines and maples, oaks and poplars. His sensitive microphone picked up a woodpecker tapping in the woods at his back.

I watched him take in my surroundings via my camera, so I slow-turned the computer to give him a quick scan of the living area and kitchen.

"Spiffy-looking place," he said. "Have you filled the new Taj with a harem yet?" His eyes sparkling with mischief, he stuck a finger in one nostril and twanged out a cartoon-Arabian melody on the other. I responded by blowing out a breath and taking a drink. He leaned nearer the camera, concern in his eyes.

"You look tired, brother. Having a hard day?"

"I'm being booted from the Taj. Seems the place is going on the market earlier than figured."

A frown. "Oh? Where will you go?"

"Miami, maybe."

"I prefer you in the Keys, Carson. You're more stable on the water."

"What?"

"You're a delicate little flower, brother. When you're not sufficiently watered, you wilt into crankiness."

"You get a D for metaphor."

"You know I'm right. How long do you have?"

"I'm still half-packed. I'll look for a place next week."

"*Hello?*" called a voice from my gate intercom. "*You in there, Alabama?*"

Jeremy frowned and canted an ear. "Is someone with you?"

"*Yo! Detective Ryder. You back there in that jungle?*"

"It's a guy I'm working with here," I said. "Gershwin. He's at the front gate."

"Tell him to get lost. Is it George or Ira?"

"*HEY, BIG RYDE! CAN YOU HEAR ME?*"

"Gotta go, brother," I said. "He's a persistent sort."

"Wait! How long does it take you to drive to Key West?"

"Under two hours. Why?"

"*I'M GONNA TRY CLIMBING THE GATE.*"

"Just curious," Jeremy said, disappearing from my screen.

I ran to the intercom. "Hang on, Gershwin, for crying out loud. I'm opening the damn gate."

Seconds later I saw him roaring up the drive on a battered motorcycle and looking from side to side in confusion. He stopped and pulled off a blue helmet, still mystified as he climbed the steps. I waved him up the steps and inside.

"*Oy caramba*, Alaba— I mean, Detective Ryder. You really live here?"

"Temporary. I'll be gone in an eyeblink."

"What, you trading it for a mud hut in the veldt?"

"Anything particular bring you here, Gershwin?"

"Did I hear the news right? Are we losing the case?"

I grunted. "Not our jurisdiction. There is no serial killer, just some horrible accident in transport. Or so I keep hearing."

He scowled. "Where does the case go now?"

"To Homeland Security for starters. Probably get passed between a half-dozen agencies until it gets buried under a blizzard of cold-case paperwork."

I sprawled the couch's length, laced my fingers behind my head, and glared at the ceiling. An idea formed and I jumped up, frantically dialing my phone. Morningstar answered.

"I haven't got to the Carosso corpse yet, Ryder. Hold your horsies and I'll look at it as soon as—"

"What kind of person would smuggle young men and

147

women – almost children – into the country as sex slaves?"

"Sick, twisted, greedy."

"Amoral?" I said.

"Totally."

"Congratulations, Dr Morningstar, you've just described a sociopath. My specific field of inquiry."

A pause as she considered my potential ploy. Then dashed my hopes.

"Hunh-unh, Ryder, nice try, but it's grabbing at straws. Homeland Security's got their paws on the case and they're keeping it."

"It was just a thought, Doc. Thanks for setting me straight."

A pause. "Between you and me and the fencepost, Ryder, I wish it could have worked. Rayles sent his team to interview me."

"And?"

"It was the B team, C maybe. A bunch of trainees getting their feet wet. I don't even think Rayles is running it, I think he delegated it to his briefcase-toter, Pinkle or whatever. I wish you guys were running this thing."

I thanked her again. I considered throwing the phone into the wall, but realized that was not only stupid but expensive. So I kicked a magazine across the room, emptied half my glass and lay back on the couch, glaring at the ceiling again. Gershwin leaned against the marble counter separating the kitchen and great room.

"I've never seen you in a shitty mood," he said. "It's depressing."

"Then you've got two choices, Ziggy: leave for happier climes or stay here and be depressed with me."

He nodded toward my glass. "Any more of that rum around?"

20

Chaku Morales walked into the main room of the club. Three women in various stages of undress cavorted on a stage above a long glass-topped bar, one performing improbable gymnastics on a gleaming pole. Morales's massive head rotated as if on gimbals, an outsized robot set on Search. He saw Orzibel near the alley door, signing an invoice for a liquor salesman. When the salesman departed, Morales walked to Orzibel and nodded at the ceiling, meaning upstairs.

"Mama Cho is here. Pissed."

Orzibel followed the behemoth to his office and stepped inside to see Leala, her eyes wet and terrified. But there was something else in them . . . anger? Beside Leala was Cho. She wore a pink and kimono-shaped blouse over a floor-length blue sheath, the skirt slit to mid-thigh. The woman jabbed a two-inch red nail at Leala.

"I want a new girl," she said, her voice like a saw cutting tin.

"What's wrong?"

"She's worthless, cry, not work. Customers lose mood. I demand a new girl and one thousand dollars."

"Why the grand?"

"For time and lost money. I got business to run, can't make money when I deal with stupid problems. Plus I lose three customers."

"I want to go home," Leala said.

Orzibel backhanded her face and dragged her screaming across the carpet to Chaku. "Take the bitch to the basement and I'll deal with her later."

Amili entered the room. "I can't work with all the noise," she said. "What is the problem?"

Cho rolled her eyes. "I have to repeat myself?"

"One of the new girls . . ." Orzibel said. "Leala. She's fucking up."

"No handjob," Cho explained, pumping the air with her fist. "Just cry."

Orzibel looked at Amili. "Mama wants a new one, which is cool. She wants a grand for her trouble, which isn't."

"Who cares what you think is cool?" Cho spat. "I make barely enough to stay open, two hundred a day a girl. I need them work all the time . . ." she rolled her fists in her eye sockets, "not cry."

"Two hundred a day a girl?" Amili asked.

"Times are tough. Everyone doing the handjob to the internet."

"Don't bullshit me, Mama," Amili said quietly. "Maybe you heard how I got started."

Cho's eyes narrowed. "What do I care?"

"You're working them twelve hours a day, sixteen when a big convention's in the city. You're taking all of their income and most of their tips and don't deny it. I figure you're clearing two hundred an hour, not a day. The two hundred a day is what you report to the IRS. How am I doing?"

"You know nothing, missy. You think you some big deal because you fuck your way up the stairs. So what . . . me too."

Amili stared evenly at Cho. "We'll replace the product by tonight. No money back because it's all part of the business. We share risk."

"Girl cries, it wrecks the dream," Cho screeched. "Johns never come back. Your lousy girl cost me permanent business and money."

"Spare me, Mama," Orzibel said. "You make more money than the Saigon McDonald's."

Cho shrugged. "OK then, I get girls somewhere else."

Amili shook her head. "Not an option, Mama. We supply your girls. You wanted an exclusive contract and you got it."

Cho's eyes tightened into slits. "Fuck contract. Girls are everywhere."

"Mama—"

"Talk is finished." She walked to the door, Chaku in the way. Cho said, "Move it, stinking buffalo man."

152

Morales looked to Orzibel, who nodded and Morales stepped aside. As she passed, Mama Cho pulled a twenty from her purse and jammed it into Chaku's shirt pocket.

"Buy some hair for your ugly head," she said, a cruel smile on her lips. "Fag boys should be pretty."

Orzibel followed Amili to her office to check the terms of Cho's contract: eighteen girls a year, monthly payments, three months left to run.

"What will we do with Cho, Orlando?" Amili said. "If she breaks the contract, others will doubt our resolve."

"We? You won't do anything, Amili, I will handle it. I handle all the dirty work very effectively, no? Perhaps it is why you did not snitch about my, uh, time with little Leala." He stepped closer and put his hand on Amili's hip. "And maybe you find me . . . interesting."

Amili put her hand over his and moved it away. "As I have said too many times, Orlando, we work together. Finding you interesting or otherwise is not a choice."

Orzibel studied Amili. "How often does the Jefé come to you, Amili? Enough to quench your fires?"

Amili sighed. "Is there a reason you are entering my private life, Orlando? Tonight, with the problems of Cho?"

Orzibel shrugged and gave up. "Cho will be handled. The problem is Leala . . . something in her nature. She weeps, she sniffles. Then, from nowhere, she fights back. Even after training Leala struck out at Madame Cho."

"Who wouldn't?"

153

"We're not making fighting dogs, Amili, we're creating animals trained to do tricks. If they have the strength to bite, they have the strength to bolt, which puts us all in danger."

Amili thought a moment. "Have Miguel Tolandoro give Leala's mother three hundred dollars and tell her Leala has sent it. We'll set up a call to Leala. Mama praises little Leala for her hard work, whatever. Maybe some head-patting will put the girl on the path."

"Your ways are too complicated for me, Amili. I say we have Mama call as Miguel is breaking her fingers."

"Who has been in Leala's shoes, Orlando?"

Orzibel's eyes flashed with anger. "While you were wearing those shoes, Amili Zelaya, who was running this business?"

"I am not diminishing your experience, Orlando. But I think Leala needs to hear her mama enjoys the money. Leila can then justify her work to herself."

Orzibel stared. "Justify?"

"It makes it easier when there is a justification," Amili said. "Only then can you believe in tomorrow."

Orlando Orzibel left the office, pulling the door at his back and muttering the word *justificación*. He was tiring of *I know this because I've been there* bullshit. It was he who had done everything, including being imprisoned at the age of twenty-four for cutting a man's throat.

Orzibel had been running a street-corner prostitution ring in one of the toughest neighborhoods in Miami, his

154

victim a rival who had stolen three of Orzibel's best money-makers. The man had lived, but Orzibel had taken a lesson from the experience.

Cut deeper.

In the span of fourteen months in the Okeechobee Correctional Institute Orzibel had killed two men and slashed pieces from others. The first one died after only one week, a hulking *mayaté cakero* who mistook Orzibel's handsome features and shining teeth for weakness. Growing up in gangs in Liberty City, Orzibel knew a dozen others in the institution, one passing him a shank, a steel bed slat with one end filed to wicked sharpness, the other wrapped with electrician's tape.

The *mayaté* and an ally came at Orzibel in a storeroom. Orzibel's blade removed a thumb from the ally before going after the main attacker. Orzibel had made sure the *mayaté* spent his last minutes in incredible pain – removal of the testes does that – ensuring that others kept their distance.

Then, after three years, release from prison. He'd worked in the clean world for several months, hating every aspect, but smiling for the social workers and parole assholes. Then, like a test, a real job: the man he'd come to know as *El Jefé* – the Chief – had a product slated for a special, one-time kind of work, but the product had been compromised by a lowly coyote. Orzibel was charged with punishing the coyote. He had devised a spectacular demonstration, even publicizing it within a certain culture.

The coyote's remains had gone into the then secret hole in the field and Orzibel had been elevated to his current position: running the ground operations of the enterprise. That, and enforcement, such as handling the punishment of the *gordo* accountant.

But just like that, Amili Zelaya had told him – Orlando Orzibel – to pat little Leala on the head and shake a finger at her: *Be good, Leala. It pleases your mother*. The woman knew how to wrap El Jefé around her perfect little fingers, but she knew nothing of taming girls who tried to resist.

Fuck Amili Zelaya and this lapse into softness, Orzibel thought. He would have Miguel pay a different kind of visit to the mother.

21

Yolanda was gone.

Her face still stinging from Orzibel's slaps, Leala stared at an empty bed, its sheets unchanged and stained with her friend's blood and urine. After the upstairs confrontation with Cho, Leala had been carried to the basement by the bald monster. He'd unlocked the mesh door and thrust her back into the warren of filthy halls and rooms. Leala had come to Yolanda's room to check on her friend. But she had disappeared.

Leala heard Yolanda's terrified voice echo in her head. *They said I would soon go elsewhere to do . . . the work.*

Thinking she heard the door open at the top of the steps, Leala froze, fearing Orzibel was coming down to continue beating her for resisting the filthy, sinful work at Cho's enterprise. But it was just another of the rats who skulked between basement drains, its feet skittering over a Tostitos bag tossed to the garbage dump of the floor.

Leala crept back to her room and lay atop the mattress, praying she would not hear the hard click of Orzibel's boots as he came down the steps to slap her face. Or worse.

Footsteps? She would hear them, right? It occurred to Leala that whenever Orzibel or the bald monster or the dangerous-looking men were in the basement, their appearance was almost always telegraphed by the thumping of feet down the steps and the clanging of the grated door.

But several times Leala had noticed something interesting: A person would appear or disappear without a stair-step or gate-opening sound. She had even discussed it with Yolanda. They had been talking and suddenly the gangster men were in the basement and throwing bottles of water into the room. How had the pair missed hearing the footfalls on the wood? The rattle of the gate?

Unless . . .

There was another way into the basement.

Amili entered the day's accounting into the laptop and locked it in the safe, the day over. She checked her watch, a vintage Piaget and a constant reminder of *him*. A few months back they'd risen from his downtown apartment bed to go to dinner, do some shopping in the Design District, then return for a second session in the bed. While outside a jewelry store he'd noted her eyes lingering on the watch and bought it without even asking the price.

When she'd protested the expense, he laughed and said be quiet or he'd buy her two of them.

Amili never told him she was studying the watch because she found it so stupidly gaudy. Though it was crusted with shining stones and special metals, inside was a machine that performed no better than a four-hundred-peso Timex. She wore it because he expected to see it on her wrist.

And she'd almost had two of the ridiculous things!

When Amili first arrived in the States, she had spent three days in the basement of the club. Orzibel had been in Honduras at the time, a meeting with Tolandoro. Amili had been rented by a now-dead sadist named Dimitri Bachinkl, who owned four massage parlors near Biscayne Boulevard. Once in Bachinkl's hands, Amili lived in a filthy bedroom with three other parlor attendants whose ten-hour shifts consisted mainly of servicing a bleary procession of penises.

Amili had resisted at first, feeling betrayed by the universe, her face implacably sullen. Ordered by Bachinkl to smile and laugh and "Do like God made woman to do," she remained obdurate until receiving a savage beating. "Use your beauty, little fool," Bachinkl had screamed, the cattle prod stinging like a fifty-thousand-volt hornet. "Use what God has given you and it will make the world easier."

Afterwards he had taken her to his stinking bed, blunting her mind with drugs as he raped her through the night. Barely able to move in the morning, Amili decided to try an experiment in the small laboratory of the massage parlor: Was Bachinkl lying? Or could the pain and brutality be reduced by heeding the Russian's words?

The next day Amili began showing her bright and even teeth in smiles and teasing pouts. She bounced her hips when she walked. She rubbed the scented oils slowly through her palms before her hands went to the customer. She swiftly learned men's rhythms, the quickening of breath, the rise of hips to her shifting strokes. She learned the words to whisper and discovered how men sought praise for the thick fullness of their fluid, even if it was only a flimsy drizzle across Amili's knuckles.

Within three weeks, Amili was the most-requested masseuse at the parlor, yet the success of her experiment proved her undoing. Customers wanted only Amili. While this brought business to the parlor, it pulled business from the other masseuses, who jumped her one night, butane lighters in hand.

"Bitch, we are going to burn some ugly into you."

Amili had escaped into the street with only her hair singed, running desperately into the night. Bachinkl had called Orzibel, who found Amili in the bushes of a Catholic church and dragged her to the basement of the club. Fearful she might have contacted the authorities, Orzibel blindfolded Amili, injected scopolomine and chained her to a bed, asking harsh questions as his knife pricked at the skin beneath her eyes. During the interrogation, Orzibel paused for whispered conversations with

160

another man, his deferential tone indicating that whoever he was talking to was a boss or *the* boss.

After an hour, Orzibel was convinced Amili had contacted no one. The men left, but paused to talk outside her closed door. Still blindfolded and bound, Amili had lain still as stone, listening.

"It's stealing all my time," the unknown man said. "It's all I do."

"Better something is stealing your time than someone stealing your money, Jefé," Orzibel had replied. "Is there no one you know . . . from your other life?"

A laugh without humor. "I can't just pull someone from the accounting department."

"Pay them highly."

"I paid the *conejo* more than he was worth, but it didn't stop him from skimming. God knows how much that bastard stole, but enough to buy a Series M BMW. Red as a fire engine. What does a three-hundred-pound bald-headed Jew need with a red Beamer?"

"Forget him, Jefé. He's forever in the hole in the world. And the fat pig had a very bad day before he got there."

"FUCK! FUCK! FUCK!"

"Easy, Jefé. It's not worth endangering your health with anger."

"I need *someone* to keep the books, Orlando! And to stay quiet."

Perhaps it was the injection or that she felt there was nothing in her life to lose. But Amili had felt her voice well up in her lungs and burst into the air. "I am good with the numbers," she had yelled into the darkness.

All sound died. Seconds ticked past and Amili felt sweat break out on her forehead. Would she be killed for eavesdropping? Amili heard a door open.

"What did you say?" asked the unknown man.

"I was training to be a *contador*, an accountant. Let me do the job."

"You are only a peasant girl," the voice said quietly. "From a village made of mud."

Amili drew every bit of courage to her voice. "How does that mean I cannot have the facility with the numbers?" she demanded. "How can you think so poorly?"

"*Caramba*," Orzibel had whispered. "Fearless. Or maybe she has gone mad."

Footsteps entered the room. "You are a beauty for sure," the voice said. "And doggone, girl, can you ever handle English."

"Because I am smart. Give me a test with numbers."

Not a sound for a full minute. She felt a hand touch her face and resisted the impulse to flinch. "My goodness," the voice had whispered. "Ain't you just something in every direction."

The footsteps retreated in a series of pauses, and Amili knew she was being studied with every pause. The door closed. Minutes later Orzibel returned and his rough behavior had turned to gruff disdain. Amili's bindings were released, though the door remained locked. Two days later she was taken from the room. Expecting to be put into another parlor or forced to dance at a club, she found herself in a tiny apartment in Little Havana.

"What am I to do here?" she asked.

"I am no longer your keeper," Orzibel had said, putting five hundred dollars on the kitchen table and departing.

A *test*, Amili figured. *I'm being watched.* She wired three hundred dollars home and used another hundred for groceries. She went outside only during the day, staying in the neighborhood and talking to no one. After a week Amili identified two men who seemed always at the edge of her vision.

Amili wondered who her watchers reported to. The answer came in the third week of her freedom. She'd come from the *mercado* with arms full of tortillas and beans and plantains, dropping them to the floor when a voice said, "Welcome home, Amili Zelaya. Do the accommodations suit you?"

She had spun to a man sitting in her living room, legs crossed and a drink in his hand. He looked relaxed. There were boxes on the floor beside him. She recognized the voice.

"It is a dream to live here, señor."

It was not a lie. There was running water, even *agua caliente*. An inside toilet. A bathing tub where water foamed in circles. Buttons that performed miracles: lights, cold air from the floor, fans spinning in the ceiling, flames from the stove . . . it was more than she had ever dreamed.

"I'm sorry to have startled you. Are you about to prepare dinner?"

163

"Yes, señor," she said, swallowing hard. "I-I would be pleased if you would join me."

"I thought we'd go out to dinner. To get acquainted, and perhaps to talk a bit of business. I know several very nice restaurants."

"I am afraid I have not the clothes for such things, señor."

"I've taken the liberty of selecting a few dresses. You're a petite, right . . . about a size four?"

Amili still owned the dresses, four lovely gowns. And the jewelry. And – for almost a year – a job in the enterprise. Her job required little beyond basic bookkeeping. There were many different accounts, each with its own *income stream*, a phrase beloved by her benefactor. Money flowed out for supplies and suppliers, profits poured in. The second half of the equation was by far the larger.

Because of the nature of the enterprise, the funds needed close tracking. On the outflow side, one did not wish to pay a bribe twice, or get double-billed for necessities. On the inflow side, one had to be assured that money arrived in the correct amount and in a regular manner. If a payment was too low or late, Amili assessed a penalty charge. Or, in the case of Mr Chalk, the freak, itemize the various medical charges and add a handling fee plus the fees lost due to the downtime of the machinery.

It was time consuming, but quite simple.

Amili phoned for a taxi and watched through the window until it arrived. For eight months she had lived near the Burgos Medical Center in a three-floor Spanish-style apartment complex built in the forties and renovated in 2007, its walls solid and perfect for privacy.

Walking to her door she drifted her fingertips across a wave of red bougainvillea cascading over the wrought-iron fence lining the sidewalk and breathed deep the elegant scent. This was the only apartment building in a neighborhood of colorful houses shaded by palms, homes without grates on the doors and windows. There were no gang signs on walls. People raised children here, good children who went to college.

And using only her wiles and the gifts of nature, she, Amili Zelaya, had risen from pulling *pitos* in a filthy parlor to a fine apartment in a decent neighborhood.

Amili entered her apartment, the shades drawn against the sun and the air cool and smelling of the sandalwood incense she'd burned this morning. She turned on a small lamp in the corner, its blue shade cut with celestial shapes. When all other lights were off, the lamp painted the ceiling with stars.

She removed her clothes, a cobalt Kate Spade jacket and pencil skirt over a chiffon blouse, peach. Her hose were dark and ended in simple black flats. She put the blouse in the wash basket and carefully hung the jacket and skirt back in her closet.

"Why do you dress like a banker and not to highlight your many charms?" Orzibel had once asked, the usual leer on his face.

"One, because I am a business person," she had replied coldly, thinking it obvious. "And two, because I do not wish my neighbors to think I am a whore."

Amili changed into a silk nightdress, pink, the kind she had dreamed of as a child. She returned to the living room, getting on her knees to retrieve the small brown pouch tucked into the springs of the couch, unzipping it and removing a syringe, a platinum spoon and a glassine bag of white powder.

She reclined on the couch, tapping white powder into the spoon and adding a few drops of purified water. She held the mix above a butane lighter until the powder combined with the water. She loaded the syringe and put her foot on the coffee table, spreading her big toe from the adjoining digit. It was a poor injection site, but hidden from all eyes.

Amili slid the needle into her flesh and watched a tiny balloon of blood pump into the glass tube. The sight of her blood made her gasp. She pushed the plunger down. An electrical charge gathered at the base of her spine, then began to climb her vertebrae. When the charge reached the base of her skull it dissolved into a high and warm musical chord that kicked her head back and filled her brain like a symphony.

She reached behind her and turned off the lamp on the end table, leaving only the lamp in the corner. The room became roofed with stars. As the ceiling stretched into the night sky of her childhood, Amili stepped from within her body and flew through the *cielo* until sleep found her and tucked her safely beneath the dark horizon of the world.

Orzibel paced his office as he dialed his phone, the heels of his boots muted in the purple shag carpeting. One wall was fully mirrored. The street-side wall was painted black and the windows hung with plush scarlet drapes. The ceiling and two walls rippled with burgundy velvet, hundreds of square meters of fabric. Orzibel had taken the idea from Elvis's game room in Graceland. Instead of Elvis's Tiffany-style shade, Orzibel had opted for a cut-glass chandelier stolen from a silent-film-era theater in the process of restoration: six feet in diameter with three levels of dangling crystals. Luckily, the ceilings were tall, so he could almost pass beneath it without ducking.

He heard a pick-up on the other end and pressed the phone to his face.

"Miguel?"

"Ay . . . is that Orlando?" Miguel Tolandoro said, his voice at the edge of slurred. Mariachis played in the background and there was the sound of talk and laughter. "The connection is . . ."

"Get outside where you can talk. Now."

"*Momentito, mi amigo.*"

A scraping of a chair and the scuffing of a phone in a palm. The sounds grew distant. "I am in the street, Orlando."

"Do you never leave the *cantinas*, Miguel?"

A wet laugh. "I am a shark on the prowl, Orlando.

167

There are young ladies here and if I am successful, they may soon be there, no?"

"I don't want *cantina* whores, Miguel. I need—"

"There is a church festival here, Orlando. The nearby villages have emptied into the streets and I have approached many sweet and simple girls who yearn for a better life. You will soon meet several of them, I expect. Why do you sound so angry, my friend?"

Orzibel closed his eyes and rubbed the bridge of his nose. "My apologies, Miguel. The day has been difficult. Do you recall Leala Rosales?"

"How can one forget such a perfect treat? So pretty and yet so smart."

"It's the smart that troubles me."

"Why, Orlando? What has the girl done?"

"She remains an independent spirit and has become a danger. I need you to make an example of her mother, and quickly. Then I will arrange a call where the mother can tell the girl what her foolish behavior has caused, and what will further happen if little daughter does not behave."

"Fingers, Orlando?"

"An eye. Not pricked, removed."

"*La mamacita* is in a tiny village thirty kilometers distant. I will pay a visit tomorrow."

"*Gracias*, Miguel. It will save me much trouble."

"*De nada*, Orlando. It is a simple task."

22

It was time to explore the basement. Leala let what she felt was an hour elapse. Judging by the increased volume from above it was late. The paper plate beside her bed held the day's ration of cold *frijoles refritos* and uncooked *tortillas de maiz*. Needing strength for what lay ahead, Leala forced the tasteless food down her throat. *The* discoteca *above me is very large*, she thought. *The basement will be very large as well.* One could not gauge its size because, behind the heavy door of fence that prohibited escaping upstairs, the basement had been chopped into many tiny rooms. There was the central hall that was two meters wide, but from it were many tight passages, like tiny dark alleys. Sometimes the alleys led to other alleys, sometimes they stopped at a wall.

It was a *laberinto*.

She headed deeper into the labyrinth, where there was

no light. Light came from bulbs in the ceiling, you pulled a string and could see. Leala waved her hand in the dark, found the string and pulled. She saw a dead end filled with fast-food bags and beer cans. An expired rat decomposed on the floor.

Leala inspected every passage that fell from the main hall, finding walls made of bricks, and walls of *concreto*. The latter would be the true walls of the foundation, the others added to make the little prisons. A passage from the basement to the outside, she reasoned, would go through a concrete wall.

Leala returned to a section of the foundation wall. The alley between it and the brick wall was as black as the bottom of a well. She took a deep breath and entered the dark, hands feeling both walls as she stepped down a path barely wider than her shoulders.

She was stepping ahead when her left hand fell into air, the wall no longer there. Leala touched ahead and to the right: walls. The path turned left. Leala followed it another several steps and nearly screamed when something touched her head. It went away, returned. She tentatively reached into the darkness.

A string. She tugged it and a bulb high in the joists came on. Another door of the heavy steel mesh was ahead, but the lock was hanging loose. The door swung open to a lit room. Against one wall were boxes labeled *Frijoles Refritos* and holding large cans of the dismal refried beans she was fed twice a day. A bin beside the boxes was over-filled with empty cans, tortilla bags and water bottles, the refuse spilling across the floor. Leala imagined the mean-eyed men filling plates with beans and tortillas before taking them to the prisoners.

The room smelled of fresh cigarette smoke. Someone had been here recently.

On the other side of the room was an opening and Leala stared down a tunnel twenty meters in length. At the far end was a series of concrete steps rising four meters, with a small platform at the top. And on the platform . . .

Yet another door.

Leala's feet moved lightly through the tunnel. The door atop the stairs would be at street level, she knew. She crept up the steps and tried the handle. The door opened to the huge, windowless room of a brick warehouse. To her left was a small room with an open door, a toilet and sink inside. Several large crates were on the far side of the room, the nearer floor was cement and open save for a big white van, the words on its side saying *A-1 Window Treatments*. Behind the van a tall door reached to the ceiling.

Leala remembered the vehicle from the day she stepped onto America, when the others rode in the van but Orzibel flattered her into the big black car. She staunched anger at herself and stepped into the room. If there was a truck door, there must be a people door. She stepped forward.

"Voy a abrir la puerta!"

A voice froze her in the center of the floor. There, to her right, a man sat inside a little room with big glass

171

windows. He was on the phone and if he turned but slightly, would see her. Leala stepped back behind the door with her beating heart so high in her throat she feared choking. The man in the windowed room had almost turned her way, but when the big door opened he had looked toward the portal.

She watched a neon green pickup truck pull next to the van, its bed stacked with brown cartons. Two men exited and Leala recognized one of them as the gangster type who brought the plates of miserable food. The men began unloading the cartons onto a two-wheeled cart. The other returned to his little office.

"*Andale*, Raoul . . . Hurry!" one man said. "Let's make the delivery and get done. My *pito* has a hot date."

"Your *pito* has a date with your hand. Why can't we take the food through the club? Why roll it all this way?"

"The *policía* might see us pushing beans and tortillas into the club and wonder what they are for. It's not a supper club. It is only a place for men to find women."

"Ha! Who would look that close?"

"It is orders from the Amili one. Things have changed since her arrival. *Muy* cautious, that one."

"I'll bet she loses that caution in a bed. I would like to get her to my—"

"Be careful of what you wish. She must surely be the property of Mister Double O."

"El Diablo! I will push the cart and wish no more."

Leala retreated down the steps and compressed herself into the recess in the wall, praying the shadows kept her covered as the men wrestled the cart down the steps and rolled by. Fortune lay on Leala's side, she thought. She had chosen to seek escape on a night when food was being delivered to the *laberinto*. Otherwise the back entrance would have been locked as tight as the front.

When the men entered the maze beneath the *discoteca* Leala ran up the steps. The watchman was not in the windowed room and the door to *el baño* was closed. Leala took a chance the man was relieving himself and ran to the office. As she had hoped, there was a door to the outside. She quietly slipped into hot air that smelled of stale beer and the exhaust of cars.

The night was painted in an electric rainbow, signs beating brightly from every direction. Leala looked for the *discoteca*, but the warehouse was between them and she was on a side street. On the corner was a building the color of a canary, PALM BREEZE MOTEL, its sign blared, HOURLY-DAILY-WEEKLY. Next to the motel lights proclaimed PAWN SHOP – OPEN 'TIL MIDNITE EVERY NITE. A bar was beside the pawnshop, no windows, just a sign saying PACKY'S HOT SPOT, BEER and LIQUOR. The street seemed paved with trash: newspapers, food wrappers, paper cups, beer cans, cigarette butts. The smell of urine and vomit rose like fog from the gutter.

A traffic signal changed down the block and the street filled with cars and trucks, horns and engines. A rusted station wagon rattled to the curb, the drunken driver leering out the window. "Hey chicka, how much *por felación*?" He mimed pushing a head into his lap.

173

"What?"

"I got twenny bucks, chicka. I meet you in the motel lot, no?"

Leala walked away as quickly as her legs would carry her, the drunk yelling at her back. The traffic was frightening and Leala turned past a closed bodega. Three men sat atop a car in its parking lot, drinking from bagged bottles. They hooted and whistled at Leala, but didn't get up.

She kept moving.

Within minutes the clubs and motels and bars turned into tiny houses on palm-fronded lots, the doors and windows grated, vehicles parked haphazardly in the street and across the pavement. Streetlamps dusted the night with a gauzy white, the air steamy and thick. It was a poor neighborhood, Leala knew, but safer than the busy avenue.

After another ten minutes the houses and lots grew larger and their portals were ungrated. The flowers and palms seemed healthier and better-attended, and even through her fear Leala smelled the sweet perfume of jacaranda and bougainvillea.

She heard a roar at her back and saw headlights veer onto the street. Leala ducked into a yard, crouching behind a tall agave until the lights passed. Struck by a crisp and pungent scent, Leala crept toward a picket fence beside a dark house. Behind it was a blue hole centering the backyard with a long plank of wood projecting across water lit blue from beneath.

La piscina. A pool for swimming.

Leala had been smelling herself and her clothing. Shooting glances at the house, she slunk to the edge of the pool and splashed the clean-smelling water over her face. When the house remained dark she edged into the cool *agua*, dress and all, taking a deep breath and dipping her head beneath the surface, staying under as long as possible, coming up for air, then submerging again, hoping the bright-smelling water was cleaning the filth from her body and her soul and renewing her for the journey ahead.

23

My phone rang and my eyes popped open. I blinked to find focus and read a blurred clock: 10:14 a.m. My hand scrabbled for the phone but my rum-afflicted eyes couldn't discern the name. "*What?*" I barked into the device, noticing I was still in yesterday's clothes.

"Not a morning person, I take it?" Morningstar's voice.

"Sorry," I said. "Not this morning, at least."

"At least you slept, Ryder. Some of us have been working all night. I just thought you'd like to hear that you were right."

"Right about what?"

"We're nearing the bottom of the column and found two seams, which I'll interpret as two additional and disparate dumping events in the cistern. Makes sense, right?"

"I, uh . . ."

"It will, Ryder. Go back to sleep."

I fumbled to my feet to face the excesses of last night's pityfest. Fuzzy recollections arrived as I showered: A diminishing bottle of Myers's. Gershwin cajoling me to the deck as he attempted conversation. Me waving it off and taking a swim, stepping on a lobster and getting my toe pinched before splashing back to shore. When I found Gershwin had left, I'd headed inside and tried to Skype Jeremy while leaning back in the chair with feet on desk and somewhere in there the chair tipped over backward and that's all I could remember.

The kitchen floor was strewn with limes for some reason. I drank a mug of coffee and headed to my car, figuring to drive to the site and see what Morningstar was talking about. My belly fought the coffee and my spinning head felt like monks had used it for gong practice.

I retreated inside, dressed in cutoffs and launched my kayak. The day was already hot and the humidity was in wet-sponge range and I was sweating like a roofer within a minute. I paddled to open water and pulled intervals – racing full-tilt boogie for a minute, arms and shoulders screaming, heart roaring in my ears – then dropping to a lower rhythm for a minute. The toxins started clearing and along with them, my head. I returned to shore a half-hour later and was feeling halfway decent by the time I arrived at the site.

Morningstar's busy night was evident in the diminution of the column, now the height of a footstool, a gray circle in the soil like a Yap Island money disk. She was on the upper level with the tables and equipment, a coterie of techs dusting and bagging and labeling. To my surprise, Gershwin sat to the side, watching the process. His eyebrows raised at my approach.

"Glad you didn't drown," he said. "The last time I saw you was splashing out into the cove. I was afraid you'd swim to open sea, but it seemed you could only go in circles."

"I'm aiming straighter today," I said. "What are you doing here?"

"Watching. Never experienced an on-site operation."

"If Rayles sees you he'll probably boot your ass back to Miami."

"Rayles wouldn't come here, Big Ryde. He'd get too much dust on his shiny shoes. He'd prefer to read the reports. Or maybe have the flunkie read them to him."

Morningstar walked up, her knee-length lab coat flapping open to show jeans and a gray tee. Her hair was cinched back in a ponytail and her knees were dusty from kneeling beside the column.

"Morning, Ryder. I hear you had difficulty accepting the loss of the case last night."

I looked at Gershwin, mouthed *Snitch*. He grinned.

"You said something about seams, Doctor?"

She cranked a finger in the *follow-me* motion and we entered the pit. A pair of techs were carefully ticking matrix from a human form, now half-removed from the concrete. The body wore what appeared to be a dress suit, much degraded.

"There was a discernible seam between JDMS and the Honduran layer," Morningstar said, "averaging two-point-one meters in depth."

"JMD . . .?"

"JDMS for John Doe, Middle Stratum." Morningstar knelt beside the circle of concrete and remains and I knelt beside her. "We're calling it middle stratum because another seam indicates a bottom layer of concrete. It's actually a bit different here, more sand in the conglomerate."

She pulled a small LED flashlight from a pocket and shone it twenty centimeters above the base. I saw a defined separation between the concrete, the lower layer having dried before the upper portion was added.

"Keep me posted," I said.

"It's not your case, Ryder. It belongs to Homeland Security and Rayles. You're long gone, remember?"

I checked to make sure no one was within hearing range. "Is it possible to send me daily reports, Doctor? Maybe without Rayles seeing where they're going?"

"Having trouble letting go?"

I looked at her without reply.

"I guess sending a few reports is within the realm of possibility," she said.

"Yo-ho-ho," called a voice from above. We looked up to see Vince Delmara's nose coming down to the pit, followed shortly thereafter by the man himself, usual dark suit and fedora.

"What brings you here, Vince?" I asked. "Didn't you hear the case has been expropriated by HS?"

He nodded at the short column. "This case, maybe. I wanted to ask the Doc if she'd found anything new I could use in the Carosso murder. Maybe match the concrete here with stuff at Carosso's home."

Confusion. "The Carosso case went back to Miami-Dade? What?"

"Those HS guys don't want the Carosso investigation, can you believe that?" Delmara said. "They said the Carosso killing was Miami-Dade's responsibility."

"Homeland Security didn't want a case that might have a link to the Hondurans?"

"That's what I got from Rayles's flunkie. He was like, 'Screw Carosso, what does a dead truck driver have to do with NatSec's investigation?' That's bureaucratese for national security, by the way, not insect love."

I shook my head. "Like I figured, the only reason they wanted the Hondurans was for the Importance Portfolio."

"Carosso's now Miami-Dade's problem. It seems like his next-door neighbor's back from a trip, and I'm going to see if she can add to what you guys dug up when the case was FCLE's. Jeez . . . I can't keep up any more."

"I've got nothing I can add, Vince," Morningstar said, answering Delmara's question. "No way I can connect the concrete here to anything Carosso might have had on his clothes. It's been months, years."

"Hope springs eternal, Doctor," Delmara sighed.

Gershwin and I followed him from the tent. A hawk

circled above, as if hoping we'd keel over and provide breakfast. Delmara pushed back his hat and wiped his sweating brow on the sleeve of his blue suit.

"It ain't even ten and I'm wilted."

"Maybe the suit? The dark fedora?"

"It's a summer suit. The hat provides shade. This has gotta be global warming."

Heat shimmered from the flat ground and I toed a half-buried iron nut from the parched sand, the nut now crusted with scaly rust. I suddenly recalled a question I'd had for Delmara.

"That first day, Vince. You said you were checking the provenance of this land tract. Anything come of that?"

"Yeah," Gershwin added. "Someone knew the cistern was here."

Delmara shook his head sadly. "I circulated the report, guess you weren't in the loop yet. This parcel, twenty-eight acres, got bought three months back by Darco Development, a consortium that builds mini malls. They ID patterns of upscale residential growth, find cheap land a couple miles past where the growth is heading . . . build and wait." He nodded toward the uncleared land. "We see scrub and buzzards, Darco sees a future population center."

"Before Darco?" Gershwin prompted.

"Owned by Allen Feldstein, a retiree who had a cab company in New Jersey and retired to Coral Gables in 2001. He bought the parcel seven years back and built a home, planning to subdivide the rest into plots . . .

never happened because Mr Feldstein stroked out a year later. Darco bought it from his widow, who's now eighty-eight."

"Maybe Feldstein knew about the cistern."

"I talked to the wife. Feldstein walked the land exactly once, a few days before signing the deal. 'He went out to see about places to put houses and getting all that junk cleared off,' is what she said. She said Feldstein wouldn't have gone out there again by himself. He was terrified of snakes."

"Before Feldstein?"

"Owned by a guy named Driscoll for almost forty years, cattle-rancher type. Never ran many cattle out here, having a bigger tract a few miles north. Might have been Driscoll who built the cistern, maybe to trap extra water for his stock. I'd have asked, but Driscoll's been dead a dozen years."

"Leaves him out. Anyone else around? Or any thing?"

"A couple miles down the road there's a dying town with a dock, bait shop and grocery, and a little restaurant-bar-gas station. I put the average age of the residents at a hundred and thirty-seven."

I knelt and scuffed my hands through the sand like it could tell me something. My fingers pulled a ten-inch bolt from the soil, rusted half through. I stood, tossed it deep into the scrubby trees, and turned to Delmara.

"So who knew the cistern was here, Vince?"

"Probably not anyone still alive."

He sighed and turned to his cruiser, off to interview the last remaining neighbor who might know Paul Carosso.

"Mind if Ziggy and I tag along?" I asked.

"Sure, come meet Hattie Doyle, though I'm doubting she has anything to add. You sure you want to waste your time?"

"It's that or talk to rental agents."

He gave me a glance but didn't ask, and we walked to his car. He pulled his keys, then paused, looking across his roof line at the Rover.

"How about you drive, Detective Ryder? I wanna see how it feels to be on a safari."

24

After reluctantly leaving the wonderful blue pool, Leala had spent the night in a nearby park, snatching shards of sleep between a pink wall and a thick growth of scarlet azalea spiked with agave. The spot was small but concealed even from the moonlight, allowing Leala to sleep naked with the thin yellow dress drying on the spikes of an agave.

When the orange sun climbed past the trees and began brightening her hiding spot, Leala continued down the street, ready to leap from sight. What would they do to her for escaping?

A memory returned and Leala's heart stopped. She wavered in the street on loosened knees. What had she been told by the Amili woman?

"If you don't behave, we will punish your mama,

Leala. If you do anything wrong, your mama will be hurt very bad. Do you understand?"

She had to call her mother. Leala ran down the block and saw two heavy women talking on the sidewalk. Pushing aside her fear, she approached.

"Pardon me, señoras. I must make a call to Honduras. How might this happen?"

The women looked at Leala's bare feet and wrinkled clothes, then at one another. "Where are you from, little girl?" a woman said, her plump arms crossed and disapproval in her eyes. "What is your story?"

"Please, good lady. There is trouble and I must tell *mi madre.*"

The women again looked at one another. Silence until one of them pointed and said, "The *abacería* down the street. You can call from there."

Leala ran until she saw a small sky-blue grocery on a corner criss-crossed with electrical and telephone wires, its walls spidered with crumbling stucco and its windows plastered with signs. One of the signs said, TELEFONO A CENTROAMERICA Y SUDAMERICA. Another, hung in the front door, said, OPEN/ABIERTO. Leala stepped inside and saw an aisle crowded with crates of bananas, mangos, papayas and limes. Other aisles held canned goods, toiletries, spices, food mixes. There was a freezer for dairy products and soda pop and beer. Items hung from the ceiling and were piled against the walls.

An old man sat behind a counter smoking a cigarette.

His yellow and wizened eyes wandered over Leala with approval.

"I would please like to make a phone call," Leala said. "It is a hurry."

"*Locale?*"

"Honduras."

The man gestured to a rack of colorful plastic cards at his back, marked by countries and denominations and time allotments. "You will need a phone card, pretty one. I can sell you a five-dollar card good for twenty minutes. It is a good deal."

"Five dollars?"

"Plus tax. Does the pretty lady wish a card?"

Leala's head had been held under water. She had been raped, beaten with a stick and kicked. She had been slapped, fed slop, forced to live with rats and make her soil in a bucket. She had been made to do terrible, nasty things time and time again. But she had not earned a single *centavo*. She had no money.

But she had received lessons in making it.

Leala looked across the grocery and when she saw they were alone, stepped to the door and turned the sign from OPEN to CLOSED. She returned and leaned on the counter to better show the tops of her breasts as her mouth hung open. *Look sexy and stupid*, Orzibel had once instructed. *It makes money.*

"I will trade you for a phone card," Leala said.

"What do you mean?" the old man frowned, looking between Leala and the door.

Leala nodded toward the rack of phone cards. She smiled and pumped her fist slowly in the air.

After earning the card, Leala instructed the old man to assist her in the call, then go outside and leave her alone. He assented quickly, needing a cigarette and time to catch his breath.

"Leala?" her mother wailed upon hearing Leala's voice. "Oh my baby!"

"Mama, shhhh. Please, Mama. I need to talk to you, fast. There are difficulties here. I am fixing them and then I will come home."

"What are you doing? Are you worki—"

"There will be time to talk later, Mama. Now you must listen."

"*You* must listen, Leala. You have to—"

"*Silencio*, Mama! You are in danger from the one who led me away. Terrible danger. Bad people wish to control me through you."

"*Madre de Dios*," Leala's mother whispered. "What do I do?"

"Go to Tegucigalpa and stay with Aunt Esmel. Do not tell anyone where you are going. How soon can you leave?"

"Maybe by the day after tomorrow if I—"

"I mean minutes, Mama."

In addition to everything else, the store also sold inexpensive clothing and shoes. Leala departed ten minutes later in a new blue cotton dress, new sandals on her feet, a bright white scarf to keep the sun from her head, and the largest pair of sunglasses on the rack. She had a colorful woven bag to carry her fruit and tortillas. Plus ten dollars in singles.

The old man was gasping as she left, his legs too weak to cross the floor, and Leala thoughtfully reversed the sign to read OPEN once again.

25

Orzibel stretched out on the couch and used one hand to pull his aloha silk shirt higher up his rib cage, the other drawing a dark-haired head closer to his body. "That's right, baby. All the way down. STOP FUCKING GAGGING! You wanna make money you gotta learn to—"

The cell phone buzzed from the glass table beside Orzibel. He snatched it up, checked the number and put the phone to his ear. "Things OK down there, Chaku? The food get deliv—" Orzibel scowled and pushed the girl roughly away, his thumb yanking toward the door. "Beat it, *puta*. School's out for now."

He put the phone back to his ear, his voice a tense whisper. "I'll be right there. Keep looking."

Orzibel jammed his shirt into his pants, zipped up and ran to the basement, where Chaku waited with three

Hispanic men in low-slung pants and bandana-wrapped heads.

"The Rosales girl is gone, Orlando," Chaku said quietly. "Vanished. We have searched the whole of the basement. Every crack."

"What? HOW?"

"Jaime and Pablo brought food and water through the tunnel last night. It's possible she concealed herself until no one could see her escape."

"What of the watchman in the warehouse?"

"He saw nothing. Neither did Jaime and Pablo."

"*Mierde!*" Orzibel's fist slammed the door. "The girl will call her mama when she gets a chance, all they ever want to do is call mama. I will contact Miguel in Honduras. When Leala calls, Mama will tell Leala to get her tight little ass back here or Mama's heart goes the way her eye did."

"Eye?" Chaku grunted.

Orzibel mimed plucking out his eye. "I will amend the threat to include death if we do not see Leala Rosales soon." Orzibel pulled his phone, paused. "Wait, Chaku . . . you have a photograph of the girl?"

Morales pulled a 3 x 5 picture from the pocket of a black velvet workout suit, a head and shoulder shot of Leala Rosales taken, as was the custom, of every piece of imported product, the photos typically used in the marketing aspect of the enterprise, giving potential employers a chance to study the goods.

"Put copies in the hands of our people," Orzibel said.

"And others whose eyes can see without tongues wagging. Say that good information will receive both my gratitude and a thousand-dollar gift. Also make it known that anyone helping this bitch will feel my steel in their bellies."

Chaku edged close. "Rosales will be somewhere in Little Havana or very close, Orlando. She will feel safer near her heritage."

"A good thought. I will handle Mama, you cast the net in the community."

The huge man cleared his throat. "You will now go upstairs and tell Amili Zelaya of the trouble, Orlando?"

Orzibel's eyes tightened into slits. "It falls on me to shovel the dung like I have always done. I will have Leala Rosales back very soon, and no one need know."

"What will you do when Rosales is returned, Orlando?"

"I will fix the problem permanently, Chaku," Orzibel said, nodding to himself as if a decision had been made. "And make big money at the same time."

Miguel Tolandoro's silver Toyota pickup led a plume of brown dust into the rural village. He was eating a piece of fried chicken and scattering chickens from the road as he wove down a street of brown dirt. Exiting the truck he tossed the bone at a pack of skinny dogs, setting off a fight. He tucked his shirttails into his pants, his voluminous belly making it a job of feel, not sight.

Tolandoro's pointed boots clicked down the cobbled alley as he passed a large four-paned window looking into a simple kitchen, three panes of glass broken out and replaced with tin and wood scraps. The next address was the one he sought, the Rosales household. It seemed the timid little Leala Rosales was proving a handful in the States, but he'd soon make the proper adjustments in the situation.

Tolandoro's rough knuckles pounded the sun-bleached wooden door and he spoke the words memorized on the drive. "Señora Rosales . . . I bring word from Leala, who is living an excellent life in America and working hard for you. She wishes you to have a gift from her labor and to call her on my telephone. May I enter your fine home?"

Nothing. Tolandoro tried again, louder. A face at the neighboring hovel peered out the remaining glass window, then disappeared. Seconds later the door opened and a wizened woman looked out, her eyes filled with anger.

"She is gone. Go away. Stop your noise."

"Where is she, old one?"

"You took her daughter, did you not?"

Tolandoro puffed out his chest and his chin. "Leala Rosales wanted to earn her fortune. It is my business to make the beautiful dreams come true. Where is the mother?"

"You are a pimp," the old woman hissed.

Tolandoro's jaw clenched and his eyes slitted. "Where is the mother, old woman? Tell me before I—"

"She has left for unknown places. She knows her daughter is gone forever. Stolen by a liar and procurer."

"Do not address me like that!"

The door slammed but the old woman continued to yell. "Filth! Pimp! Stealer of babies!"

Miguel Tolandoro started away, but halted after three steps to snatch a rock from the gutter. He turned and smashed it through the last window, which would now need covering to keep out the flies.

"Live in the dark, crone," Tolandoro called through the hole before striding back to his vehicle.

26

Hattie Doyle was in her seventies, wore a pink housedress, fluffy matching mules, and too much lipstick. After apologizing for hair in curlers – "I gotta set it ev'ry day or it looks like I'm wearin' a windstorm up there" – she invited us into her home, small and tidy and filled with inexpensive souvenirs from places like Rock City, Nashville and Branson. Ms Doyle was a transplant from the coal fields of West Virginia whose husband, Delbert, had died three years back from black lung.

She held a cigarette in one hand, an ashtray in the other, and nodded toward the former Carosso household, eighty feet distant over a chain-link fence threaded with moon vines. A sickly twelve-foot palm tottered in Carosso's side yard, held in place by two-by-fours.

"Mr Paul had some ornery-looking critters over there at times, men mostly," Ms Doyle remembered between sucks on the smoke. "A few ladies who didn't really look much like ladies, if you gennelmen get my drift. They'd barbecue burgers out back and get drunked-up. I figured they was folks he worked with at the concrete plant."

"Did you speak to him very much, ma'am?" Delmara asked.

"A little. Mr Paul, he weren't a big talker."

"He have this crowd over much, the ornery critters?"

"Purty regular, twict a month or so.' She paused in thought, tapping the cigarette on the tray. "'Cept I never saw them there when he had his niece visitin'."

"Niece?"

"A year or so back. He had his niece come and stay with him for a couple months. He was keepin' the girl while her parents went through tough times. It was sad."

"Tell me about the niece, Ms Doyle."

She frowned through curling blue smoke. "Hardly ever saw her cuz she stayed inside. Sixteen or thereabouts. Pretty li'l thing, skinny as you git, though. Big sad eyes."

"Caucasian?"

She shrugged. "Musta been a mix to be his blood niece, with Mesican or Cuban or whatever. I been livin' in Floridy almost eight years an' I sure cain't tell. Them people seems able to, but I cain't."

"The girl never came out? Went places?"

"I only found out she was over there when she came busting out the door onct, cryin' her eyes out. Mr Paul grabbed her up in his arms and carried her back inside. He looked over and saw me watching. That's when he come and told me the story."

"About tough times?"

She stubbed out the smoke and shook her head. "The father – he musta been the white one – had cancer in his backside, y'know, and was dying. But since he couldn't be like a man to her no more, the mother had found herself a boyfriend and wanted the daddy to sign the papers so she could get married to the boyfriend. When Mr C told me, he 'bout near busted down crying and I understood the troubles that poor girl was going through. And now I understand about the parties being stopped whilst the girl was livin' there."

"The barbecues?"

"Makes sense, you think about it," Miz Doyle said, lighting another smoke. "As young and pretty as that li'l girl was, Mr Paul didn't want them rough types around her, bad influences and all. Musta been why he kep' her in the house all the time: He was watchin' out for her."

I shot a glance at Gershwin. His eyes crossed and his mouth dropped in mock amazement.

"Did you get the niece's name?" Vince asked.

"He never brought her to the fence to be formerly innerduced, but I once or twict heard some yellin' from over there. I think that poor child's name was Zora."

I looked at Gershwin, rolling his eyes. *Zorra* was Spanish for slut.

That seemed to be the extent of Miz Doyle's recollection of Paul Carosso. Still, the trip added new knowledge to our scant portfolio.

"What a fine humanitarian Paul Carosso is turning out to be," Vince said as I headed back to the site and his vehicle. "Caring for a distraught young girl like that."

Gershwin was in the back seat and leaned close. "Funny, the only relatives we found didn't want anything to do with Carosso. They lived in New Jersey and seemed real happy to have a lot of landscape between them and him. Right, Big Ryde?"

Delmara turned the proboscis my way. "Big Ryde?"

"Don't bring it up," I said. "A phase he's going through. I find it interesting that the niece was visiting about the time the Hondurans were put in the cistern, given Morningstar's estimates."

"What you thinking?" Delmara asked. "About the young lady and the timing?"

"I dunno yet. You got anything, Zigs?" I shot a glance into the rearview. He leaned back, crossed his arms and looked out the window.

"All I know is I'm coming back to Ms Doyle's house tomorrow."

"For what?" I asked.

"I'm gonna sell that lady the Brooklyn Bridge. Twice."

Arriving at the site, we noted that Gershwin had been wrong about Rayles visiting. When we dropped Delmara at his cruiser the HS honcho and his pet poodle were just leaving the tent.

"Is there a reason you're here, Detective Ryder?" Rayles called while the shiny shoes flashed toward us.

"Been out with our good buddy Vince here." I didn't mention we'd gone along on the interview and Delmara, an intuitive sort, didn't mention it either.

"Funny your using the excavation site as your meeting point," Pinker said, giving me his standard hard eye.

"Funny ha-ha, or otherwise?" I asked, head canted in innocent curiosity.

"Not funny at all," Rayles said, stepping up. "I expect you've got a lot on your new plate at FCLE, Detective. I'm not planning on seeing you here again, correct?"

27

Hands on her ample hips, Consuelo Amardara stared at the food between Gershwin and me as if it were too Spartan for her liking. "If that's not enough I can bring a nice slice of cake."

"I think we're fine, Miz Amardara," I said, reaching for my Consuelo's Delight. I had planned to order a beer, but she had the drink in my hands before we'd settled into the back booth. After the bushwhacking by Rayles, we'd retreated to Tiki Tiki to review our only road into the case: Carosso. Amardara had already loaded the table with tortillas, matzo balls, carnitas, chunks of baked salami, garlic dills, guacamole and chips, ceviche, sliced limes, pickled herring and three kinds of salsa. It seemed the kitchen at Tiki Tiki was also used for Ms Amardara's sideline businesses: catering for Jewish or Latino events, presumably even Polynesian.

Carosso was now Miami-Dade's case and Delmara seemed happy for any input we could supply. To me it seemed a tremendous oversight by Rayles's people, but I was happy to have a road into the trafficking case, no matter how slender. We revisited Carosso's financial records, still intrigued by the anomalous two grand deposited in Carosso's account thirteen months back.

Gershwin drizzled a matzo ball with lime and salsa picante and popped it in his mouth. "Maybe Carosso got a big payoff and spent it on something, had two grand left."

"I don't think the guy owned anything that cost more than fifty bucks."

"Maybe he has stuff elsewhere. An offshore account."

"I doubt Carosso had that kind of fiscal sophistication. But then, I don't know how much he made helping ditch a batch of dead bodies. Maybe he owed someone a favor."

Gershwin's turn to think. "Reverse it," he said, flipping his hands over one another. "Maybe he got a favor instead of money. Or a favor with a little sugar added to the pot."

His point dawned as I was sipping my drink, slowing today's rum intake by using a pink straw. "Like his own personal slave, maybe? A young toy to play with for a couple months?"

"Maybe it was enough to make Carosso fill his truck with dead bodies and drive to the cistern. That's a huge chance for an ex-con. If caught, he'd have spent twenty years in the iron-bar Hilton."

I couldn't think well, sitting and jamming food into my mouth. I stood and began pacing, but Ms Amardara zeroed in on my motion like a hawk on a mouse. "Sit, Detective!" she called, patting a hand in the *down* motion. "Don't strain your legs. I'll bring you a fresh drink."

I glanced at the drink in my hand; she thought I was looking for a refill. "It's fine, Miz Amard—"

"Connie!" she shrieked. "It's Connie."

"It's fine, Connie. I'm just stretching."

"Then stretch, *stretch*. You need something, anything, wave. An eyeblink and I'll be there."

I smiled and retreated to the restroom, thinking in the quiet for a couple minutes before coming back to the booth, careful not to blink or do anything that might be construed as a wave. "It's pure speculation . . ." I said as I sat, "but if the girl was a gift, it could mean someone knew Carosso well enough to pull his secret strings. And that person was either one of the traffickers or tight with them."

"Someone Carosso worked with?" Gershwin said. "A buddy at the plant?"

I looked at my watch. "Redi-flow will be closed by the time we get there. I think we kick off tomorrow with another talk with Mr Kazankis. Could you pass the tortillas?"

Leala knew her escape would have been noticed by now and every eye turned her way held potential danger. The day's project had been finding a hiding place. She'd noticed empty houses fronted with signs saying POR SALE, or POR SALE – FORECLOSURE. Her first thought was to break a window and slip inside, but that was the work of a thief and Leala was not a thief.

She had been passing such a house – which, like many, had a yard where the plants and lawn were untended and the house seemed to be sinking into the mouth of a green monster – and saw the roof tip of a building in the rear. There was an alley behind the house and the gate opened with a nervous creak.

The building was a tiny shed with no lock. It smelled of petrol and in the corner was a lawnmower with a missing wheel. A rake and shovel hung from pegs on the wall alongside a bicycle wheel with a flat tire. There were two oily cases of Corona beer bottles, empty, and a rotting cardboard box filled with mechanical parts from the inside of a car.

But there was soft light through one dusty window and room on the concrete floor to stretch out. The backyard was overgrown with palms and palmettos and the ground was covered with fallen fronds. Staying low, Leala gathered the fronds and used them to make a pallet on the hard floor. It was crunchy, but softer than the *concreto*.

Leala took a siesta through the heat of the day then wandered down a tight dirt alley between fenced backyards and tiny garages, some with doors open. The cars inside were older, some with their hoods up, as if gasping for air.

The alley emptied into a wide avenue with a bright building on the corner, its faded sign saying *Lavandería*, laundromat. The long window was filled with signs taped on the inside. Leala pulled her scarf tight to her face and ran to see if the signs *en español* had anything she could use.

A lost dog, *nothing*. Cars for sale, *nothing*. A festival at a local church, nothing now, but Leala noted the nearing date and time as a potential for food. There were signs for appearances by bands, *nothing*. Homes for sale, *nothing*. A man who did the quiropráctico, *nothing*. Leala's wary eyes shot from the signage to the street and back again. At the very bottom edge of the window, four words caught Leala's eye:

ARE YOU IN TROUBLE?

Leala crouched to the text mostly hidden beneath another sign that had been in place earlier.

Have you been brought here illegally? Are you . . .

That was all she could read. Leala stepped inside the *lavandería*. Two men in their mid twenties were leaning against the wall smoking cigarettes and talking to an older woman folding clothes. When the men's eyes riveted to her, Leala's heart froze, but she made herself move to the window.

Pretending she was looking outside, her thumbnail severed the clear tape holding the sign in the window. It was paper and she dropped it in her bag. She turned to find one of the men blocking her way. He stunk of tobacco and even at his young age his teeth were brown.

"You bring no laundry?" he smirked. "Nothing to clean?"

"I am awaiting the bus," Leala said.

The man started laughing. The second man walked over, a grin on his flat face. "Why would a bus stop here, pretty one?"

Leala gave the man her most assertive stare. "I am new. In my country the buses stop at the *lavandería*."

"And do the planes land at the *taquerias*?" he asked. More laughter from the men, one now angling to study her rump.

"Paulo! Barzano!"

The voice of the woman folding clothes filled the room, like glass breaking. The men snapped to her, eyes wide.

"*Qué, Mama?*"

They sounded like children.

"Leave the señorita alone," the woman ordered, shooting a glance at Leala. "Come help me fold, do some work for a change."

Leala bolted out the door. Her feet carried her quickly back into the alley, where she continued reading in the bright sunlight.

. . . being held against your will? Made to do things against your will? Have you been told of a debt you must pay or a service you must fulfill?

If you are in these kinds of trouble, there is a

204

place for help. No policía, no Federales, no Inmigración . . . just an organization that knows your troubles and how to help you escape them. Call the number below. You do not have to leave your name. Even if you are scared, call . . . we want to keep you safe.

There was a big telephone number, below it a drawing of a chain being smashed by a fist. The words beneath that said, *The Human Anti-Trafficking Project, Victoree Johnson, director.*

Leala refolded the paper and retreated to her hiding place to kneel in the light from the window and read it again and again.

It had to be a trap.

"Sh-she was in here today, sir, the girl you seek. A fellow came in and showed me a ph-photo."

The old man's hands shook as he spoke. A woman entered the grocery with a shopping bag over her arm. When she saw the men at the counter she quickly retreated, crossing herself as she hustled down the pavement.

"When?"

"Not two hours ago, señor."

"She made a call, did she not?"

"Si, señor. To Honduras. I sold her a card for five dollars."

Orzibel spun to Chaku Morales. "Where could she get money?"

205

Chaku shrugged, Orzibel turned to the elderly clerk. "Did she buy anything?"

"A dress, a scarf. Sandals. Sunglasses. Some fruit and tortillas and a bag to put them in."

"Which way did she go when she left the store?"

"That way, I think. Toward Flagler."

"Describe her new clothes, old man. Every detail. What was she wearing?"

"W-will I get the money?"

"Did you not hear my question?" Orzibel said, the knife suddenly in his hand.

28

Morning came. I called Kazankis at Redi-flow, the man answering the phone telling me he wasn't in but he'd tell the boss I called. Trucks rumbled in the background. Kazankis phoned back twelve minutes later, apologizing.

"I'm out of the office until noon. Got to inspect a pour. Then I'm dealing with some business I hope might interest you, Detective."

"What might that be, sir?"

"A wise man never promises until he can deliver. Might I expect you at half-past twelve?"

"We'll be there."

I called Gershwin. He was having breakfast at Tiki Tiki and would meet me downtown. Next I dialed the number that replayed messages on my office phone and had but one, from Roy.

"Hey buddy, how's the house-hunting going? Good, I

hope. Don't want my favorite psycho-hunting dick sleeping beneath an underpass."

I hadn't done anything about a new place. I called Gershwin and told him I'd be delayed a bit. On my way to Miami I pulled into several homes with For Sale signs visible. Most of the signs had attached boxes holding hand-out sheets of the properties' prices and particulars. A pattern emerged: anything vaguely resembling a decent place to live cost twice what I'd figured I could pay. It seemed that, in the Keys at least, my simple taste far exceeded my wallet. Or maybe I was spoiled by living on Dauphin Island and at my current jungle-equipped address.

The fruitlessness of my pursuit depressed me and I blew it from my head with high-decibel Jimmy Buffet on the drive in. I wasn't particularly a Buffet fan, but suspected driving without at least one Buffet CD in your vehicle was grounds for a ticket in the Keys.

When I arrived the office was empty, the crew out on various cases and Roy somewhere else. He'd left a stack of real-estate publications on my chair. Gershwin breezed in ten minutes later peeling a banana. He jammed most of it in his mouth, tossed the peel over his shoulder into the trash bin, shot me a thumbs up.

"Whass op, Big Rybe?" he said around a mouthful of banana.

I started to say something, realized the futility, shifted to business. "We have a meeting with Kazankis at twelve-thirty. He said he might have something interesting. We'll see."

"What until then?" Gershwin asked, sucking his fingertips.

I tossed him a few of the real-estate mags, kept several for myself. "Go through these and circle anything under three hundred thou that's not a rathole."

"The sand about to run out on your tropical paradise?"

"I think I'm down to three grains. Get circling."

29

Victoree Johnson was clearing her desk, trying to stay abreast of files and alerts from similar organizations across the globe. The phone rang and she noted it wasn't her university line.

"Human Anti-Trafficking Project, this is Victoree."

Nothing. Victoree Johnson knew the silence of fear. "Are you in trouble, my friend?" she whispered. Still nothing. She tried again in Spanish.

Silence for several seconds. Then a tiny shaking voice. "I think I am in trouble big."

"Can you talk? Is it safe?"

"At this moment."

"Tell me of the trouble."

"I-I came here on a big ship, in a metal box. I was taken to a bad place and made to do things that sickened me. But if I didn't I was hurt. Bad people want to hurt my mama in Honduras."

Victoree Johnson frowned. *Honduras*. The detective sent her way by Doctor Morningstar was investigating that terrible case from Honduras. Johnson had agreed with Morningstar's assessment of Ryder: *He seems to have brains.*

"Can you warn her?" Johnson asked. "Your mother?"

"I did. I told her to run to Tegucigalpa. I pray she is safe."

"Good, that's very good. But you are not safe?"

"I ran from them. They are looking for me, I know."

"Can you tell me your name?"

"Lea . . . Leala."

"Can I meet you, Leala?"

"I-I don't think I w-want to . . ."

Easy, Johnson cautioned herself. *Don't spook her; she's afraid she's being drawn into a trap. I would have been.*

"It's all right, Leala," Johnson said quickly. "It's not necessary. You have my number. Keep it safe."

Johnson thought about what else she might offer the girl in this initial contact. There was something about the man Ryder, more than the intellect, a depth. They'd spoken after discussing trafficking, his thoughts reflecting knowledge of people, the highest angels and lowest demons. In policemen, such knowledge either made one jaded or driven. Ryder seemed much the latter. That might make him a potent ally to people like her caller.

"Here's another phone number," she said, not quite certain why she was breaking pattern. "A man who might help."

"Who is this man?"

Johnson decided on the truth. "He is a detective in—"

"NO! Your sign said no *policía*."

"He is not a *federale* or from *inmigración*. He cares not of citizenship, only safety. He is a special detective from a special place called FCLE. He represents the state of Florida, not the big government. He is studying people from Honduras, people you know, perhaps. Have any of your friends disap—"

"NO *POLICÍA*! NO *POLICÍA*!"

"I'm not telling you to call him. I'm giving you a phone number. You should have more than one number. Throw it away if it frightens you."

Victoree Johnson recited Ryder's cell number. The girl had been so heavily indoctrinated against the police that even writing down a number frightened her. "Tell me more about yourself, Leala. Where were you held? And where are you now?"

"I . . . I must go."

The girl was spooking. The mention of Ryder had been a mistake. "*Momentito*, Leala!" Johnson said. "*Por favor, mi amiga*. Can you please at least tell me—"

The line went dead.

Once again we pulled past the defunct rental concern, over the tracks, and onto the spreading Redi-flow lot.

212

Kazankis was out his door before we'd exited ours. "Come in, gentlemen. I've taken the liberty of ordering lunch."

I looked at Gershwin. He'd just been complaining about his empty belly. How could such a beanpole eat like a famished lion?

"We hadn't really planned on—"

"Cuban sandwiches," Kazankis patted his stomach. "Layers of spicy pork on bread made an hour ago."

Gershwin moaned. I said, "Sure. We'll eat."

Kazankis led us to a lunch room, Spartan, like you'd expect in a concrete-supply concern: a long table, plastic chairs, a wall calendar from a truck-transmission company. A big red fire extinguisher hung from the wall beside a stained refrigerator. The bag of chow centered the table and Kazankis distributed paper-wrapped sandwiches and bags of tortilla chips. He opened the fridge to display several types of soda and I opted for Seven-Up, Gershwin for a papaya beverage. Kazankis grabbed himself a Diet Pepsi and sat, saying a quick grace. "You been here long, Mr Kazankis?" I said when he'd finished, making conversation as I gnawed the sandwich, a big, fat pile of delicious. "This location?"

"My daddy had a crane business, leasing. I started with him when I was eighteen, running the lot while he stayed inside mostly, bum leg from the big war made his walking difficult. Cranes were getting larger and more sophisticated, especially the self-assembling units. Plus you had to rent a lot of acreage to store all that stuff.

213

About the time he retired, a lot of road-building was happening, so I got into concrete. In addition to pouring, we lease portable mixing factories assembled on construction sites."

I nodded out the window as one truck left the mixing tower and another took its place. In a far corner of the lot a hoist was loading a huge, convoluted box inset with pipes and valves onto a semi-trailer, part of a mixing plant.

"Which brings me to your late driver, Carosso. Did he have any close friends here. Or anyone he spent time with?"

A sigh, like a disappointed parent. "Paul was a lone wolf, not sociable. It was Paul's soul that concerned me. Some guys here, we form a bond in the Lord, a fellowship. But Paul never seemed to find the Spirit."

Gershwin raised an eyebrow. "Any thoughts why?"

"Some people can't let go of the past, Detective Gershwin. Or maybe the past isn't done with them yet, I don't claim the wisdom to know. But Paul never had the look of a man who truly wanted to break with his past, and it always troubled me."

"You're saying he wanted to return to crime?" I said.

"I'm saying maybe I misread him in prison. I think the idea of easy money kept calling his name." He paused, seemed to look inward. "I guess I'm saying yes, I must have failed with Paul."

"You mentioned having something interesting for me, Mr Kazankis?"

It snapped him from his dark moment. "Ah, yes. Some men, even our successes, have a hard time releasing their pasts. Not committing crimes, but the codes of such a life. Not telling about suspicious things they've seen."

"Ratting," Gershwin said, taking a sip of liquid papaya. "It's bad form in the crime crowd."

"I was speaking to employees about Paul. One man looked unsettled and I knew he had something to say. We prayed past it and I've asked him here."

Kazankis went to the door and waved in a fiftyish man, medium height with small brown eyes in a round face made rounder by frontal balding. His hands twitched at his waist and he wore a blue uniform with the company logo on a shirt pocket.

"Thomas Scaggs, gentlemen. He works in the conveyor tower and has a wide view of the whole yard and out to the road."

Kazankis gestured the man to sit. Scaggs looked nervous, boxed into himself. No one offered handshakes. "Now, Mr Kazankis?" Scaggs said, looking at Kazankis as if he needed permission.

"What you saw, Thomas. Everything."

"A-a few times I saw Carosso out front by the gate, looking down the road. Then a big black SUV pulled up, two guys inside. Paul went over and they talked. Each time they handed him something and he jammed it in his pants."

"What did you think?" I asked. "Drugs?"

He looked at me for a split second, then at the floor. "It could have just been a bet that hit."

"A bookie that delivers way out here?" Gershwin said. Scaggs shrugged.

"How many times did you see this, Mr Scaggs?" I asked.

He frowned heavily, like I was requesting the fast solution of a quadratic equation. "Uh . . . five-six times, maybe. Over a couple years."

"That long? You're sure?"

"I got a promotion to the tower two years back this month. I saw Paul and the black car my first week."

"Could you see into the vehicle, sir?" I continued.

"It was a black man driving, that I know. The other man was a white guy, big. Wore sunglasses. A suit, too."

"You see the license tags?" asked Gershwin.

"Hunh-up. Way too far."

It turned out to be all Scaggs had; not a lot, but it suggested Carosso was into something before he ran the truck full of bodies to the cistern, which I was ninety-five per cent sure he'd done. And maybe Carosso was more tightly connected to trafficking than we'd figured.

"Thank you for your help, Mr Scaggs," I said, but I was speaking to his disappearing back. Kazankis looked my way, his eyes expectant.

"I hope that helps you in some way. I wish I had more to tell you about Paul's relationships, but he had no relationships."

Gershwin shook his head. "No one has even been to his house?"

Kazankis gestured to the room around us. "I never

216

once saw Paul eat lunch here with the others. I can't imagine Paul having guests from Redi-flow. Most workers here couldn't tell you the color of Paul's eyes. I know," he confessed. "I asked."

I stood. But before we left, I had one final piece of info to impart.

"Speaking of guests, Mr Kazankis, we heard Paul Carosso supposedly had a niece living with him last year. He ever mention such a thing?"

Kazankis frowned. "I don't recall Paul having a close family. I check because family can be a powerful influence in redemption."

"We have an interesting description of the girl: mid teens, probably Hispanic. Sometimes agitated. Almost never out of the house."

Kazankis started to speak, but was stopped by a thought that furrowed his brow. "You're saying what I think you're saying?"

"If you're thinking the worst, then I expect so."

All Kazankis could do was stare, his hand clenching at the air, like he was trying to find something to hold on to. "Gracious Lord, no. Not a little girl." He turned fearful eyes to me. "Paul's in Hell, isn't he?"

"Not my field of expertise."

Kazankis walked stiffly to his window and looked out over the yard. The portable concrete factory was pulling away, but Kazankis's eyes were in the past. "I was Paul's vehicle from incarceration," he whispered. "His road to more sin."

"The fault was Carosso's, Mr Kazankis. Your intentions were honorable."

Kazankis turned with his broad hands out and searching for ours. "Pray with me, gentlemen. Pray for a sinner and for the innocents who bear the sin."

"I'm, uh, more inclined to my own forms of expression, Mr Kazankis."

"Of course. Excuse me . . ." He dropped to his knees with hands clasped. Tears streamed down his cheeks. I had intended to thank him for lunch and tell him we were likely finished with our visits here, but instead I nodded toward the door and Gershwin and I tiptoed away, quietly retreating from Kazankis's misery.

When we hit the lot and I switched my phone back on I found two voicemails, Victoree Johnson asking me to call her, the same from Doctor Morningstar. The din on the lot was oppressive, so I drove across the tracks to return the calls, parking beside a battered tank big enough to hold the Rover. Gershwin stepped out to heed the call of nature.

"I just got a call from a terrified young woman who said her name was Leala," Johnson said. "She claimed she'd been smuggled here on a ship, then escaped from people holding her against her will. She was from Honduras. Listen, Detective, I uh – I gave the girl your number. I'm not sure why, just in case, I guess."

"But I don't speak—"

"Leala, if that's her real name, has quite good English. I doubt she'll call, but . . ."

"If she calls, how should I respond?"

"She's been heavily conditioned to fear the police. That's all I can tell you. You'll have to be guided by intuition."

I watched an empty semi-tractor pull from the Rediflow lot and angle our way, engine roaring. Didn't the damn things have mufflers? "Thanks for the heads-up," I yelled over the din. "It goes without saying that—"

"Yes. If she calls me again, I will let you know."

The truck pulled by and rumbled past the building and down a dirt road cutting through the treeline. I dialed Morningstar.

"We're finished," she said. "Two more bodies pulled from the column."

"Congratulations."

"You in the area, Ryder? I think you'll be interested by what we found."

30

"I have seen such a woman not two hours ago. She wore sunglasses, a scarf, and her dress was a blue like the sky."

"Where did you behold this woman, friend?"

"There was talk of money, no?"

"I can't yet know if this is the woman we seek. Here is a good faith offer, one hundred dollars. There's much more to come should your help result in finding this woman. She has . . . problems. Her family wants her to get assistance."

"Sad. She looked in good health, a pretty one, I think."

"Where did you see her?"

"Do you know the ice-cream store near the cemetery? With the cell phones – not so many places have phone booths. There is one still there, on the outside of the store. She was on the phone. When her call was done she stepped into the alley and ran in the direction of the cemetery."

"Where were you that you could see her?"

"In the store, eating ice cream."

"Now you can get a hundred dollars' worth of ice cream. Don't eat it too fast, *amigo*, you'll get a headache. Pay the man, Chaku."

When we arrived at the site the only vehicles were from the med and forensics labs. The air was as still as stone, and nearly as heavy, a wave of humidity adding to the late summer heat and we booked for the cool atmosphere of the tent.

My first glance went to the pit. Empty, the column now borne in hundreds of evidence bags. Morningstar stood beside one of the tables on the upper level, conferring with a tech. I waved as we approached. "Good morning, Doctor, I—"

She snapped her fingers and the tech filled them with several photos. "This is the head of John Doe Middle Stratum. You'll note that the neck flesh is ossified by the concrete, but you can't hide a slash like that. The victim was slit ear to ear. It also seems the hands were severed on this victim. They're on their way to the lab. A severed hand means thievery in the Muslim world, right?"

"Biblical, too, maybe, given the Old Testament. Any ID on the body?"

"None. But the clothing was somewhat intact. He wore a suit, silk. We have a label from the jacket, an expensive Italian make. We have shoes as well, also Italian and pricey."

"What was that guy doing underneath a cargo of dirt-poor Hondurans?" I mused.

"Slumming?" Gershwin ventured.

"Now for JDBS, our bottom victim," Morningside said. "The first body dumped in the pit and more ossified than the Hondurans. I figure our bottom John Doe was down there for a couple years, so maybe a year before the others." The tech anticipated the fingersnap by getting there first, handing the doc a dark plastic bag, large. "Glove up, Ryder," she said and I resisted dropping my mouth in awe: Morningstar was letting me handle evidence. I snapped the latex in place and the doc reached into the bag and handed me its contents.

"A skull," I said unnecessarily, turning it in my hands and noting the lower mandible was missing. "Or what's left of one."

"Wait. More to come."

The tech took the skull from my hands as Morningstar opened her hand and revealed an object resembling a petrified thumb until I looked closer.

"Is this what I think it is?" I asked, grimacing.

"Yep. A penis."

"It fell off the body?"

"We removed it from the oral cavity of the skull. Go ahead, take a look. It won't bite."

I lifted the severed member. I had held but one penis before and felt uncomfortable holding this one, even though it seemed more statue than human. "The preservation is rather remarkable," Morningstar said. "Don't you think?"

The urethra seemed to stare at me and I looked away.

"I guess."

"Check the base. There's no tearing of the flesh nor internal tissue. Probably removed by a razor-sharp knife. Zip . . . and it was gone."

The *zip* did me in. I set the penis on the table.

"Any idea as to meaning?" Morningstar said. "The oral placement?"

"In certain circles it means the penis has been places it shouldn't. The only other time I've seen this was when a gang boss discovered his wife fooling around. He had lover-boy brought in and removed his equipment with a kitchen knife, jammed it in the guy's mouth and put a bullet in his head. The, uh, surgery was not very neat."

"Torture, you think in this case?" she asked. "Or an example?"

"An example would mean a victim was shown around as a warning to others."

I recalled my personal encounter. The gangster had assembled friends of the victim at gunpoint, forcing them to behold his work. When the horrendous story hit the streets the boss became one of the most feared monsters around. It was a double-edged sword, because word eventually made its way to the cops. The boss was now doing life in Holman Prison and I hoped it was a short one.

"So someone might know?" Morningstar asked.

"Or have heard about it. That's all it takes to create a street mythology. Mess with my woman, steal from me, this is what happens."

Morningstar looked me in the eye. "The bottom victims give no indication of being trafficked. They appear to be separate incidents. Think it'll change the situation with Homeland Security?"

I felt a rising excitement. "I'll let you know," I said, turning toward the exit. "You should probably expect a call from Roy."

I kept my expectations in check as we headed to Miami and didn't mention my hopes to Gershwin. I didn't want to call Roy with the information, but convey the news in person. I also expected I'd have to do a sales job, perhaps with Morningstar's help, but she seemed on my side, finding HomeSec's investigation lackadaisical and almost inept thus far.

We parked and headed to Roy's office, and found the door wide as usual. Roy wasn't a closed-door kind of guy. "There's my man," Roy said as I knocked on his door frame. "I left some real-estate brochures in your office, though you've probably already found a—"

"You should call Morningstar, Roy," I interrupted, running on hope and adrenalin. "She's out at the site."

"Is there a problem?"

"Not any more, maybe."

Roy frowned and was talking to Morningstar in seconds. Or listening, mainly. After a minute he tapped the phone off and gave me a raised eyebrow. "I under-stand what you're trying to do. But most of the column . . ."

"Yes indeed, Roy. But I can live with dual ownership."

What I was proposing was not something Roy wanted in his day, but the big hands clapped together in a deci-sion made. "I'll have the interested parties pow-wow at the site. Rayles ain't gonna be a happy pup, you know that, don't you?"

Like a bouncing ball, we headed back to the site. Roy, Gershwin and I arrived first, the HomeSec twins a minute later. Morningstar handed them a copy and photos of her latest findings, then retreated to the fringe of the conversation.

"What does all this mean?" Rayles asked me, scanning the report. I saw him wince and figured he'd got to the amputated penis part. "I'm afraid I don't understand."

"It's in the files, Major. There were two bodies in the lower section of concrete, both hideously mutilated, one sexually. I can show you mutilations on the actual bodies if you wish. They're over in the—"

"I'll trust the photos."

"The bottom line is that the assault was savage and meant to create extreme pain and fear, the kind of action I associate with a psychotic mind."

"And this leads you to think—"

"That it's our case, FCLE. At least the two bodies in the lower section of the column. You can have the upper section." I smiled with all the charm and bonhomie I could muster. "We'll investigate the case together, Major, like a team."

The look on Rayles's face told me my idea was not bringing joy to his day. He looked to Roy. "Your thoughts, Captain McDermott?"

"Detective Ryder has a point," Roy deadpanned. "He's looking forward to working with you, Major."

Rayles was irritated, not, I figured, at sharing a case that would go nowhere from a national security point of view, but at being bested by a guy whose credentials lacked the gravitas of a command at Gitmo.

"It's inefficient," he said. "Meetings alone would be problematic."

"I'll come to your department every morning to review findings, Major. How's the coffee at HomeSec?"

He was now looking less angry than ill.

"Or . . ." I said as if the idea had just occurred, "FCLE can handle both investigations. If you're looking for efficiency, Major Rayles, I think that may be the best solution."

I watched Rayles mentally juggle his options for several seconds. Though his chin was on full and clenching jut, his words came out in an even tone. "Given that the investigation was initiated by FCLE and the bulk of the investigative material has been generated by FCLE, the appropriate response is that jurisdiction reverts to FCLE. For the time being, at least."

Rayles's assistant, Robert Pinker, eyeballed his boss. If anything, he looked more pissed off than Rayles.

"That's it, Major?" Pinker snapped. "The guy wins? You're gonna hand it back just like that?"

"It's a criminal investigation, Mr Pinker," I corrected. "Not a competition."

Pinker moved close and looked ready to swing on me. A surprised Rayles stepped between us, eyeballing Pinker. "Detective Ryder is correct, Robert. We'll leave the investigation to the capable hands of the FCLE."

The *capable* was nice, though a political frippery, like congressfolks addressing each other as *honorable colleague* when all they wanted was to gut one another. Rayles turned to leave, but paused to turn back, needing to end with a note of command.

"I expect to be copied on every aspect of the case, Ryder," he instructed. "Do you read me?"

"In triplicate," I said, holding up my fingers in the Boy Scout salute.

We were back on the case.

31

Minard Chalk is sleeping in his expansive home in Key West, sweat beading on his brow, the red silk sheets jumbled from his tossing and turning. The white suit worn at Orchids restaurant is hanging in the closet and freshly laundered. Every day Chalk leaves the house at one-fifteen p.m. for lunch at one of the nearby restaurants. The staff arrives at one-twenty to gather laundry for dry cleaning, drop off fresh laundry, and to pick up, dust and vacuum. A prepared dinner is left behind, as well as a snack for later in the evening. The dinner and snack combined must not tally beyond eight hundred and sixty-five calories.

The staff must be gone by two-thirty. Chalk never returns before three-fifteen. When Chalk is at one of the other residences – Seattle, San Clemente, Minneapolis – the house receives a total cleaning.

Chalk is dreaming of a girl. He does not want this

dream, but his moaning, rolling body cannot fight it off. He always loses to the dream.

The girl's name is Xaviera Teresa Santinell and her sixteen-year-old skin seems to glow with its perfection. Her hair is as black as polished coal and her eyes as gentle as the eyes of a faun. She is dressed in a simple pink dress that ends well above her knees. Her legs are long and slender and when she stands with one small foot on the ground and the other cocked in the air behind her, she reminds the young Minard Chalk of a beautiful flamingo. Xaviera moves through the Chalks' sprawling San Clemente household like a vision, an ethereal presence in the eyes of Chalk, eleven years old.

Minard Chalk is in love. He's been in love for four months, since his eyes first fell across Xaviera, entering the Chalk household beside her mother, the Chalks' newest housekeeper. The previous housekeeper, Maria, had disappeared after a shouting match with Mrs Chalk, a door slamming as she ran crying from the home. Mrs Chalk is a demanding woman who goes through several house staffers annually.

They are alone, Minard and Xaviera. Her mother is visiting relatives in Los Angeles and Chalk's parents are in Spain or Italy or wherever the jets fly, though Minard has never been further than a private academy in New Mexico. The Chalks do not vacation with Minard because it makes them look old enough to have a child of that age.

Sometimes when all the parents are gone Xaviera has her friends over, other teenage girls who swim in the pools – one inside and one outside – and giggle into one another's ears. They wear tiny swimming suits and move like cats. When they use dirty words it makes the eavesdropping Minard feel sweetly crawly inside, though he doesn't know why.

Later, in his room, he repeats their words and feels sweetly crawly yet again.

"Fucking. Boobies. Pussy. Dick. Rubbers."

Minard has been watching Xaviera from the furthest shadows of a darkened room across the hall from the room Xaviera had been dusting. She has just done something truly amazing: plucked a feather from the duster and lay down on the wide bed in the guest room, dusting herself where Minard could not see, below her belly button, her pink dress hiked high on long legs ending at pink tennis shoes. Her hair is tied in a red silk bow and splays across the bed, dark locks cascading over the side. Her pink tongue pokes from lips like a fresh rose. The sun blazes through the window across the room and the space seems filled with golden light.

She turns and sees him watching. Her eyes widen. The sun explodes and the room turns to pure white.

Minard rolls and moans and his fingers dig into the pillow.

The room shivers back into view, at first just an outline of Xaviera, then filling with color. She is cross-legged on the bed now, the feather on the floor. Chalk's hand covers his genitals over his khaki shorts.

"Come here, little one," says the rose mouth of Xaviera. "I want you to show me what's under your hand."

"I . . . I . . . I . . ." Minard Chalk's breath has frozen in his throat.

"Don't be frightened, little dove. Maybe we can have a trade."

"T-t-trade?"

"If you show me what's in your hand, I might show you what's in mine. Would you like that?"

Xaviera's hands are cupping her breasts. Her teeth shine like stars. The girl's hands fall from her breasts, their points visible under the thin fabric. Minard wants to stare at the tiny perfect moons but knows that is rude.

"You do this a lot, do you not?" Xaviera says, her voice as quiet as a prayer. "Watch me?"

His eyes drop to the floor. His tongue is a rock in his mouth.

"I've seen you, Minard. I know all of your watching places. You've watched me since the day I arrived, no?"

"It just l-l-looks like I'm . . ."

"Shhh, Minard. I'm not angry. I like to be watched."

"R-really?"

A pink finger slips to one of the moons and brushes over it. "It makes me feel special. Why do you like to watch me?"

"Because I-I love you."

"You're so smart, Minard. Don't shake your head, everyone knows it. Tell me in smart words how much you love me."

The boy tries to search his mind but he's frozen by the girl's beauty. Twenty years away Minard Chalk moans into his pillow.

"I-I can't."

"You don't really love me then," she says, her face dropping. Even sad she is so beautiful that Chalk wants to cry.

"I do, Xaviera. I really do. I-I want to marry you."

"What? I didn't hear you. Tell me louder."

He swallows hard and takes a deep breath. "I love you and I want to marry you," he says, his voice filling the room.

A wide smile. "Oh? What will we do, Minard? If we are married?"

"Go to another country. China, maybe. Or Australia."

"Why so far?"

"To be happy."

"I think you should kiss me, Minard. Will that make you happy?"

The boy's mouth drops open. He has practiced kissing in the mirror a hundred times. The world turns to stillness as he leans forward with his lips on fire. But her hand touches his chest and holds him back.

"Not on my mouth, my dove. Kiss me down here. On my panties."

She scoots forward on the bed and opens her long legs. Her panties are revealed, cotton, as white as snow. The amazed Chalk begins to bend.

"No, Minard. Don't lean down. Get on your knees and kiss me with your tongue."

His knees are on the floor and her thighs graze his ears. His tongue reaches out and licks at her panties. Xaviera shifts her hips, angling them higher. "Yes. Eat it, Minard. Eat it like candy." She laughs happily.

"What?"

"Keep going like that. But . . . uh, make some noise."

"Mmuuum . . ." Minard moans as he kisses and licks at the panties. "Mummph." If he died now there would be no regrets; his life ended in perfection.

Xaviera giggles strangely, like hearing a joke. "Are you hard?" she asks.

"What?"

"Your dick, Minard. Is it big and hard?"

"Y-y-yes."

"Stand up and open your pants. I want to see it."

He stands and with trembling hands lowers his shorts and briefs. His erect penis is small and uncircumcised and curves downward, the hood extending past the tip like a rumpled wizard's hat. Her hand reaches down and her middle finger gently strokes the top of his penis from his body to the tip of the hat.

"When will it get big?" she frowns.

"It . . . it is."

"There's all this skin, Minard. Why don't you fill up your skin?"

"I . . . what?"

Minard Chalk feels a pain like his thing has caught fire. He screams and his eyes snap open to see Xaviera's fingers closed tight on his flap, pinching hard. He tries to jump away but excruciating pain holds him in place. His hands go to her wrist but she squeezes harder still. It's like teeth have closed on his thing.

Wild laughter fills the air. The slatted door of the long closet rolls open and a half-dozen of Xaviera's friends pour out, pointing at the spectacle and howling. They have been watching everything.

"*Dios mio*, is that a *pito* or a crayon?"

"Stretch it out, Xavie! Nasty little Minnie. This will teach you to spy on Xavie."

"That's it, Dolores, his name will be Minnie! Minnie-Minnie-Miney, why is your *pito* so tiny?"

With a yip of laughter Xaviera releases Minard's penis. His face is on fire as he bolts to the basement to hide in a corner until Xaviera and her friends scamper out the door. Alternately screaming curses and crying, Minard Chalk runs upstairs and flushes four of his mother's earrings down the toilet. When his parents return Xaviera's mother is accused of theft and fired.

Though he never sees Xaviera again, her laughter never leaves his brain.

"Minnie-Minnie-Miney, why is your pito so tiny?"

When Chalk wakes – the sheets, as always, soaked with sweat and, oddly, semen – he will phone a number in Miami and close a recently discussed deal.

With the HomeSec twins out of our hair – at least for now – we could catch up on the latest from the front or, in this case, the pit. Roy had a meeting in Tallahassee

234

and booked for the airport to catch one of the department's Cessnas, another gift from the drug lords.

"So we've got two bodies," I recapped to Gershwin and Morningstar. "One with a neatly severed penis in its mouth and a severed head, and the other with his hands removed and throat cut."

"But the chopped-off hands were in the matrix," Gershwin said. "So it wasn't to hide fingerprints. By the way, Doctor . . ."

"I just heard from the lab," Morningstar said. "The skin got dissolved. But whoever killed the vics was someone who keeps a sharp blade nearby. Of course, your Carosso body . . ."

"Yep," I nodded. "Blade again."

We had a perp who liked to use a knife, a truly ugly inclination. I pulled my cell and called Vince Delmara.

"How you doing, Vince?"

"I'm doing scut work at a sleazebag massage parlor off I-95. The Taste of Heaven, how do you like that? Place burned down last night, looks like arson. Or maybe a concerned citizen doing the city a favor."

"Anyone hurt?"

"A bouncer got burned bad hustling the chickadees out. Naturally, nobody's saying a thing. I don't know whether to hand the case off to the fire investigator or Vice. Whatcha need, Detective?"

"How's your snitch network, Vince?"

"A thousand tiny stars shining in the dark, Detective. Some a lot dimmer than others."

I asked if he could check his snitches for anyone known for using a blade. There were plenty of bad people who favored knives, but the one we sought would be border-line or fully sociopathic, the type to kill for an audience to enhance his reputation.

"I'll put out the word."

"And I'll copy you FCLE reports of everything we dig up. And what we have to date."

I could hear his grin. "Cooperation *and* information? You're an odd guy, Ryder." He rang off. There was little for Gershwin and me to do but keep digging. Vince Delmara would work the Miami-Dade snitch angle, trying to find if anyone out there knew of a cutter.

It was a long shot.

32

Leala lay in her hideaway, the muted light telling her the sun was fading. It was hot and Leala had shed her dress to keep from spoiling its freshness. She wiped her brow with the scarf, ate her last banana and waited until night arrived.

The door creaked open and her eyes checked the house, still black, still safe. Cars and motorcycles roared on nearby streets and when a vehicle swerved into the alley Leala slipped into shadows, grateful for trash cans to squat behind.

She slipped to the house with the pool and slid into the cool blue water. It was bitter on her lips but delicious against her skin. She was submerging when the night exploded into light, hard and white and everywhere.

"Someone's out there!" a voice screamed from the

house. "Someone's in the pool! YOU! GET OUT OF HERE!"

An alarm was tripped and a sonic blade knifed the air. *Zeee-yup, zeee-yup, zeee-yup.* Leala grabbed her dress, running naked across the grass and out the gate. Shaking uncontrollably, she threw the dress over her head and shook it into place, sprinting across front yards before dashing toward the alley. Dogs were barking now, each alerting the other to an intruder in the neighborhood.

Orzibel and Morales were crisscrossing the grid of blocks forming Little Havana and searching for Leala. Orzibel grinned. "Did I tell you, Chaku? Cho called Amili an hour after our match man left, probably while the flames were highest. Said she'd like to continue our business relationship."

Morales snorted and slapped the steering wheel in delight. Orzibel went back to scanning the street. He paused and canted his head toward the window.

"What is all that noise, Chaku? Roll down the windows."

Hot air poured into the cool vehicle. Orzibel stuck his head out the window, listening. "Head down the street. Toward the sounds."

Morales turned onto the cross street. His eyes stared in disbelief as a flash of blue crossed a hundred meters ahead.

"Her!" Morales yelled. "There, by the white house."

"Go!"

The big engine roared, tires squealing as it spun and headed in the reverse direction. "She's jumping that fence," Orzibel said. Morales stood on the brakes, Orzibel's feet hitting pavement before the vehicle halted.

"Come here NOW or I will kill your *madre*!" he screamed, seeing a small body tumbling over a fence and disappearing between a house and a garage.

"She's going for the alley. Head her off, Chaku!"

Morales burned rubber around the end of the block. "Come to me, bitch!" Orzibel howled. "Or I'll SLICE OFF YOUR FACE!"

Lights flicked off in nearby houses. Doors were locked and residents scurried to central rooms where bullets couldn't reach. There had been gang wars and gunshots were familiar. The police were rarely called, for fear of retribution. Orzibel pushed at shrubs and bushes, checking for a crouching girl. Nothing.

Morales nodded across the street, an old man brave enough to step to his porch. "Someone's gonna call the cops, Orlando. They might get to her ahead of us."

The pair retreated into the vehicle. "She's here, Chaku," Orzibel said, staring out the window. "She found a garage, an empty house, a boat in a backyard." They passed a corner holding a closed and shuttered grocery, three junkies jittering on the steps. The wretches were everywhere. Orzibel stared at the junkies as they passed, a fingertip tapping his lips as he thought.

"I'm doing this all wrong, Chaku. Go to the local

junkies. Tell them the right information buys a month's worth of the finest scag."

Morales wheeled around the corner, checked his rear-view. "The junkies hear many lies, Orlando. It would be best to have the drug in hand. And give a taste to a select few so they might tell others of the quality."

Orzibel grinned and pulled out his cell phone. "Brilliant thinking, my large friend. I will schedule a meeting with Pablo Gonsalves. Dangle pure H before the junkies and they will scour the streets like starving rats."

Leala sat shaking in the corner of the shed. One knee screamed in pain from a fall over fence to a brick patio. Her left palm hurt from a cut, left by the ragged top of a metal gate. Her hair was still soaking wet.

"Come here NOW or I will kill your madre!"

It had been so terribly close. One time Leala had been beneath a van as the huge man's feet had slapped past. Had he slowed in his run he would have heard Leala's ragged, gasping breaths. When he turned past a corner she had continued to run, jumping from shadow to shadow until she had reached the shed.

"Come to me, bitch. Or I'll SLICE OFF YOUR FACE!"

She couldn't hide much longer, the pool proved there were eyes everywhere, even behind darkened windows. Leala clutched herself tight, but even though the night was as steamy as a jungle, she continued to shake. In the morning she would call the woman from the poster again. Her only chance of escape was in trusting someone.

It would have to be Victoree Johnson.

"To what do I owe the honor of a visit from such a successful businessman?" Pablo Gonsalves said. "Sit, Orlando Orzibel, and tell me why I am so favored."

Gonsalves was dark-skinned, in his forties and hugely obese, his small bright eyes peering over cheeks like bags of pudding, his outsized lips wet and floating over a frog's chin that became his chest. His black silk shirt opened to display a golden crucifix as large as a saucer nestling in a cleavage many women would have envied.

Gonsalves hunkered at a back table on the balcony of the club in Miami Beach, the cavernous room almost empty, another hour before the trust-fund babies queued at the front door. Three *cholos* sat at the round table, gophers and bodyguards, large, but not as large as Chaku Morales, who stood a dozen feet away and watched as Orzibel neared the table. Gonsalves seemed high on something, Orzibel noted, the man's eyes glassy and his words carefully controlled.

Orzibel saw the tiny glass half-filled with a green liqueur, absinthe, the real deal. On the floor below a smattering of dancers gyrated to thudding techno-pop as lights flashed pink and orange and green. The DJ sat in a booth in a corner, a black man in a white and sequined suit with a Miami Dolphins ball cap slung sideways on his head. The music was loud, but the upstairs speakers were turned down, allowing normal conversation.

"I need something, *amigo*," Orzibel said, bowing a millimeter as he sat. There were protocols and though he, Orlando Orzibel, bowed to no man on his turf, this was the turf of Pablo Gonsalves and respect was to be shown. That's why Orzibel allowed himself and Chaku to be patted down. It was not disrespect, only caution.

"We are friends?" Gonsalves said. "I am not complaining, of course. But how comes this alliance when we have never spoken to this day?"

"We have not spoken in words, Don Gonsalves, but in business. Our enterprise purchases various business supplies from Tiny Chingala on Bastion Street. Tiny is an employee of yours, no?"

An enigmatic smile from Gonsalves. The fat fingers picked up the miniature glass and brought it to the outsize lips, sipping as delicately as a mosquito. He set the glass down and raised an eyebrow.

"Tiny Chingala has many offerings, Señor Orzibel. Why do you not go to him?"

Orzibel laced his fingers and leaned forward. "His heroin is diluted and necessarily so. It extends the product for a clientele of limited means."

"Purity is expensive. Go on."

"You have higher-quality products, Don Gonsalves. Items for those whose wealth is so vast prices cease to matter. I wish to purchase . . . let's say ten grams of the best heroin, uncut."

242

Gonsalves regarded Orzibel for a three-count. "*Para una dama?*" he asked. *For a lady?*

Orzibel did not understand the question. But perhaps the absinthe-soaked *elefante* was addled. He shook his head. "I seek information and wish to enlist eyes on the street. Junkies: The eyes that wander endlessly."

Wet laughter from Gonsalves. "The product you seek is something street users only touch in their dreams. When do you wish your goods?"

"Time is of the essence, Don Gonsalves."

Gonsalves quoted a price and Orzibel nodded. The fat man gestured and one of the hulking minions disappeared as Gonsalves emptied the glass of absinthe. Orzibel resisted the urge to scowl; he never allowed himself to be affected by substances when working. Gonsalves was weak.

The *cholo* was back a minute later. The fat man pocketed money, Orzibel drugs. "*Gracias*," Orzibel said, standing from the table.

"*Momem-to*," Gonsalves slurred, a fat hand rising. "I know that you work with the beautiful Amili Zelaya. The rumors are that you two are . . . involved." Gonsalves said it strangely, as if suggesting there was something curious at play.

They weren't, not physically, though not due to lack of trying. Still, Orzibel knew of the street-level rumors and did nothing to dissuade them. It made him look good. He flashed his brightest smile. "Amili and I are . . . even more than co-workers."

"So you know her every secret?" The fat man's eyes seemed even more glazed, his lips more engorged.

What is this fat, impaired fool getting at? Gossip?

"Amili and I have one blood," Orzibel lied, crossing index and middle fingers beside his face. "There are no secrets between us."

Gonsalves gestured a bodyguard near and whispered in his ear. The man was gone for scant moments. Orzibel saw something dropped from behind into Gonsalves's hand. When it rose, there was a tiny parcel in his fingers. It was the size of an earring box and wrapped in the paper of one of West Palm's most exclusive jewelers.

"Señorita Zelaya is a very busy lady, I think, and you can save her this month's trip, Don Orzibel. Please deliver this to your *amiga*. As you know, the pretty lady needs her dreams, too."

Orzibel's hands closed around the package. He bowed just enough to satisfy protocol and backed away.

33

A rooster awakened Leala in the morning and for a moment she thought she was back in her village, safe, her mama cooking breakfast. But instead of the scent of wood smoke and tortillas she smelled the oily rags in the corner of her hideout and rain about to fall. She pushed the door open and saw dark and low clouds above, a lone gull wheeling in the air. The rooster, no further than a couple houses away, crowed again, followed by the sound of an engine cranking into life. A dog began barking. The neighborhood was waking up.

How far to the telephone? Leala thought, her mind tracing the distance to the ice-cream store. Is it worth the attempt?

Sí. Something had to be done today.

Leala rummaged in her purse for a rumpled bill and

a few remaining coins. She combed her hair with her fingers, shook her dress until the worst wrinkles fell away, then tied on her scarf and crept between brush to the alley.

The *helado* shop was ten minutes distant and Leala passed no one on the way, averting her face as sparse traffic passed. A bus passed her by, then slowed and stopped for two women who had been standing beside the street. The bus hissed away.

The ice-cream store was closed. Leala thumbed coins into the phone until hearing a chime. Hoping it meant the call was accepted, Leala entered the number in her memory. As the phone rang, she practiced words in her head.

"I have nowhere to go. I will do whatever you wish. Please help me."

A click, a pause . . .

A voice: "This is Victoree. I am out of town until Monday. Please leave a message."

Leala stared at the phone as if it had betrayed her. Should she wait until Monday? What to do?

Would she survive?

She turned to see a man a dozen paces behind, skinny as a stick with filthy hair hanging like snakes from his head. He stared at Leala through bloodshot eyes.

"*Pardóneme*," Leala said, averting her face and slipping past the staring man. Even passing two meters away the man smelled bad and Leala wondered if the stench came from his arms, red and inflamed on the insides. He was a junkie, she knew, having seen them in her days in

246

Tegucigalpa. He was sick with drugs and the need of them.

She watched the man make his call and continue down the street. Leala had to be bold. There was one thing she might do. But she had to find out certain things first. She had to see a man, a detection *hombre* named Ryder.

But first she had to find out where he was, where he worked.

In the distance, above the trees and low housetops Leala could see the skyline of Miami, terrifying in its height and breadth. Just aiming eyes at the city stole her breath. But it wasn't far, three kilometers if that. Certainly the man she needed to see worked in one of the tall buildings.

She would go into the city. Just to see. That was all. Leala waited beside a garage until another bus appeared. She darted to the street holding her dwindling money in one hand and waving at the bus with the other.

Leala sat behind the driver who, as if he'd seen it often before, pointed at the money in Leala's hand to indicate correct payment. The driver was Hispanic, with a wide and open face and a cheery manner. The bus entered the city, passing from sunshine into the shadows of towering buildings. When the bus stopped at a light Leala leaned forward. "Excuse me, Señor. I seek the building that houses the *policía*. Do you know such a place?"

Be nearby, her heart hoped.

"Miami-Dade *Policía*, señorita?"

Leala frowned, not expecting a choice. She tried to

recall Johnson's words: *He is a special detective from the state of Florida* . . .

"Is there a Florida *policía*?" Leala asked. "Special ones that do the detection?"

The light changed and the bus pulled forward. "You are probably talking about the Florida State Police, or maybe the FCLE, who are—"

"That's it!" Leala said, recalling the odd sequence of letters. "Is it in the city?"

The driver nodded. "I have a regular, a gentleman who does maintenance there. He usually takes the bus after this one, which arrives at seven forty-five."

"Drop me where you drop the gentleman, *por favor*," Leala said. "And point me in the way he goes."

At seven fifteen a.m., Ernesto "Chaku" Morales strode into the downtown Miami health club with his black gym bag over a granite shoulder, his small, tight eyes scanning the vast room. A white fan the size of a helicopter's rotors spun overhead as men and women pumped free weights on the floor. Others used machines or ran the encircling track. Rap-beat dance tracks pounded from speakers in the ceiling.

Chaku Morales didn't visit the locker room. He simply stripped off his turquoise jumpsuit, revealing a brief scarlet bodysuit that embraced every cut, every ripple of muscle. His genitals stood out like a fist in a driving glove. Eyes drifted to the hulking entrant, some lingering in shaded curiosity, others turning away in fear or shame.

Morales fell forward, catching himself on his fingertips and warming up with pushups before progressing to squats and crunches. After an effortless ten minutes he crossed the room to a weight bench in a far corner, loading the holder with a hundred pounds of barbell carried one-handed from the rack. He lay on the bench and began his warm-up reps, the ham-thick biceps engorging with the push, relaxing at the bottom.

"Need a spot?" a voice said from behind.

Chaku Morales nodded. He looked from side to side and saw that he and the voice were alone. Morales continued to pump, speaking as the weight came down, stopping as it lifted.

"Have you had enough time to find out . . ." The weight went up, started down. ". . . what is going on?"

"There's a new guy sticking his nose into things. Some hotshot from Mobile."

"Hotshot?" Morales said.

"Carson Ryder. The guy solves things, a specialist. A lot of people are in prison because of him and now he's in Miami."

Morales pumped harder. The veins in his arms stood out like the burrows of miniature moles. "You have advice about what . . . can be done?" he grunted. "Can the hotshot be convinced to go blind to certain things?"

"I know these types. He can't be bought, a believer."

"Leverage?" Morales grunted.

"No wife, kids, not even fucking anyone at present."

"Advice?"

249

"I'll keep an eye out. If he starts down a road dangerous to us all, you might have to take him off the board."

"But someone else takes his place, isn't that" – Morales pushed the barbell above him like it was a broom – "what happens?"

"A new nose will be sniffing the air, true. But this Ryder guy has a unique nose. You don't want it near the business. You don't want it near Miami. It's a dangerous nose."

"I will pass this on. *Gracias*."

"Nice spotting for you, buddy."

Morales watched his spotter disappear into the locker room and emerge a minute later in khakis and blue polo shirt, neither man acknowledging the other as the spotter disappeared out the door. Morales followed ten minutes later. He knew Orlando Orzibel well enough to hear the man's response before he told him the news and advice:

"Why wait, Chaku? Let's take Ryder off the board now, and be done with him."

34

I hit the department a bit past nine and headed to the investigative section to finally introduce myself to the rest of the dicks, then grudgingly seek a place to live. But I arrived to find the place as empty as a politician's promises and I realized it was Friday and everyone was on the streets trying to get far enough ahead to take a couple days off.

Pushing dark thoughts to the back of my head, I took the stairs up a floor to my office, passing the small whiteboard giving the crew's current whereabouts, Canseco in Jacksonville, Degan in Boca, Valdez listed as DO, Day Off. Tatum was in town, just not here. I pined for one of my so-called colleagues to pass me in the hall, say something like, *Got a tough case with a perp in Fort Myers, looking like a psycho. Gotta couple minutes to kick it around, bud?*

All was silence save for the sound of a radio nearby, an announcer giving the forecast.

"... *rain giving way to clearing skies and the heat and humidity returning ...*"

I headed to my corner office until stopped by hearing my name, and turned to see Bobby Erickson, a retired Florida State Police Sergeant who worked the phones. He proudly wore his dress blues daily, but had bad feet so Roy allowed him to wear slippers, big pillows of tan suede with fleece pushing up around his ankles. Erickson was short and round and looked perpetually concerned, lips pursed, eyes in a frown over half-glasses. He seemed to bear me no animosity and I figured I hadn't waylaid any of his money.

"Morning, Bobby," I said. "Whatcha need?"

"A woman came to the downstairs desk a half hour ago. She asked if there was a detection man named Señor Ryder in this building."

"Detection man?"

"The desk folks have your name, of course. They phoned up here but I told them you hadn't arrived yet, expected soon. When they went to tell that to the woman, she was gone."

"A half-hour ago?"

"There's more. Five minutes later this note was left at the desk. It was delivered by a clerk with the assessor's office, asked to deliver it by a woman resembling the one at the desk."

I opened the folded note, my name on the outside.

MET AT A POOL FOR SWIMING PLESE 10 TO-DAY

it said in a flowing hand more precise than the spelling.

"Met at a swimming pool at ten?" I scowled. "Met what?"

Erickson eyeballed the note. "Maybe it's meet. You're supposed to meet her at the swimming pool."

"Where's a swimming pool around here?"

He shrugged and pushed the lips out further. "Got me."

I started away but he called again. "Almost forgot, Detective. She asked what you looked like."

Though I hadn't seen surveillance at the entry, I figured it was there, just nicely tucked away. "There are cameras at the entry, right? How can I get a look?"

"The surveillance center's in the basement. But unless it's an emergency it's gonna take an hour to pull the stuff."

Erickson padded away on his tan cushions. I gazed out windows, wondering if there was a nearby hotel with a pool. My eyes wandered the plaza, wide walkways overhung with shade trees, people strolling or sitting the steps around the fountain, a center spray of water into a shallow circle pool of . . .

Pool. Was that what my caller meant?

I checked my watch, saw 9.56, and elevatored down to the wide promenade. The pavement was damp from rain but the sky was breaking through in the west, a bright blue shout through tattered cumulus. Gulls darted above the trees as pedestrians moved below. I crossed to the fountain – swimming pool? – and surveyed the surroundings: Business types bustling to work, joggers, a man pushing a food cart, a long-haired kid sitting a bench and tuning a guitar, a busload of school kids wrangled by a trio of teachers, probably visiting the center as part of a class in government.

I sprinted to the far side of the fountain to scope things from that angle. No one seemed interested in me. I continued to circle the pool, hands in my pockets, studying everyone within sight. More office workers. A trio of teens playing hacky-sack. A group of tourists, German by their voices, cameras strung around necks craning toward the skyline.

I heard footsteps and turned to see a woman passing behind me, face hidden beneath a pulled-low white scarf and large sunglasses, age indeterminate, but youthful in her profile. The blue dress needed a session at the ironing board and she seemed to have a slight limp.

"Miss?" I called. "Excuse me, miss?"

She turned. "*Si?*"

I jammed my hands in my pockets and smiled benignly. "I'm Carson Ryder. Does that mean anything to you?"

A pause. The shades seemed riveted on me.

"*No hablo inglés, señor.*"

"Sorry," I said. She continued away.

Leala moved quickly from the plaza, needing time to weigh information. The man was a gringo, bad. But he was not a hulking, stoop-shouldered monster, probably

254

good. He was actually nice looking, slender, with dark hair and eyes. Still, there was something that seemed threatening about the man, but it did not seem directed at her. Perhaps it was his eyes, scanning all directions at once. Or maybe it was how he walked, almost carelessly but with surprising speed. She had seen him exit the building, but had looked away when distracted by a vendor. When she looked back, he was on the far side of the pool.

Cats did that sort of thing, and cats could not be trusted.

But when he'd spoken, there was no threat in his voice, only curiosity. That was good. Could such an *hombre* with such a concerned voice be bad in his heart? Or were he and the woman named Victoree wolves in disguise?

What was true, what was a lie?

Questions without answers. Leala passed a large building, her eyes catching the sign, seeing the word *Library*. That meant the building was a *biblioteca*, a place where the books lived. There was a *biblioteca* in the village six kilometers distant and Leala's mother made sure Leala got there once a month for books.

Books held the answers.

She turned and darted inside, shaking back her hair and straightening her spine, acting like she belonged with the people entering the long building. She was halfway across the wide floor when her eyes saw a flash of uniform against a far wall: a *guardia*! He was looking right at her. Leala felt her knees loosen and her breath turn to ice. *Keep moving*, her mind said. Do not look his way. You are just one of many seekers of knowledge. She saw a huge counter with several workers behind it. One was a young man, not much older than her, shuffling books into a pile. She took a deep breath and stood before him.

"Help you?" he asked.

Leala had her story ready, created in the twenty steps it took to cross the floor. "I-I am an *estudiante* visiting from Honduras. May I see into the books? It is proper for me?"

A smile. "Certainly. What are you looking for?"

Leala handed him the poster from the laundromat. If Victoree Johnson was a trap to catch illegals, there would be nothing about her in the library. Would anyone be so tricky as to put a trap in books?

"I seek the *informacíon* to this project. The who is it that they are." Leala added a phrase from her class, one used by Americans a good deal. "And so forth and so on."

The man paused to digest Leala's words. "You're doing research, then?"

"*Si*," she nodded. That was the word. "I am to do the research."

The young man read the poster, nodded as he handed the poster back. "Aha. The director, Ms Johnson, gave two talks here. Quite unsettling, as you might expect."

Leala felt her eyes widen. Was she receiving a confirmation without having to figure out which book might tell her? The library was huge, big enough to hold her entire

256

village, every house, every plot of land, every pig and every chicken.

"The director, then . . . she *es verdad*?" Leala said. "One that is real?"

"Pardon, miss?"

Leala knew her English was falling apart. Was the *guardia* listening? Could he tell she was a criminal?

"Victoree Johnson was here?" Leala asked, shooting a glance at the guard. He looked like he was yawning, but it might be a trick. "Señorita Johnson is the real woman?"

"As you get, I expect. I was in the front row of the audience and . . ." the man paused, his eye narrowing. "Are you all right, miss?" he asked.

The man's eyes had turned into question marks. All he had to do was point at Leala and yell "Criminal!" and the *guardia* would throw a net over Leala and pull her away to be raped and tortured. She shot a concerned look at her bare wrist and slapped her forehead.

"*Dios mio* . . . I am *mas* late to an appointment. I will return in the *mañana*." Leala pushed a bright smile to her face and turned for the door.

"You're not wearing a watch," the man called to her back.

But Leala was outside and ducking between and around pedestrians. She sprinted across the street, hastening down another block to a bus stop on the opposite side of the street from where she was dropped off. She boarded a westward-bound bus, the direction of

257

her safe place. She paid her fare and sat behind the driver, her mind racing.

"Damn," I muttered, studying the surveillance video and watching a pretty teenage girl in a white scarf and blue dress speaking to one of the clerks at the Clark Center's info desk. The building's security office was in the basement, and the chief of security, a square-jawed ex-cop named Talbot, stood beside me as a minion ran a playback from a camera at the front desk.

"I'm to speak to Señor Ryder," the woman was saying, her soft voice picked up by one of the sensitive mics mounted in the desk. "He said I am to . . . to meet him in the lobby. But I cannot know who is he. Es possible you show me a *fotografía* please?"

I watched the clerk pop my ID pic onto the screen, turn it to the woman. She was the one I had the fleeting interaction with on the plaza. She must have been terrified to be in a government building that housed a major police agency, but she held herself with amazing aplomb, the façade dropping for a split second as a uniformed cop walked to the desk. When the girl's eyes saw the cop they widened as her shoulders tightened. When the cop turned away and the girl's face re-assumed the mask of concerned citizen, standing on tip-toe to study my photo before thanking the clerk and retreating.

Her story about having a meeting with me – at my request – and needing to ID me in the crowded lobby was pitch-perfect, delivered with sincere confusion and disarming innocence. Whoever the girl was, she had brains and bravery . . . getting me outside so she could look me over.

Had I passed a test? Failed?

"Someone you know?" Talbot asked.

"Someone I'd like to." I thanked him for pulling the video and headed back upstairs, nothing to do but go back to my office and hope the girl phoned.

35

The establishment known as O's Cupboard sat a block off Duval and one of the delights of the workers was seeing the faces of middle-aged Midwestern tourist ladies stepping inside expecting a trendy bistro and beholding racks of rubber bondage suits, whips and riding crops, X-rated videos, and a display counter of dildoes and vibrators.

Spyder Rockwylde, né Bruce Hastings, was in the back room finishing lunch. He tossed the sloppy remains of the tuna salad sandwich into the trash can in the corner. He belched and stepped into the tiny high-fenced court-yard out back and polished off the joint he'd started before work, then paused in the high sun to pull up his skin-tight black tee to admire his latest tattoo, a Gibson Les Paul guitar running from his pubic hair to his sternum.

Too cool.

He heard the door pull shut as he entered the front

section, seeing his shift partner and drummer – when he could borrow a kit – pushing the drawer closed on the register. Billy T. Rexx, né Kent Buttram, jumped back up on a stool and tugged at the inch-round black plug distending his ear lobe.

"Yo, Spyd . . . just made two hundred-eighty bucks," he smiled, holding up a fifty. "And a tip just for ringing things up. The man said to split it with you."

Rockwylde smiled. There was only one customer who tipped: Babyface Sanders.

Neither knew the customer's real name, the moniker coming from the man's childlike visage and affectation for white suits à la Colonel Sanders. Both enjoyed inventing backgrounds for customers and speculated Babyface was the secret love child of Harlan Sanders and the Chucky character of horror-flick fame.

"Babyface load up on more freaky teeny flickies?" Rexx asked, referring to the man's devotion to Hispanic porn flicks featuring the most youthful-looking actors, preferably movies involving simulated kidnap and rape.

"Bought all the latest titles," Rockwylde said. "And this time he bought the Avenger Twelve."

"Fuck me," Rexx said, checking the display case and seeing a dust-free pattern where the device, a lifelike though hugely outsized rubber penis held in place by a wide leather belt – a strap-on, in the lingo – had resided. "The Babyface jumped up a notch since last time." He paused and frowned. "You don't think a weirdo like Babyface is gonna actually, uh . . ."

Rockwylde laughed. "No fucking way. This place is the guy's girlfriend."

"Then what's the Babyface gonna use it for?"

"Early Halloween shopping, maybe," Rockwylde grinned. "He's going as a horse."

I did catch-up paperwork in the office, hoping Leala would contact me. Gershwin arrived at eleven-thirty and I told him of my near-miss with the girl.

"A dozen feet away?" he said, pulling off a banana-yellow blazer and hanging it from the back of his chair, his blue tee freshly laundered. The jeans looked new and the skate kicks had been replaced by sedate black cross-trainers. He'd upped his fashion game, either to look more professional or because he'd run out of clean tees and jeans.

"I had no idea who she was."

"You think she's the key, Jefé?"

"All I know is that she's in bad trouble."

My phone rang and I had it to my eyes before the second ring, saw the caller was Vince Delmara. I switched gears, hoping his snitch network had come up golden. *Give me something, anything.*

"Vince . . . tell me a snitch came through."

"*Nada* on a blade man. You know the problem there, right?"

"You rat out a knife pro, the knife starts looking for you."

"The worse the guy is, the less likely we'll hear

anything. Hey . . . I do have some good news. I get to close a MP case, Detective. The lab just confirmed dental records on a corpse named Perlman, Bennet J. Some called him Benny the Books."

"Bookmaker?" I asked. Though it didn't affect me, I was always buoyed by someone else's success.

"Book*keeper*. Got his CPA degree from Indiana University in '84, got hired by a manufacturing company in Elkhart, Indiana. I guess he found the winters a tad frosty and moved to Miami in 1990 and went to work for a private brokerage firm, long gone. Reason the firm died was the top dogs were running a pyramid."

"Uh-oh," I said.

"Perlman was keeping a fake set of records for the investors and FEC, one for his bosses. When the FEC took down the company – with help from FCLE, I should mention – the boyo lost his CPA accreditation and couldn't get the big gigs. He played Bobby Cratchit for a couple of slinky bail bondsmen around town, then turned up not turning up. Like for last year's family reunion. Not a sighting or financial transaction since. I figure Perlman fucked someone over and went swimming with the sharks."

"What makes you think that?"

"Perlman claimed the bail-bond accounts as his employment, doing basic payables and receivables. True, and they paid him thirty-two grand last year. But Mr P. has a big red Benz gathering dust outside his condo. And a flat-screen TV you could play handball off of."

"Expensive tastes, your Mr Perlman."

A barking laugh. "*Your* Mr Perlman, Detective. He is, or was, JDMS in the cistern. Second from the bottom. Wanna see where Perlman lived before he moved to the concrete condo?"

Benny Perlman had lived in a complex in North Miami, a four-layer pink and aquamarine cake with six units per layer, each with a long balcony, a palm-shadowed swimming pool in back, numbered parking slots to the side. We pulled into the lot and saw Delmara relaxing against a red Mercedes beneath a carport, the paint dulled by dust and its tires soft from sitting.

Delmara patted the Benz. "Two years back Perlman bought it second-hand off a two-year lease. It still cost seventy-three thou."

"Not bad for a man making under forty," Gershwin said. "But as an accountant, you expect him to be good with a budget, right?"

"Stellar," Delmara said. "Given that Perlman was paying fifteen grand a year on the condo and upkeep." He tipped back the hat and pointed down the opposite side of the street to a restaurant named The Cascades. "Toney joint, three bright stars in the Michelin. Big bucks, in other words. Credit-card records show the Perlster ate there three or four times a week."

"They must have been sad when he stopped showing up," I said. "Anything else come from the cards?"

"Only that his biggies in life were eating and drinking

and a pretty car." Delmara pulled his fedora and brushed the crown with his palm. "How about we head inside? You're gonna love it."

Perlman's second-floor door opened to cool air and the scent of cleanser. The dark blue carpet held the streaks of a recent vacuuming. The living room boasted the huge screen noted by Delmara, before it one of those goofy, overblown loungers touted in airline publications, pillow-thick cushions, arms and foot-rest, the monstrosity about the size of a double bed and having angle and massage settings, plus a folding platform for food and drink that currently held controllers for a PlayStation, Xbox and Wii, all running through the screen. I'd seen smaller screens at art-house cinemas.

"Pull the fridge closer, install a toilet, and I could live in a chair like that," Gershwin said.

"Perlman had a shitload of DVDs," Delmara said. "Eighties porn was big, a classicist. He also had a yen for space opera: *Star Wars* and *Star Trek* and so forth. Plus all the Disney animation flicks."

"A boy at heart," I said, imagining the hours Perlman must have spent in the geeky dream-chair switching between Captain Kirk, the Lion King, and Marilyn Chambers. I squatted to study a stack of DVDs set between the Wii and PlayStation boxes, all oddly without dust.

"This place looks like it was cleaned yesterday," I noted.

Delmara nodded. "Mr Perlman's sister has been paying a housekeeper for weekly cleaning. She's convinced baby brother ran off to Mexico with a hottie girlfriend but he'll be back when he comes to his senses."

I glanced at the chair set-up and doubted Perlman had ever had a girlfriend. Gershwin came in from the bedroom, frowning.

"No reading material," he said. "Zero."

"Maybe he didn't like reading," Delmara said.

"I mean no accounting bulletins. My uncle Pete's a CPA, has to read a shitload of IRS updates to tax laws. He's got them everywhere, even by the crapper. Perlman's got nothing like that. Probably means whatever funds he was accounting weren't being reported."

We tossed the condo and found nothing to indicate where or how Benny the Book lived so nicely on thirty-two grand a year. It was a sad kind of place, and I pictured Perlman as an oversized child who rented his services to whoever paid him the bucks, and never asked questions about what the numbers added up to. We went back outside after a fruitless hour.

"Got one other thing," Delmara said, pulling a page from his dark jacket. "Traffic citations Perlman's Benz gathered. Parkings and speedings, mainly, bullshit stuff. You wanna check them out?"

"Might be a pattern there, Big Ryde," Gershwin said.

"Sure, Vince," I said, taking the copy of the cites. "The boy and I will see if they mean anything."

"Boy?" Gershwin said. "Ouch, Detective Ryder. Snap."

Gershwin scanned the seven addresses where the Benz had been parked overtime or picked up a speeding citation. "All over town," he said. "Except for the two speeding cites, which were on I-95 between exits eight and ten, and two parking tix . . . one for parking too close to a hydrant, another for parking in a loading zone. They're on the same block."

There are names for the location where we ended up. Some call it the Strip, to others it's the Combat Zone. Some cities euphemistically refer to it as Nightclub Row, or Clubtown. I called such places Dregsville, because it's where the dregs of society felt most at home: shot'n'beer bars, strip joints, pawn shops, used-car lots, liquor stores, storefront sandwich shops, hot-pillow motels; there was always a bail-bondsman's office nearby. These establishments were interspersed with windowless warehouses and car-parts outlets and whitewashed shops selling second-hand tires, the sad stacks of balding rubber protected by high fences encircled with razor wire, like ten-buck tires were worth stealing.

"What do you call this neighborhood, Ziggy?" I asked.

"Technically, it's part of Hialeah, but this part I call Shitsville."

"No argument there. Where'd the cites get issued?"

Gershwin pointed at a fire hydrant. "The hydrant cite was here." We continued slowly for another block and he had me pull to the curb. "And there's the loading zone where he got ticketed."

"Times?"

"Both Friday mornings, one at eight-fifteen, the other at nine twenty-five."

We got out. The smell of urine rose from a gutter clogged with cigarette butts, fast-food wrappers, broken liquor bottles, crack vials and used condoms. A bus roared past and added its oily exhaust smell to the miasma.

"What a hellhole," I said, scanning the block, seeing a warehouse on the far side, flanked by a two-story strip club called the Paraíso, beside it a broken-down motel. Closer was a closed *taqueria* and a muffler outlet. On the other end of the block stood another strip joint called the Pink Pussycat, another brick warehouse, and a pawnbroker. I watched a skinny, miniskirted hooker step from between two buildings, make us – they were as fast to ID cops as I was – then turn and disappear into the bricks. "What brought Perlman here?" I wondered aloud.

"Getting his knob polished," Gershwin said.

"On Friday mornings?"

"Yeah, I've never been horny on a Friday morning, Detective. I save it for Tuesdays and Thursdays between two-seventeen and three twenty-two a.m."

I ignored the sarcasm as probably warranted and nodded toward the Paraiso. "Think he was looking for love at one of the titty bars?"

"They don't open that early. Gotta have time to mop up the previous evening's diseases. Think Perl-O-Man might have been keeping the books for one of these joints?"

I waited until traffic on the four-lane was stopped by

lights and stepped into the street to study all the businesses. The lights changed and cars rushed my way.

"I don't see any of these ratholes bringing in enough money to need an accountant," I said, jumping from the street as a garbage truck rumbled by, the driver giving me a blast of horn. "Unless they're selling more than lap dances and tires."

"We can always ask. I'm sure they'll be happy to answer our questions."

"Right now I got just one question, Ziggy," I said.

"What did Perlman do to end up in a cistern beneath a stack of Hondurans?"

"Nope. Perlman's hacked-off hands tell us he stole something. My question is, Who did he steal it from?"

We jumped inside the Rover and I watched the rearview for an opportunity, squealing out a U-turn. I was looking into oncoming traffic when I snapped my head to follow a dented gray sedan rushing past in the oncoming lane, the suited, tie-wearing driver now seeming to duck away as he slipped on a pair of shades.

"What?" Gershwin asked, seeing the swerving trajectory of my gaze.

"That guy in the beater gray Caprice," I said, looking in the mirror as the car turned a hard right without signaling. "I swear he looked just like Lonnie Canseco."

"A Latin-lover type?"

"I know, not exactly a rarity in Miami. Plus there was a woman beside him, blonde like Valdez, but her face turned away."

"Canseco's in Jacksonville," Gershwin said. "And Valdez is off today. It's on the board at the department. Besides . . ."

"Yeah," I realized, still shooting glances at the rearview. "I haven't exactly spent a lot of quality time with my colleagues. I'm amazed I can remember their names."

36

Gershwin and I retraced our steps to the department. I passed Degan's office and saw him at his desk, sleeves rolled up, the huge revolver in a shoulder rig and looking like an upholstered cannon. A case file was spread across the desk. Tatum stood beside the hulking Degan. Instead of tormenting a Styrofoam cup, he was shuffling pages in a file. I stuck my head in the door.

"Roy in today?" I asked.

"Jacksonville," Degan grunted. "In tomorrow."

"Hot case?" I asked, nodding at the file.

Tatum shrugged, not looking at me. "Counterfeiters."

"I thought you were in Boca Raton today, Detective Degan."

"Guess I got back." He didn't look up.

Six words from two colleagues, I tapped the door frame and continued down the hall. "You know

McDermott's in Jacksonville," Gershwin said. "You told me that yesterday. What's with the question?"

"Just gauging today's enmity quotient."

"And?"

I waggled a hand. "Chilly but not frosty. I think they're starting to love us."

"Yeah. And tomorrow's forecast is for twelve feet of snow."

We went to the office and I kept my phone close, but nothing from the girl. I tried not to think of her brave face at the information desk a dozen stories below my feet, but kept wondering how she was surviving. Twice I stood from my desk and went to the window. *Call me*, I thought, trying to beam my thoughts through the city. *Call me*.

My friend Clair Peltier – physician, pathologist, scientist – believed in synchronicity: hidden interstices below time and space where wishes, dreams, actions and events formed linkages unfathomable to the human mind. Clair might say that if I wished hard enough, I could create a ripple in the bosons that would nudge Leala to a phone.

My bosons weren't rippling, and I was at the window a third time when my cell rang, Delmara. "We need walkie-talkies," he said. "So I don't have to dial every time I have something cool for you."

"I'll get Roy to buy us some. What you got, buddy?"

"A guy got busted yesterday for a smash and grab, Blaine Mullard. For some reason Mullard asked to see me, hoping I could get him a break. I asked what he had to trade. It's a story you'll want to hear."

"Mullard's not your snitch?"

"Never heard of him before. I checked the others in the can with the guy, nobody there I knew. It's kinda strange that Mullard called me."

"Maybe the cop he usually snitches to cut him loose for lying."

"Possible. The guy's a walking ball of nose drool. I had Mullard transferred to a holding cell here, so run on over."

We were at Delmara's mid-Miami Division HQ in fifteen minutes. Delmara led us to an interrogation room, a twelve-by-twelve box with bland blue walls, a single table, four simple chairs, and a gray wastebasket in the corner. A horizontal mirror filled one wall, a one-way, behind it a room where interested parties observed conversations. The observation room would smell of coffee and perspiration and tobacco and no amount of cleaning could ever dislodge those signature odors.

The occupant of the interrogation room was a small and twitchy man in his early thirties, his brown hair long and ragged, his cheeks hollow and pocked with acne scars not concealed under the wispy attempt at a beard. His brown eyes were tiny and seemed to operate on independent gimbals, the left one finding me before the right one did.

"These are the guys you need to talk to, Blaine," Vince said. "Tell them what you started to tell me, and maybe it'll buy goodwill with the DA."

Mullard swallowed hard. "It c-can't g-get out that I'm t-talking or I'll b-b-be dead."

273

Mullard's fingers twiddled at a button on the front of the soiled black shirt shrouding his bone-thin frame, the body of a man whose primary nourishment was junk food and methedrine. I figured his stutter was exacerbated by nerves and withdrawal.

Delmara put a shiny loafer on a chair beside the man and laid a hand gently on his shoulder. "You'll be fine, Blaine. Your words will never leave this room."

"Oh yeah?" Mullard challenged, pointing at the mirror. "Wh-who's back there?"

"No one, Blaine. These two gentlemen would customarily be watching from behind the glass, but that would be subterfuge, right?"

"Wh-what's a s-s-sutter-fuge?"

"A cheap trick, Blaine. By having these gentlemen here rather than behind the glass, I'm showing you the only other people who will hear your story."

The guy was in his thirties but chronologically an adolescent, likely a permanent condition. I'd seen hundreds of Blaine Mullards, directionless, doomed by savage or absent parenting, and assuming the liquid mores of whatever group or gang they found in early teens, their nascent personalities and individualism replaced by a street culture that lacked any concept of responsibility or future.

"I huh-heard you was a good dude, D-Detective D-Del-m-mara. That you might help me slip the beef."

Delmara shot me a look. "Who told you that, Blaine?"

"I-I-I . . . it's just s-something a guy said. I don't remember his name."

"Some guy you met in jail?"

"If y-y-you can't help m-me I guh-got to . . ."

Mullard started to rise but Delmara's hand gently pressed the man back into his chair. "OK . . . so my rep got to you. But you've fucked up a bit, my man. Busting into a vehicle in broad daylight, snatching a laptop as a cruiser came down the block."

"I-I-I . . ."

Delmara did empathy. "I know how it was . . . you were hurting and needed to score. The true idiot was the one who left the laptop on the seat, right? An unwarranted temptation."

Mullard nodded vigorously. "Y-you don't leave a c-computer laying in puh-plain sight. It's s-s-stupid. Wh-what's wrong with p-people?"

"Look, Blaine, I think I can convince the prosecutor that the temptation was too strong. You'll have to do some time, but weeks, not months, right? Maybe in a program. Clean sheets, hot food, counseling you can sleep through."

A puppy smile. "Y-y-you're a g-good dude, Duh-Detective Del-ma-m-mara. Like I heard."

"But you've got to tell the story. That's the trade."

Delmara patted Mullard again and sat. Gershwin and I followed. Mullard picked at his beard. "I h-heard this a f-few times. It's on the street but no one says it ou-ou-out loud. There's this guy, a p-p-pimp. He had a woman, owned her, she was pure, y'know. Undone."

"You mean a virgin?" I said.

275

"Some c-c-chick in her t-teens. Came here in a truck fresh from some Mexican f-farm or whatever. Never even s-saw a dick. The p-pimp was gonna sell her to some guy who paid buh-big bucks for a weekend with the chick. The g-guy wanted t-to open the b-bitch up, y'know." Mullard gave me a grin like we were conspiratorial children. "Puh-party time."

I kept the grimace from my face. "When was this, Blaine? Recently?"

"I-it's bub-been a while. A couple years, at least."

"Go on, bud," Delmara said.

"A-anyway, some coyote on the c-crew bringing this ch-chicklet to town got drunked up and horny. He can't help himself, buh-bangs the bitch. She's ruined, so big bucks good-bye. The gangster who owned her stayed cool, told the crew boy he owed him twelve grand. The guy's a low-level smuggler, says he c-can't pay it all right then. So the gangster man says, 'It's cool, c-come to my place and we'll puh-put together a p-payment p-plan.' So the coyote goes to the g-guy's place. Buh-buh-buh . . ." The nerves ramped up.

"Take it easy, Blaine," Vince crooned. "One word at a time, bud."

"Bu-but instead of a payment plan th-the g-guy is there with a h-huge bald fuh-fucker who strips the c-coyote's clothes off and t-t-tapes the guy to a chair wi-wi-wi . . ."

"Shhhhh. Easy."

"With his dick and buh-balls hanging over the e-edge

of the chair. Then the guy puh-puh-pulls out a long buh-black knife and kisses it."

"Kisses it?"

Mullard mimed bringing a knife to his lips and kissing it slow and lovingly. "Then he took th-th-that black fuckin' blade and slices all the coyote's junk off. He does it r-real slow and the gangster fuh-fucker's smiling while he d-does it. And then he he he . . ."

"He what?"

"He has the huge bald dude hold up a mirror so the coyote can see his face as the guy jams the coyote's p-p-pecker into his mouth. He . . . the guy . . . the m-m-man, he he . . ."

Mullard was patting at his eyes in disbelief of something. I recalled a similar torture from years back in South Alabama, a psychopath who wanted to be sure a husband watched his wife's rape.

"The gangster cut off the coyote's eyelids so he had to watch, right, Blaine?"

Mullard started gagging. Vince smoothly moved a waste can into place and the guy spewed thin brown gruel into the bucket.

"Others were there, right, Blaine?" I asked when the sickness passed and Mullard was wiping his mouth on the back of a dirty hand. "An audience. The torture was supposed to be a lesson."

The unhinged eyes stared at me. "M-m-motherfuckin', yes. A s-s-s-serious lesson."

"Do you have a name, Blaine? For the knife man?"

A long inward squint. Even the eyes stopped moving. "Sometimes when the story gets told he's called Double Ought. Or maybe that was someone else."

Mullard wavered on the chair, his energy draining. "Anything else?" I pushed. Again Mullard retreated into his head for snatches of conversation or street lore, a difficult task, I figured, given the prodigious amounts of drugs the man had ingested over the course of a sad and small life.

"Uh, uh . . . someone m-might have once said he wuh-worked in a club or something like that. Or maybe it was a strip j-joint. Was it a strip joint?"

"You're telling the story, bud."

"Oh, sure."

I looked at the guy, head heavy with the weight of his rancid recollections, his breath smelling of rotting teeth and vomit. From here, I knew, he would invent memories just to go to a cell, do his time, and get back to suicide by street life.

Vince shot me a glance; he knew it, too. The guy was empty.

"We're finished here," I said, reaching over and giving the man's shoulder a squeeze. It felt like a Tinker-toy connection. "Thanks, Blaine."

He grinned lazily and looked at me as if he was wondering who I was and might I have a laptop he could steal. A uniform came and led Mullard back to his cell. The three of us leaned the wall by a water cooler.

"Double Ought?" I said. "Sounds like a gang handle. Double Ought make any connections, Vince?"

"I think of double-ought buckshot, the heavy-gauge stuff."

I saw Gershwin frowning over pursed lips. "Got a thought in there, Ziggy?"

"If the gangster's a blade man, how does he get a handle you'd use for a shotgun killer?"

"Nice thought," Delmara said. "I'll talk to our gang people, see if they have anything." He paused, pushing back the fedora. "It's so weird, but cool, you think about it. You're looking for a blade man, Mullard calls me with his story."

"Freaky," Gershwin agreed.

"Yeah . . ." Delmara said, shaking his head in disbelief. "It's like someone beamed him to me."

37

It was past two when we left the precinct house and drove to Tiki Tiki for lunch. I once looked into my rear-view and saw a couple that looked like Degan and Valdez. When I slowed, so did they, turning off at the next light.

No way, I thought. You're getting flaky.

Ms Amardara hovered less, thankfully, staying in the kitchen to supervise a catering job for three hundred people. Ziggy and I shared its largesse, making sandwiches from *ropa vieja* and chomping pickled jalapeños. A minute of resolute *No's* by Gershwin had restrained her from pushing a dozen-item banquet cart to our table.

"I'm gonna operate on the assumption the coyote is John Doe Bottom Layer," I said, sandwich in one hand, papaya juice in the other. "It fits Morningstar's time frame and Mullard's time speculation."

"Mullard's brain is gooey. But I'll buy in."

"So we got a guy with a knife who kills a coyote. Though it happens two years ago, it revolves around human smuggling. He goes into the ground first. One year later Mr Knife gets ripped off by Perlman, so he removes the accountant's hands as punishment. I figure a sadist like this guy probably watched Perlman howl for a bit, then sliced his throat."

"Ouch. Bet the Perlster wished he'd been watching Johnny Wadd beaming aboard Princess Jasmin while Mr Spock locked on."

"No doubt," I said. "And somewhere around that time the shipment of Hondurans went bad. It must have been right after Perlman got whacked—"

"Because he got dumped in the cistern first."

"Yep. A separate incident. Next came the Honduran problem, when Carosso got called: 'Hey Paul, could you come over here with a truck full of concrete? We need you fast.'"

Gershwin nodded and sucked a gulp of mango soda. "Carosso shows up and loads bodies into the mixer, an inspired solution. The mixture goes down the hole and it's all over. 'Cept no one figured on developers."

I stared aimlessly into the restaurant. The lunch crowd was gone, the ubiquitous Bert and Lenny kvetching at the bar, the ladies playing their mah-jongg. I heard clatter from the kitchen and snatches of Amardara's voice as she orchestrated the proceedings.

"You in there, Big Ryde?" Gershwin asked after I'd spent a stretch in the ponder zone.

"I'm still bugged about who knew the cistern was there. The damn thing is in the middle of the center of the nexus of nowhere and surrounded by brush, besides."

"That why you stare at the brush and kick at the ground at the site? Pissed off that it's got secrets?"

I grunted, not having noticed. "Maybe. Subconsciously."

"Could it have been Carosso? He drove the truck there, after all."

"Nothing links Carosso to the area, never lived nearby, never pulled a job below Fort Pierce. Miami and points south were outside his comfort zone."

Criminals, especially the dullards, tended to operate in circumscribed locales, places they knew and were comfortable within. I put Carosso in that batch.

"But Delmara did the due diligence," Gershwin said. "A rancher had it for years, then it was owned by a guy who didn't go near the parcel, afraid a python would bite his tootsies."

"Someone knew. We figure that out, we've got a window into this thing."

I started the thousand-yard stare again.

"You're not going to be happy until we visit the site again, are you?" Gershwin said.

We stepped outside and found the sky was a roiling, unsettled gray as an afternoon thunderhead swept over the city, the sun buried and the air thick with the smell of incoming rain. The gulls seemed lost in the imposed twilight, wheeling without purpose or joy, and winging for cover amidst the low buildings of the neighbor-hood.

Gershwin and I walked the gangplank toward the lot, the tiki torches flickering in the freshening breeze. I saw the usual vehicles in the lot, the two six-passenger golf carts used by the Jewish folks from the nearby retirement center, and Amardara's bright red Caddie. It fit, the retirees were the only clientele in the restaurant.

No, my mind said, another vehicle was at the side of the building, tucked behind a corner planting of foliage and palms. I studied the vehicle, a white panel van with the engine rumbling. The van shivered on its springs, like weight was shifting inside and the darkened passenger-side window rolled halfway down. A raindrop pinged off of my forehead as the truck started to move. Something made me throw out my arm and stop Ziggy in his tracks. "Down!" I screamed as the van charged. I saw shivering bursts of flame and dove into the shallow pool of the fountain. Gershwin crouched behind a palmetto as bullets shredded the foliage and whined off the rock border of the pool.

"Jesus," Gershwin said, eight feet away and pulling his hat tight to his head.

It started to rain, hard. I stuck my head up for a split second and a burst sent me back down. The van was under fifty feet away and approaching.

"*Vamos*," a voice yelled. "Go and kill him."

Lightning lit, thunder answered. Rain poured down my forehead as I heard the van's side door roll open and

283

footsteps on the ground, splashing. They were coming for us. I jabbed my head up and down again, saw the van being used as a barricade, two or three men behind as it moved in, wipers beating.

A burst of fire turned the rock beside me into dust and I flattened against the bottom of the pool, warm water filling my nostrils and choking me. I jabbed the barrel of my weapon above the short wall and fired three blind shots, hoping to slow them for a few seconds. I'd been ambushed twice before; you might save yourself if you had time to think. The trouble was you never got it.

My shots took return fire. A lot of it. Rounds stripped through the palmetto in front of Gershwin. I wiped rain from my eyes.

"You OK, Zigs?"

"Can you get them to concentrate on you, Big Ryde?"

He pointed to the nearest stone bench, better cover. Another round of fire pushed me below the water. A goldfish wriggled beneath my chin. I stripped off my soaked jacket and felt a round sizzle past my elbow. I balled the jacket in my hands, set to mimic what countless cowboys had done in hundreds of westerns: throw their hat as a distraction, kind of.

I rolled on my back and clutched the jacket like a football. I willed every bit of strength into my arm and whipped the jacket the other direction from Gershwin, hoping every eye followed the sudden motion. I rolled to my stomach as I threw the garment, two-handing my weapon above the wall and firing low and fast. The Glock had fourteen remaining rounds and I burned through them in seconds.

A glance showed Gershwin rolling to the bench, a dozen feet to his side. The shroud of rain helping keep him hidden.

I heard shots from my side, Gershwin pulling off rounds before he flattened behind a bench splintering under returning fire. But underneath the shots I heard screaming. The firing drizzled to a stop. More screams ended with a door slamming and the sizzle of tires on drenched asphalt as the assailants pulled into the street and raced away, lost in dense rain.

I sat up as Gershwin approached, gun at his side. He was trying to find something witty to say, but his brain was aboil with adrenalin and he had no breath, besides.

Been there.

Chaku Morales stuck the phone back in his pocket and turned to Orzibel, who was pacing his office and scowling.

"There is news?" Orzibel said.

Morales shook his head. "It's uncertain whether Ryder is dead. There was not time to look for a body."

"But he was shot, no?"

"It's not known. But Valdone is shot in the face and dying. Montega has a bullet in his chest. It did not pass through and could be anywhere inside him."

"Fuck them," Orzibel hissed. "They failed me. I pay thousands of dollars to buy failure."

"Ryder might be dead, Orlando. No one knows yet."

"He *will* be dead. If not today, tomorrow. The police . . . they know nothing?"

"The escape was clean, the plates stolen. The van is in the warehouse and will be painted another color."

Orzibel paced and considered the situation. He was a warrior and Miami was his battlefield. If Ryder had somehow survived, it was a small battle, no? The war was the thing. He always won . . . he was Orlando Orzibel. The thought buoyed him and he congratulated himself on his calm in battle.

"Call the man and find out if Ryder is dead or wounded, Chaku. If he is alive, it won't be for long. Perhaps the distraction will give us more room to find Leala Rosales. So maybe it is a good thing, hey? Let us get back to business."

Morales nodded. "Mr Chalk? Did you again hear from him?"

Orzibel made the OK sign with thumb and forefinger. "The deal is done. Now it's only a matter of time."

A half-hour passed and the taped-off Tiki Tiki grounds were a scramble of activity. The rain had come and gone, ten minutes of pounding replaced by blue sky and benevolent cumulus as fluffy as cotton. Ziggy and I had given our statements and regained our feet. He was inside with Ms Amardara, who was less unnerved than angry anyone would wish Zigs harm, and I was showing Roy the courtyard where we'd made our stand.

"What's Polynesian for OK Corral?" he said.

"Dunno. I'm just happy you don't have to ask it about Boot Hill."

"Not your Boot Hill at any rate. We've got blood out on the lot, and plenty of it. Someone got hit." Roy smiled, the thought pleasing him. "We're checking hospitals, of course."

"Gershwin made the hits, I'll bet. I was firing blind. He rolled from the palmetto to the bench, got a better angle. Gershwin was cool as ice all the way."

"That's why I brought him on board."

"You didn't. He was thrust on you."

Roy snapped his fingers. "Oh yeah. That." The eyes studied me. "So what have you done that makes you a target, bud?"

I shrugged. "No idea, but I'm a threat to someone. Thing is, Roy, there aren't many people who know what I'm into. Hell, I'm barely on the books."

Roy considered my words. "That bothers me. It's like someone has insider info. You've kept all this real low-key, right?"

I nodded. "And we haven't blundered into anything I'd consider a strong lead."

Roy pulled a cigar for twirling. "Whoever did this is scared of what you might find, a cautious type. I'm gonna put walls around you, a detail."

"Thanks, but no bodyguards, Roy. Gershwin and I need room to move. We'll be cautious."

"You're getting a couple units at your place. At night, at least."

"I can live with that."

"Found new digs yet?"

"Uh, getting close."

He whapped my shoulder and retreated to a vehicle on the far side of the lot, got inside. There were two others in the vehicle, I noted, Tatum and Degan. They didn't even get out to see how I was. I saw Degan's eye scanning the battlefield and was waiting for them to light on me so I could fire a one-fingered flare, but heard footsteps at my back and turned as Deb Clayton ran up, pixie hair beneath a blue cap announcing FORENSICS UNIT.

"You heard about the blood, right? Come take a look."

I followed her a dozen steps into the lot, saw the pool of red diluted by the rain, one side tracking off in twin rows. "Heel marks," I said. "One of the assailants was dragged away."

"Figured you'd seen it before. Doubt y'all had time to get a tag number."

I laughed and shook my head. "I saw a white work van, smoked windows, eight to ten years old. Then the shooting started."

She did a one-eighty turn. Techs had gridded out the lot and set numbers, photographing all the shell casings where they lay. We stepped past a young female tech crouching with a Nikon, clicking like a fashion photog.

"True gangland style," Clayton said. "More shells than Sanibel."

"It's why they prefer rapid-fire weaponry. Country

288

guys can go out in the woods and practice precision shooting all day long. Inner-city gang types are lousy shots, so they spray-shoot and hope they hit something. More often than not it's an innocent bystander."

Clayton shook her head and trotted off to supervise something. I saw Morningstar walk up wearing a simple white linen dress, the material stopping just above her knees. She twirled sunglasses in her long fingers.

"You're all the buzz, Ryder. I had to come see the scene and, uh . . ."

She paused. I had just survived a close-range assassination attempt and was feeling bolder than usual and winked.

"To see if your favorite imported detective was all right?"

She looked at me like I'd lapsed into gibberish. "To make sure the blood evidence got handled correctly. I heard about the rain and it was on an asphalt parking lot. That means grease and petroleum and other adulterants."

"Oh? You didn't care if the blood was mine or not?"

She put the shades on and stared at me through expressionless black. "Sometimes you make sense, Detective, sometimes you don't." She started away, paused, turned. "But I'm happy you survived."

"As long as I keep making sense?"

She backpedaled and spun away. "Actually, I'm beginning to prefer when you don't."

"*Oy caramba,*" said a voice at my shoulder, Gershwin. "The doctor lady has wheels."

"Consuelo all right?" I asked, ignoring his reference to Morningstar. "Not distraught about the damage?"

"Auntie has plenty of insurance. But I'd hate to be one of our attackers if she got hold of them. Ever see a roast suckling pig?"

"I'd help baste. Where were we before we were sitting ducks, Zigs?"

"You wanted to look at the cistern site. Or do you need a nap after the big dance?"

38

Leala had taken a wrong turn. The streets were growing dirtier and there were bars and nightclubs and fences on the windows and the smell of drinking and garbage made the air feel like oil on her face. Cars were on the street, growling, honking, radios blasting rock, rap, mariachi. There were taxicabs as well, as yellow as flame.

She pushed back into the vestibule of a store with wood where once were windows. If she'd been smarter, she'd have bought a map, and not blundered into this busy, dirty area.

She decided to re-trace her steps one block over, cutting down a slender side street. At the corner was a drive-in *taqueria*, its window thick glass with orders passed through a little door. A tall and skinny Hispanic man was at the window, a sequined cowboy hat on his head and sequins on his white cowboy shirt. His trousers were tight and black and he wore white boots. Leala had seen such men when visiting Tegucigalpa . . .

He was a *proxeneta*, a pimp.

Leala backed up until hidden by the corner of a building while the pimp received a bag of food and drinks. He complained about something and whoever was behind the window told him to *irse* in the style that meant *get lost, loser.* The pimp cursed at the window and spat on it, turning and striding back to the big car. Leala shot a look inside and saw four women, all crushed together in the back seat so the man could own the front.

One of the women was Yolanda.

Leala almost gasped aloud as she watched the man pass out a taco and drink to each of the women. Yolanda shook her head, *no*, but the man barked something and she took the food.

The car screeched from the curb, heading down the block and stopping at a red light. Leala started to run after it but realized the futility. She saw a taxicab and waved it to a halt. Leala climbed into the back seat, pointing forward, breathless. "Please, sir. You must follow that black car."

The driver was a heavy man with a mustache like a line drawn over his lip. He spoke in the Caribbean manner.

"The pimpmobile, hon? Why? You get lef' behind?"

"Please to follow black car."

"You gotta the *dinero*, girl?"

Leala threw all her remaining bills at the man and he pulled away, following as the pimp crossed Flagler, went right another several blocks. Leala's mind registered the street: it would lead her back to her safe place. Get Yolanda, run, wait until Monday and call Johnson.

The neighborhood grew even worse. Bars lined the street. They passed a burned-out shell of a car. Windows were broken or filled with wood. Once-bright paint was faded toward memory. A skinny dog vomited yellow froth as two women laughed from the steps of a dirty building. The women were barely dressed, their faces painted like corpses.

The car holding Yolanda pulled to the curb. Yolanda and a second girl exited, both in tiny skirts and tube tops and high-heeled boots that climbed to skinny knees.

"Stop," Leala told the driver. "I must get out."

Leala jumped from the cab and flattened against a brick building. When the black car drove away she ran to her friend.

"Yolanda! I found a woman who might help us. Her name is Victoree—"

Yolanda turned, her eyes wide with fear. "Go away, Leala. You are in great danger."

"You must come with me," Leala pleaded.

"They will kill *mi madre* if I do not do as they say. They are filth and they are making me into filth. Go fast, run."

"Not without you." Leala grabbed Yolanda's arm, but Yolanda yanked it away. Yolanda's companion looked between the two and slunk off as if the drama was a threat to her life.

"What are you doing?" Leala said. "I came to save you."

"I am here for ever, Leala," Yolanda said. "Get away."

Leala saw motion and turned to see two young men with hollow eyes and ragged, dirty clothes, one black, one white. They stared with open mouths. The white junkie pointed. "IT'S HER!" he screamed. "WE GET THE STUFF!"

The junkies circled like wolves, backing Leala into the vestibule of a vacant storefront. The black one pulled a small knife from his pocket.

"Easy, chicka," he said. "Stop right there and you don't get cut, right?"

Leala feinted left and jumped to the right, but the knife was ahead of her. The other junkie pulled a gun from his pants, small and rusty, the grips gone from the handle, now just a frame wrapped with string.

"Keep your mouth shut and don't move, chicka," he told her. To the junkie with the knife he said, "Keep her there and I'll call the number."

Leala held up her hands in surrender as her eyes searched for escape. But there was none: the vestibule surrounded her on three sides and the junkies held the fourth.

Then, seemingly for no reason, the white junkie spun across the pavement and fell to the ground, landing atop the gun.

294

"THE FUCK YOU DOIN' WITH MY BITCH?" a voice yelled.

Leala looked up to see the big-hatted pimp, his car twenty meters away, the door wide. He held a bat like the kind used for the *béisbol*, but smaller. The junkie with the knife retreated.

The pimp stared at Leala. "You ain't my . . ." his mouth moved from surprise to gold-toothed grin. "Are you the one they're looking for? It's you, ain't it? Baby, you gonna make me money an' all I got to do is make a call."

Leala spun to escape but the pimp was on her, one hand clamped over her mouth, pulling her to his body, his dirty breath against her cheek. Yolanda grabbed the pimp's arm, pulling with all her might, but the pimp grinned as his fist caught Yolanda in the mouth. She tumbled backwards to the pavement.

"NO!" a voice screeched. Leala felt the arms loosen on her throat. She struggled loose as the pimp staggered backwards, the black junkie hanging from his neck and stabbing wildly at the pimp's face with the little knife. The cowboy hat tumbled to the pavement.

"She's ours, bitch," the junkie yelled. "WE SAW HER FIRST!"

The pimp swatted the junkie away, blood streaming from torn cheeks as he lurched back to find room to swing the bat. The white junkie stumbled to his feet and stood in front of the pimp, pulling the trigger on the pistol. All it did was click. He hit the pimp across the face with the gun, which broke into pieces, the magazine tumbling one way, the frame another. The pimp slashed with the bat, catching the junkie's arm. A scream. The black junkie sunk his knife into the pimp's forearm, the blade breaking off as the bat rolled into the street. The pimp roared as the white junkie began kicking at the pimp's groin. The pimp caught him in the nose with a fist as a kick landed. Both went down. The junkie, nose pouring blood, screeched and fell atop the pimp, slapping desperately at everything in reach as the black junkie furiously kicked at the pimp's legs.

Leala staggered to her feet and looked at Yolanda, moaning on the ground but alive, beside her the grunting, screaming, furious tangle of pimp and junkies. Yolanda waved her away.

"Run, Leala," she gasped, blood streaming from her nose. "Run to save your soul."

Leala turned and ran. She was too frightened to look back and did not see the black junkie break from the tangle and turn after her with a phone in his hand.

39

There were still a couple hours of daylight, so I opted for the cistern site, one reason being its potential for opening up the case, the other being that the locale was peaceful and rural and after this afternoon's mayhem, some quiet was called for. I also liked that the landscape made it hard for anyone to sneak up on us.

With the column dismantled and carted to the lab, all that remained was a forlorn rectangular depression with the bottom now swampy from the afternoon rain and, it being Florida, probably breeding mosquitos the size of fruit bats. Beside it was the mound of excavated earth. The construction would begin anew on Monday and I hoped the first job was filling the grave.

I parked a dozen paces from the pit. Somehow on our journey a six-pack of Newcastle Brown Ale had fallen into Gershwin's lap and we exited with bottles in hand.

"You think the answers are here?" Gershwin asked, looking out over low, gnarled trees and desert-brown soil.

"One of them, at least."

"How do we find it?"

"We feel strongly and it finds us."

Gershwin gave me a look but said nothing. I waited until my bottle was emptied and meandered into the brush to stand on a rotting few inches of stump. A black clot of vultures broke from a nearby tree and tumbled to a further one, content to watch and hope for death. Gershwin walked up with a two-foot length of iron.

"Where'd you get the shillelagh?" I asked.

He swung it like a ball bat. "Poking from the ground."

I jumped from the stump and kicked at sandy soil studded with prickly pear, my mind seeing the agonized swimmer in the stone. I pictured her stroking free of the earth, face breaking the ground as her hands pulled desperately toward the light. And then she disappeared into crumbled dirt and a walnut-sized locknut pushing from the land. I kicked it free and picked it up, thumbing dirt from the hole, ready to launch it toward the vulture tree, send the bastards fleeing.

But stopped. In my wandering around the former tent, I'd picked up a couple other locknuts and a bolt or two. A shard of tempered metal.

What were they from? How did they get here? When?

I fixed my eyes on the dirt and walked circles. After a few minutes I saw a rust-colored vine coiling from a clump of weeds. I pulled . . . not a vine, a section of baling wire that left a slender furrow as it tore free. Gershwin walked up bouncing a rusty, heavy-duty clamp in his palm.

"You know, Big Ryde, I've been thinking . . ."

"Me too," I said, pulling my phone. "What else is down there?"

The forensics folks showed up within an hour, led by Deb Clayton, her day to pull a double. The sun was turning the western sky to layers of pink and purple and the trees grew long shadows.

"You have the metal detectors?" I asked.

She smiled, not looking the least bit tired after an afternoon working the scene at Tiki Tiki. "Six, highly sensitive for ferrous and non-ferrous. They'll detect a nickel at eighteen inches. We looking for nickels?"

"You're looking for stuff like this," I said, holding up the wire, steel bar and clamp. "Supposedly this land has always been vacant. But something was here."

"You find those subsurface?"

"Partially. We're wondering what else is down there."

"Where'd you start scratching? We should probably begin there."

Ziggy took the Rover and made a run for coffee and snacks, always appreciated, and I showed Clayton the general area where we'd found the scraps. The sun dropping fast, Clayton's team set up a generator and three banks of high-intensity lamps and went out waving detectors over the hard ground.

I saw headlights closing, a red sports-racked Outback pulling beside me. Vivian Morningstar jumped out wearing lightweight running shorts and one of those advertising-intensive shirts given to participants in sporting events. Her feet were in neon-green running shoes. "I don't recall requesting a pathologist," I said. "Even such a highly decorated one."

"A two-shift day," she said, stretching her back. "I break them with a run to clear my head. When Deb asked could she borrow the ME's two metal detectors, I got curious about my site."

"Your site?"

She nodded at the pit. "I release the site to the developer on Monday. 'Til then, I own it." She flashed me a grin. "So whatcha looking for in such a hurry?"

I explained that it was a fishing expedition and showed her the relics Gershwin and I had unearthed.

"We found a couple things like that when the excavation started. I set them aside in case they meant something." She led me to the rear of the mound. Atop a plastic sheet were two long bolts and another heavy-duty clamp. "What's the stuff mean?"

I knelt and studied the clamp, the kind I'd seen on hydraulic hoses. "Probably nothing. The rancher drove a piece of machinery here years back and it fell apart. Still . . ."

"I'm starting to understand you, Ryder, a bit obsessive."

We leaned against Morningstar's vehicle and watched

the techs work. If I'd hoped for a case-breaker to leap from the soil, it wasn't happening. After thirty minutes and hundreds of square meters covered, all we had was a rusty flange and a five-foot length of cable.

I heard my Rover in the distance and saw it zooming through the trees like Gershwin thought he was in the Daytona 500. He wasn't coming down the usual path to the pit, but a couple dozen meters to the east.

"Damn," Morningstar said. "He's moving."

"He bangs up my ride he'll spend eternity in Vehicle Theft," I muttered. The Rover finished the final hundred feet of its trip at a cautious pace, pulling beside Morningstar's cruiser. Gershwin jumped out with a bag cradled in each arm. "The burrito king has arrived," he proclaimed. "And I've got about a gallon of coffee in the back."

"Where'd you find the chow?"

"A little bar-restaurant a couple miles west. It's an old-timey joint, but good stuff, homemade while I waited." He passed out paper-wrapped burritos to nearby company. Morningstar grabbed a chicken and black bean and watched the techs sweep the ground. Gershwin grinned at her and elbowed me.

"You call her?" he whispered. "Or she just in the area?"

"She's still in charge of the site. And she's interested."

"I know what interests the Doc," he grinned.

"What was with that piece of driving coming in?" I said to change the subject. "I thought you'd wrap around a tree. Why not use the path?"

301

"I *was* driving a path," he protested. "Like a lane."

"There's no road there."

"I saw a natural opening to the east of the one everyone's been using. It's rugged – you bump over some stumps, but that's what the jungle buggy's built for, no?"

I'm not sure if I was dubious or curious.

"Show me."

He retraced his path to the paved road and circled around, the headlamps transforming the vegetation into a pattern of dark and light. In the daytime the landscape blended into a panorama of sameness. At night the headlamps suggested an entry into the low trees and scruffy bushes. He was right about the stumps as well. There were only a few but they seemed to step a path through the heavier growth.

"See?" he said. "What do you think caused it?"

I crouched beside a desiccated stump and picked at it with a fingernail. Another was five meters distant, another two beyond that, and so on. There was just enough room to drive a vehicle without scratching the doors.

I stood, slapping wood chips from my palms and picturing a crew taking down trees with chainsaws, behind them a Cat dozer scraping away the brush. The path was like a fire lane in a forest, passable if you didn't mind a bumpy ride.

But where had the road led?

I jumped in the driver's seat, waving Gershwin aboard. "Let's head past the pit site and see where this goes."

We bounced down the lightly demarked path until the

brush scratched at the Rover. I eased into a clearing, if that's what it could be called, lighter growth. It was just a hundred or so paces from the cistern.

I ran back and pointed the area out to Clayton. "Let's try over there," I said. "And cross your fingers."

The team reset in a line at the edge of the clearing and began walking. In addition to a buzz sounding in the earphones, a yellow light blinked atop the detectors when an object was located. By the time the team was a dozen steps into the hunt the lights were blinking like fireflies and I could hear the stronger audio signals. Whenever a tech with a detector yelled, *Strike!* a pair raced in with a shovel and sifting screen.

Within a half-hour the team had unearthed a bushel of smaller objects, plus three L-shaped pieces of rusted steel, two, four and eight feet long, a hole at both ends and obviously structural in purpose. Clayton crouched in light with the finds arrayed on a plastic sheet, studying each piece with a magnifier.

"Wish we still had the field lab set up," she said.

"Why?"

"Might help read this—"

She handed me a gray strip of thin aluminum, a tag once affixed to another object. I took the glass and saw meaningless runes.

"Wait," Clayton said. "Let's try something."

She spat on the tag and wiped it on her jacket. The runes were now a strip of numbers and some kind of logo. "Science," she grinned.

It was past ten and the mosquitos were ignoring the DEET so I closed down the operation. Clayton said she'd study the tag in the morning, but I expected she'd be on it yet tonight. When the final forensics van pulled away, I turned to Gershwin.

"This place you got the chow. Where?"

"At the end of the two-lane, the edge of the 'glades, an old village or the bones of one centered by a combo gas station and bar-restaurant. I don't think I saw anyone under a hundred years old."

"Why'd you go there and not toward civilization?" I said.

"When I came to watch the dig I overshot the road. Ended up there asking directions and grabbed a burrito."

"Old guys, you say?"

"Even older than you, kemo sabe."

"Let's go see what the old heads remember."

Orzibel was in a back booth at the club. Onstage, a pair of women mimed sex with lolling tongues and grinding hips. Few seats remained at the long bar, most filled with men in business garb, conventioneers. The majority would only drink, Orzibel knew. But a few would get heated up by the dancers and seek personal entertainment, ending up at the motel across the street, more money moving from their wallets to the enterprise.

Similar scenes were being replayed across Florida. And that didn't take into account the products working in factories and private homes, mainly the males and women too ugly for the clubs and whorehouses and massage parlors. Every piece of product generated a weekly or monthly fee, depending on the contract. In return, fresh girls were sent out on a regular basis, and all their costs were handled by the enterprise.

Brilliant . . . though too much tilted toward El Jefé on the money side. What work did he do, really? Jefé had a whole other life . . . how hard *could* he work? It was Orzibel who set up the shipping times with Miguel Tolandoro and who maintained order: chopping off the works of the guy screwing Jefé's then-favorite whore, removing the hands and slicing the neck of the *gordo* Perlman, removing Carosso from the world – and handling similar but lesser operations on a daily basis. El Jefé negotiated the terms with the customers, not in person but through Amili Zelaya, who also kept the contracts, tracked the product, and handled all of the accounting from her quiet office and tiny computer.

Jefé stayed clear of almost everything that might connect him to the enterprise, which was smart, of course, but why should he make so much money when Orlando Orzibel and Amili Zelaya did most of the work?

Orzibel saw a flash of motion to his right, Chaku waving from the entryway as a fresh clot of convention-eers staggered inside, hooting when they saw the girls writhing on the stage. He followed Morales upstairs to his office and closed the door, the music shivering through the floor.

"You were at the health club?" Orzibel said as Morales

tossed his duffle into the corner. "You heard something from our man inside the system?"

"Ryder is unharmed."

"Fuck!"

"The source did not think the operation was well planned. He said . . ." Morales frowned and paused.

"What did he say? WHAT?"

"He asked who set the clowns loose."

Orzibel's dark eyes blazed as he strode across the room. "*Bastardo!* I should go to his fancy downtown office and slice off his—"

"I told him about the girl, Orlando. That she escaped."

Orzibel spun. "You did what?"

"The man's job means ears on the street. Big ears. He'd heard we sought some form of information. He said he should have been told from the start."

Orzibel shut his eyes. Forced himself to be calm. If their insider's ears had heard of Leala's escape, could not the information soon reach El Jefé? That would be a very bad complication in his plans.

"Yes, yes . . . I did not expect little Leala to elude us for so long. Did he speak of her?"

"Only that we must catch her fast. And that she must never escape again."

A phone rang from Chaku Morales's plush blue warm-up jacket, a burner purchased to broadcast its number to the junkies and others looking for Leala Rosales. "What?" he said into the phone. He froze, asked, "Where?" He listened, said, "We're on our way."

Morales closed the phone, dropped it to the floor and crushed it beneath a massive heel. Its use was over.

"We have her, Orlando. Leala Rosales."

"A junkie spotted her?"

A nod. "He followed her to a shed behind an empty house. She is there now. Shall we go and grab our prize?"

Orzibel pulled back the sleeve of his leather jacket and checked the time.

"You take care of it, Chaku. I have a meeting I cannot ignore."

40

The restaurant, a single-story ramshackle assemblage named The Fishing Hole, sat where the asphalt crumbled into gravel. There was a half-decayed trailer court behind it and tiny pastel houses on the far side of the street. The restaurant's sign boasted *Air Conditioned!* like it had been invented yesterday. A faded Texaco sign was nailed to the side of the building.

It was like looking at the south Everglades, circa 1950.

We parked at the edge of the shell lot, a few battered pickup trucks closer to the door. I peeked through the window, seeing pine walls hung with taxidermied fish, a short wooden bar and a dozen tables. Patsy Cline was singing about walking after midnight. Two men sat at the bar as a guy behind it flipped meat on a grill. Three other guys played cards at a table, a pile of coins centering the tableau. The cook-bartender was maybe fifty and no one else looked under eighty.

I figured if I went in flashing tin I'd make them nervous. Two cops would be worse. I jogged back to the Rover. "You're staying here," I told Gershwin. "It's old guys night."

"Drink your Geritol, Big Ryde. Go get 'em."

I entered the bar tentatively, a genial guy a little lost and a lot thirsty. "Howdy," I said, my Alabama accent dialed to ten. "Good to see y'all still open."

"'Til midnight," the barkeep said.

"That ol' rain reach out heah today?" I asked.

"Ten minutes of fallin', two hours a turnin' to steam. Get you something?"

Not the place to ask for a Bass. "Bud."

I looked at the card players and nodded, nods came back. "What brings you out here?" the barkeep asked.

"Yeah," one of the guys at the card table asked, a slender man wearing a brown Stetson over a deeply wrinkled face, his low-lidded eyes and bolo tie giving him a resemblance to Roy Rogers. "It ain't zactly like we're in the travel brochures."

Laughter, me joining in. I jammed my thumb toward the development. "A big dozer's busted at the construction site down the way. I came in from Tampa, gotta get that sumbitch up an' runnin' by Monday."

"What's wrong wit' it?" one of the players asked as he pushed a couple nickels to the pile.

I shrugged. "Somethin' electrical. I drove out to look

at it tonight, see if I needed to call for parts. Got dark on me."

"Yeah," Roy Rogers chuckled, thumbing a few coins to the pile and checking his cards. "Night does that."

"Had me a flashlight and time to kill. I ended up wandering around, that or go back to the motel and watch the Weather Channel."

"Ain't nothin' left on that land, was there?"

I shook my head. "Nope. Guess the shopping center people were the first to see somethin' useful in that scrubby ol' parcel. Prob'ly useless since the dinosaurs."

The hand was over. Roy reached out and pulled his winnings close, about three bucks from the look of it. The others flipped cards to the table.

"You're wrong there, buddy," Roy said, setting his coins in stacks. "It was owned from a long time back." He scraped his chair around to face me, happy to set a stranger straight. "Walt Driscoll owned forty or so acres, ran some cattle there from the late sixties to early eighties. Walt was a buddy. I spoke at his funeral."

I took a sip of beer and affected benign curiosity. "Walkin' that parcel tonight? I nearly fell into a big ol' hole in the ground. Driscoll ever mention a well or cistern on the land? If I'd gone down that sumbitch I don't believe Lassie coulda found me."

Laughter, but it was an easy room to play. Roy tipped back the hat and the eye crinkles deepened as he scratched his stubbled chin. "'Y'know, I recall Walt digging some-thing for groundwater to seep into. A stash for the

310

occasional drought. Wasn't long after that Walt got into Brahma bulls and moved the herd to his main ranch by Okeechobee."

"Better forage, I expect." I fake-yawned. "Land go dead after that?"

"Walt made a few bucks from the land rental. More, I expect, when he sold it to some New York Jew. The guy was gonna build houses, but died."

I knew about Feldstein, but this was the first I'd heard of the land being rented out. "Rental?" I asked. "To another rancher?"

A shrug. "Some company used it to store stuff until it was needed. Derricks, or maybe it was scaffolds. Stacks of long metal frames. There were a couple ol' trailers parked out there as well, prob'ly to haul the stuff. It was a buncha years back."

I drank the rest of my beer and knocked the bar with my knuckles. "Thanks for the history, gennulmen."

"Enjoy the Weather Channel, mister."

I stood a couple rounds for the house which, judging by the response, was a rare experience. I drove away to a pull-off along the road, telling Gershwin what I'd dug up, then pulled my phone and called Delmara. I heard sounds in the background, muted voices and a jazz tune.

"Question, Vince. You mentioned the cab-company owner who bought Driscoll's parcel, remember?"

"Not well. But I'm here in Scully's with my trusty briefcase by my side. My wife won't let me in the door until I've had a couple pops."

"Good woman. You mentioned the cab guy's wife saying something. What was it?"

"Lemme check, lemme check." A briefcase snapped open. Pages rattled for a minute. "Yep . . . Myrna Feldstein. What she said was hubby walked the parcel exactly once to see if he could get all that stuff cleared off."

Stuff? *Stuff!*

"Thanks, Vince. I owe you a bottle of whatever you're drinking."

"Shit. I went bottom shelf. How 'bout I lie?"

I assured him he was drinking single-malt and rang off. I turned to Gershwin, tapping a rhythm on his thighs to burn off nervous energy.

"Damn, Zigs. I'd figured Feldstein was talking about brush, clearing it off for houses. He was talking about clearing out some kind of equipment that looked to the guy at the bar like derrick superstructure or scaffolding."

"Which you think it was?"

"Neither. I think the land was rented as an overflow lot for crane towers and booms. They take up a lot of room."

"Cranes?" Gershwin frowned. "Where have I heard that before?"

"Our preacher man out at Redi-flow, Ziggy. Kazankis's daddy had a rental-crane biz, remember? Olympia."

"The old Olympia building's by Redi-flow, Big Ryde. Miles from here."

"Doesn't matter. All Kazankis needed was a few acres of cheap land to store the big crane parts. This is actually

312

closer to Miami, where I figure the bulk of the cranes got hauled to."

Gershwin went still as stone. I saw him making the connections in his head and considering the implications.

"We go see Kazankis now?"

"Not with the hazy recollections of one old card sharp to go on. Let's see what Clayton comes up with. And let's put the microscope on salvation man before we talk. I want to see into his holy pores."

George Kazankis sat at the wooden desk in his shadowed office, penciling on a spreadsheet under the amber glow of a desk lamp. Outside his window the light on the high tower blazed over the black cross and the conveyor assemblies resembled skeletal remains set against the stars. He rose and checked the main room a second time just to be sure: a half-dozen empty desks; he was alone.

Kazankis returned to his office. Hearing tires on the gravel lot, he walked to the front door, flipping off the lock and alarm. A black Escalade pulled to the door, the moon reflected bright and full across the windshield, as though the vehicle was propelled by celestial forces. The driver's door opened and Orlando Orzibel uncurled from the Escalade and walked to Kazankis.

"You wanted to see me, Jefé?" Orzibel said.

Kazankis raised an eyebrow at the Escalade. "You drove here by yourself, Orlando?"

"Chaku had to handle a problem."

"Anything important enough for me to know about?"

Orzibel flicked the question away with the back of his hand. "*Nada*. A client at a strip club missed a payment."

Kazankis nodded. "The usual bullshit. Morales will handle things, right?"

"If he doesn't, I will. What do you wish from me, Jefé?"

Kazankis beckoned Orzibel inside. The pair walked the short hall to Kazankis's office. He resat at his desk and stared at Orzibel.

"I seek reassurance, Orlando."

Orzibel stiffened. "What do you mean, Jefé?"

"We've had problems recently. Ivy Hatton. The discovery of the bodies. Then I see a news story about two cops ambushed at a restaurant."

"I can explain, Jefé. The attack was a—"

Kazankis's raised hand cut Orzibel short. "If it doesn't affect me directly, I don't want to hear about it, Orlando. There's a fresh shipment due tomorrow and all I need to hear is that I've no cause for worry about anything."

"No worries, Jefé. All pay-offs are made. Joleo and Ivy Hatton's replacement, Landis, will pick up the box between Customs shifts. It will be delivered to the hut and . . ."

"My special drivers will meet them," Kazankis finished with a nod. "Mr Scaggs and Mr Salazer will deposit the product in your specified places. And I expect you'll take product downtown for local use."

"Like I said, Jefé, nothing has changed."

"How about Landis, the new guy I sent as Ivy Hatton's replacement? You sure he knows his part?"

"Joleo tells them everything they need to know."

Kazankis's eyes narrowed. "Joleo didn't fucking tell Ivy how to keep his mouth shut, now did he?"

"I think he did, Jefé. Many times. But Ivy did not listen."

"Fuckin' Ivy looked and talked tough in prison," Kazankis said, shaking his head. "He kept to himself. So I made him one of my special salvations. But Ivy took to drink and drugs, Orlando. It made him soft in the body and weak in the mind."

"I did not notice the problem until I heard of his loose mouth in the bar, Jefé."

Kazankis stood from his desk and walked to Orzibel, his voice suddenly as cold as death. "Dammit, you gotta keep closer track on them, Orlando, y'hear me? You gotta watch everything."

Orzibel's jaw clenched but his gaze dropped to the floor. "It won't happen again, Jefé."

Kazankis stared at Orzibel a long moment. His voice warmed up. "How many we got coming in the new shipment, Orlando? You always check with Tolandoro, right?"

Orzibel paused. "Miguel says there are, uh . . . nineteen new products on the way."

"Nineteen? You don't sound sure."

"I almost said eighteen, but Miguel found another at the last moment. A fifteen-year-old girl he claims is a true beauty."

315

A hint of a smile drifted over Kazankis's lips. "That young? A true beauty?"

Orzibel flashed a grin. "Miguel has a good eye."

"Maybe you can bring her by my house before you put her to work, Orlando. If she's that pretty."

A knowing wink from Orzibel. "*Si*, Jefé. I think I know what you like."

41

Leala sat in the darkness and listened to the pounding of her heart. She had made it back to the shed, but felt strange, even beyond the ugliness with Yolanda and the pimp. It was like eyes following her, but when she'd turned, nothing, though once she had sworn she saw a shadow dart through the alley at her back.

There was but one thing to do: call the Ryder *hombre* and tell him where she was. Even going to a gringo prison had to be better than moving through the streets like a rat. At least there would be food and a roof and fewer bugs than where she currently slept.

It was late, but she would call Señor Ryder.

Leala stepped from the shed, wincing as a foot crunched over a dry frond. The house was as black as always. A dog barked in the distance and traffic hissed, honked and roared on the wide avenue two blocks over.

Leala closed the door and stepped gingerly across the thick grass. Again a frond crunched. But behind her, not beneath her. Leala felt her body wrapped in iron bands that lifted her into the air as a huge hand covered her scream.

It was over.

Midnight neared and Amili cleared her desk and put away the computer. A shipment arrived tomorrow and there was much to do, but her skin itched and her belly roiled with sick motion and she needed to hide from the world.

She heard familiar footsteps climbing the stairs and held her breath, hoping Orzibel and the hulking Morales would pass by. But knocking came to her door, impatient. She sighed, said, "Enter."

Orzibel entered the room as if it were his, not Amili's. He leaned against the wall, a long black line: hair, shirt, vest, pants, boots, all a vampiric *noir*. But the brightness of his smile bordered on angelic.

"I have the girl in the basement, Leala Rosales. She was hiding in a shed not more than three kilometers distant."

"She escaped and you did not tell me?"

"It is my job to handle such things."

Amili leaned back in her desk chair, looking relaxed though the need of an injection crawled in her veins. "This proves what I have been thinking, Orlando. The best thing is for Rosales to return to her village. We give her some dollars and she becomes a part of the past."

"We lose money? That is a bad business model, Amili."

"It serves everyone best if Leala goes home."

Orzibel raised a dark eyebrow, as if intrigued by a puzzle. "I thought I knew a woman named Amili Zelaya," he said. "Now I'm uncertain. Are you having second thoughts about the career you have chosen? The career you fucked your way into and fuck to keep?"

"Careful with your tongue, Orlando. And never presume to know my mind."

"I'm not sure if you know it any more. Leala Rosales is not returning to her little village. She has cost much in time and effort and I intend to have her pay it back."

"How do you plan on that?"

Orzibel produced a smile as cold as the bottom of the ocean. "I am selling her to Mr Chalk."

Amili's eyes flashed. "Absolutely not. The man has rabies."

Orzibel ignored Amili. "Upon delivery we receive one hundred and twenty-five thousand dollars. Some time later we will send someone to pick up and dispense with the . . . leftovers."

"You'll do no such insane thing, Orlando. It goes beyond all bounds."

Orzibel uncurled from the wall and advanced. "Yes I will, little Amili Zelaya. And not only will Mr Chalk pay us to remove our problem, it will never be recorded on your books. You have not submitted the reports for this month. To El Jefé, Leala Rosales does not exist. That's how it will stay: You will remove her from all accounts, her arrival, the rental by Cho . . . everything. When Mr Chalk's payment arrives, you will not record that either."

"You have gone mad, Orlando."

"You, for being such a good little girl, may have twenty-five thousand of Leala's price. My generosity marks the start of our . . . what are the words, splinter enterprise?"

"*Our* enterprise?"

"Kazankis – let us break the rules for once and use his name – takes small risks and makes huge profit. I take huge risks and make small profit. I realize he invented the enterprise and devised a clever way to find the right workers, but I am worth far more than I am getting. That is about to change."

Amili studied Orzibel. "You forget my closeness to El Jefé, Orlando. For your sake I hope you are joking. But it is in poor taste."

"Do you see laughter on this face? Or is it delight at bringing you a gift, sweet Amili?"

"Gift?"

Orzibel made a show of patting at his pockets. "Where is it . . . Ah, here we go." He produced the gift-wrapped package from his jacket.

Amili froze, then regained herself. "And just what is that?"

Orzibel set the package on the desk and used his forefinger to push it slowly to Amili. "Your gift from Pablo Gonsalves."

"I know nothing of such a man."

"He seemed to know you very well, Amili. He wanted you to have this, something about you needing your dreams."

Amili pretended to find a memory and her smile appeared. "Ah, Gonsalves, the poor man. I met him once and now he tries to buy my charms with baubles. As if I wish to be flattered by a—"

"No, no, conchita. I opened the package. It holds several grams of heroin, extremely pure. Gonsalves called it your monthly gift. That's a *muy grande* habit, Amili."

"This is all a lie and a set-up," Amili hissed. "Get out of here before I call—"

Orzibel flicked his head. In the span of a breath Morales had grabbed Amili and taken her to the couch, pressing her small body deep into the cushions.

"What . . . is . . . this?" Amili choked, the big man weighing her down. "You are . . . sealing your doom."

Orzibel grabbed Amili's leg and pulled off a shoe. His knife flashed and parted the fabric of her hose without nicking skin. He tore the nylon from her foot and held it to the light.

"What is this crust between your pretty toes, Amili? Punctures and scabs. And on the other foot as well, I expect. You have the feet of a hidden addict, a housewife junkie. El Jefé has no problems with drugs for the product, but will not tolerate it in his employees. When he discovers his bookkeeper is a junkie you will be gone within seconds." Orzibel grinned. "Maybe he'll ask me to hide you, Amili. Would you like that?"

Morales removed himself from Amili and left the office, closing the door at his back. Amili sat upright and straightened her hair as if it would restore normalcy to her life.

"What is it you want, Orlando?"

"Miguel Tolandoro has sent us twenty-three products. I told Jefé we were getting nineteen, and you will record nineteen in your precious books. El Jefé has no way to discover we are diverting workers to rent or sell on our own. This will occur with every future shipment, and will start with tonight's erasure of Leala Rosales from all records. Her erasure is your second task."

Amili frowned. "Second? What do you wish first?"

"I have been denied your comfort for too long, my little junk princess. That will change, starting now."

Orzibel grinned and unzipped his pants.

With all governmental offices closed, there was nothing to be done tonight. We needed an early start in the morning so we went to Gershwin's digs, a 1940s-era apartment building on the southern edge of Little Havana.

"Price is right," he said, opening the door. "The building's owned by my uncle Saul and he's a generous sort. To relatives, at least."

It was a two-bedroom unit, one for sleeping, the other Gershwin's workout room, free weights, exercise ball and so forth. The living room, dining room and kitchen were one long space with a couch and chairs and television at one end, stove and fridge and sink at the other. The front window was filled with potted plants. Poster art was on the white walls, bright representations of local festivals and events. It was a comfortable space.

"Want me to see if a unit's available?" Gershwin asked. "You gotta get gone from your little wilderness real soon, *nu*?"

My soon-to-disappear paradise. I sighed. "I don't wanna discuss it now, but yeah . . . ask Uncle Saul."

My cell rang in my pocket. I checked the caller: Deb Clayton. "Just had to check that tag, right?" I said.

"Seems we're both a bit obsessive. The tag's from something made by the Maschinot Crane Works in Newark. There's an ID number and a date, 1977. All I could get."

"It might be enough," I said.

Gershwin was pacing one end of the apartment to the other, wired on adrenalin. But I'd been in this position more often than he had. "We're gonna tear into Kazankis like a buzzsaw tomorrow," I said, tilting back on the couch. "Sleep and get ready."

"Tough day, Gramps?" he grinned. "Need me to fetch your slippers?"

"Get me a pillow and set the alarm for six a.m.," I said, kicking off my shoes. "And don't even think you'll be able to keep up with me."

42

Six in the morning rolled in fast. We showered and sucked down coffee and jammed leftover pastrami and tortillas in our mouths, chasing it with cold latkes. I wore yesterday's pants, since Gershwin's waist was two inches skinnier than mine, but I borrowed a blue button-down and socks. He had a fresh pack of bikini briefs, which I bought for ten bucks, a lot of money for so little cloth.

Freshly dressed and semi-rested, we booked for the office and I waited until seven before making the call. Luckily they started early at the Maschinot Crane Works. "We keep records of everything," Candi Zefferelli told me after I summarized our situation. "Summa our cranes are decades old and still workin' like champs."

She sounded a bit like a character on *Jersey Shore*, but hey, it was Newark. I read the number deciphered by Clayton.

"Gimme couple minutes," she said. "See what I can dofahya."

It took less than one. "That tag you found? Musta fallen offa turret assembly for a fi'teen-ton crane. The turret got bought March a 1978, delivuhed in April to Olympia Equipment Rental in Florida. Got signed for by a man named Avram Kazankis." She spelled it out. "Sorry, but that's all I gahfuhya."

"Wrong," I told Ms Zefferelli. "You have my heart forever."

I turned to an expectant Gershwin. "The tag came from a crane assembly delivered to one Avram Kazankis in 1978."

"Georgie's daddy," Gershwin said. We punched knuckles.

"According to Kazankis, his father had a bad leg. What you want to bet Georgie was in charge of clearing the leased land?"

"Finding a big hole in the ground," Gershwin said, finger-drumming a riff on his desktop. "He knew."

I heard Roy's voice booming down the hall. It was time to see how much clout my new boss had. And how much autonomy I had.

I stuck my head in his office. "I need a chopper, Roy. Do-able?"

He frowned. But his only question was, "How many you seating?"

"Zigs and me."

"A little one, then. They're easier. Every time I need

one of the big chops, the damn Governor's got his ass in it. No one's gonna shoot at you with missiles, are they?"

"Hope not."

He picked up his phone and spoke for a few seconds before zinging the phone back to the cradle. "One's being gassed up. The heliport's on the roof."

Within minutes we were strapped in with mic-equipped helmets around our cabezas, Miami turning to a distant skyline as the land became gridded subdivisions set into green land broken by brown stretches of farm field. I was amazed open land existed in Florida, thinking the last piece of arable Floridian earth was in a museum somewhere.

After a bit the low sprawl of the Okeechobee prison appeared, a grid of gray boxes at first, then we saw the rec area and ball field and towers and high-wire fences topped with wire that could filet meat. The warden knew George Kazankis well enough to use the man's first name, Kazankis visiting twice a year on average, his rehabilitation programs seemingly beneficial. I was curious at how Kazankis made his picks.

"I never figured out George's reasoning for his selections," Warden Pruit Sloan said. Sloan was a big, brown-suited guy in his sixties, square as a refrigerator, with longish gray hair and eyebrows that looked like tufts of dirty cotton over mobile brown eyes. "George has a high success rate, so I never argued. But his candidates were all over the board."

"How so, sir?"

"Mainly it was guys working hard on rehabilitation. But now and then George would sponsor a candidate I never figured would get straight."

"They stood out?"

"Some of them were freaking scary. Hardcores. But they were at the end of their stretch and George figured he could save them."

"You know Paul Carosso?"

A nod. "Don't know why Carosso appealed to George. Carosso was a loner with all the personality of a clam. Did max time because he wouldn't inform on a guy already doing life. Not real bright."

"But loyal," I noted. "Not a bad trait in an employee."

The Parole Board had faxed a list of cons selected for Kazankis's program over the years. I passed it to Sloan. "We're kind of in a hurry, Warden. Could you check the bad boys on this list? Just pencil-mark the ones you never figured for salvation."

He scrutinized the list. Gershwin had told me Sloan had been with the prison for twenty years. I figured he knew most of Kazankis's cons from day one.

"You want their records?" Sloan said, picking up a pencil. "I can have copies made pronto."

We went buzzing back to Miami with dense clouds in the western sky, but a strong wind seemed to be pushing them quickly over the horizon. Gershwin and I passed the time reading Sloan's paperwork on the men Kazankis had sponsored.

327

"He spends a lot of time with the prison personnel and the cons," Gershwin said. "Gets a lot of background, sees a lot of records, hears a load of scuttlebutt. Then picks the cream of the crop, so to speak."

"I bet most want to go straight, Zigs, how Kazankis keeps up the illusion. But every now and then I figure he finds a prize. A guy with a trade he needs. Like a knife psycho."

"Here's Carosso's pages," Gershwin said. "Everything down to cellmates: Two years with Frank Turner, four and a half with Ambrose White, two months with a guy named Orlando Orzibel. Then Carosso's out and under the Bible-thumping tutelage of Kazankis."

"Any cellies match with Kazankis hires?"

Gershwin cross-checked as I studied the landscape. Miami lay twenty miles or so distant, looking like a prosperous Oz on the shores of an emerald sea.

"Got a match," Gershwin said, checking against parole records, picking up where the prison records left off. "The Orlando Orzibel guy. He was also a sponsored release by Kazankis."

"What's the PB say about Mister Oh-Oh?" I asked. I heard myself, paused, looked at Gershwin.

"Oh-Oh," I repeated.

"DOUBLE OUGHT!" he yelled. I saw the pilot wince beneath his amplified headset.

I scanned the pages, heart pounding. "Orzibel went to work for Kazankis three and a half years ago. He hit all his meetings with his parole officer. The reports from

328

Kazankis were glowing: Model employee, hard and dedicated worker, always on time. Even so, Mr Oh-Oh left the employ of Redi-flow after only eight months, just as he went off parole."

"Going where?"

"Said he planned to work in the entertainment industry."

I grabbed the chopper's land link and called Warden Sloan.

"I thought Orzibel the oddest of Kazankis's choices." Sloan said. "A good-looking SOB, big smile, articulate, but . . ."

I noted Sloan was no longer calling Kazankis by his first name.

"Never turn your back on him?"

"We suspected Orzibel of nasty incidents, two killings among them. One victim got his genitals carved off. Another, a rock-bodied psychotic fuck, by the way, got his neck slit. Of course . . ."

"No one saw a thing."

"While I'm amazed Kazankis sponsored a borderline sociopath like Orzibel," Sloan said, "I'm more amazed someone as violence-prone wasn't back inside within two weeks."

"Maybe Mr Oh-Oh got to keep cutting people apart," I theorized. "But found he could get paid for it."

Amili looked from her desk to the couch, currently occupied by Juan Guzman, one of Orzibel's lieutenants. He was heavy, with dull eyes and bad skin. His fat and tattooed fingers twiddled at a video game on his phone. Another *cholo* leaned against the wall and stared at the ceiling.

"Are you to watch me all the day?" she asked Guzman.

"I apologize, Señorita, but it is Señor Orzibel's request. You must stay in my sight and not use the phone."

Amili studied herself in the mirror above her credenza. Who was this woman? She had two subhumans watching her, Orzibel's foul seed within her. Music came through the floor and below danced young girls she had helped bring here under all manner of lies. There were so many others as well, stretching into Alabama and up to Georgia.

But today was the first time she had sent one to certain death.

There had been a plan once, hadn't there? Conceived in those first days when she'd slowly gained small pieces of freedom. When she'd moved into the enterprise she'd realized both the limits of her life and its unique access. The plan was how she had kept her sanity. That and the drug . . . the only way she had found to sleep without nightmares.

Had the plan been a lie she'd made to herself, a way to live in long-ago dreams? A justification? There was little she could change in the Today, she had told herself time and time again. It was all for Tomorrow. Gifts came from El Jefé, raises, designer clothing, a nicer place to live. For Tomorrow, Amili had told herself. I'm doing this for Tomorrow. For many Tomorrows.

She closed her eyes against the image in the mirror and turned to Guzman. "I must do my work."

"*Si*. But you must do it here without using the phone."

Amili thought for a long moment. She frowned at Guzman. "It is a delivery day, you know that? The money."

His mouth drooped open. "Uh, *si*. I think."

"I must prepare the records for the bank. You have been given importance, so perhaps you understand."

Guzman's chin jutted with pride. "*Si*. I understand."

No, Amili thought. *You do not*. She withdrew her computer and began preparing the records.

It was becoming Tomorrow.

43

The sky was a searing blue as the chopper roared south and banked toward Miami, now a distant cluster of jagged forms breaking the horizon. I wondered what we could accomplish at our desks. We were doing damned good at present: pulling the case together a half-mile in the air with little more than snippets of history, some inside information from a prison warden, and a lap full of records. I suddenly needed a sense of place and tapped the pilot on his shoulder.

"Think you could spare time to fly over a concrete plant below Homestead?"

The pilot's eyes shot a quizzical look. "You're a Senior Investigator from FCLE, sir. You don't ask, you tell."

Well, damn, I thought. *Score one for Roy.* We banked into a sky blazing with promise as I turned to Gershwin with more pieces assembling in my head. "Kazankis worked us like puppets, Ziggy. Expressing sorrow about Carosso while pointing us directly at him."

"Who gave Carosso the occasional packages? The guys Scaggs saw from the Redi-flow tower?"

"Pure fiction, I'll bet. Scaggs was likely one of Kazankis's hardcores shoveling more dirt on Carosso. Packages, my ass, Kazankis invented the solution while we were in his office: lay the action off on Carosso, make him a lone wolf. When Carosso got his throat cut, Redi-flow became a dead end."

"Brilliant. And cold."

"Five minutes to destination," the pilot said. We were riding the edge of the 'glades southward. The subdivisions were replaced by lone roads and solitary buildings. I saw Homestead to the east, the cistern site nearby. A minute later I saw the branch between the main highway and the road to the Red-flow complex.

"Glasses?" I asked the pilot, hands cupped around my eyes.

"Binocs under the seat. Gyro-stabilized. You can see up someone's ass from a thousand yards."

I pressed them to my eyes, finding the high water tank of Redi-flow, the cross sailing over the compound. "Stay back," I cautioned. "Don't want to spook anyone."

He pointed to another chopper a couple miles away. "We're in the flight lanes of helicopter tours of the 'glades, sir. They're used to choppers."

We flew closer. I ID'd the Redi-flow building and the closed Olympia Equipment structure nearby. I saw an old Quonset hut a thousand meters south. The treeline kept it hidden from ground view.

"Swing south." I frowned. "Let's check that q-hut."

The semi-truck rumbled down the sandy lane in the South Florida coastal backcountry, a battered red tractor pulling the kind of intermodal container loaded on ships.

"You looked worried a few miles back, Joleo," Landis said. "Any reason?"

"Ain't nothing. I thought we was being followed but looks like we're clean. I get wired up. Nerves."

"This how it's supposed to be?" Landis asked, nodding to the spare, scrubby land. "Just us and nothing else."

"Quiet and peaceful. I climb atop the cab and keep watch while you open the trailer. It's gonna stink. The guy I told you about – Mr Orzibel – he'll come and inspect the load, and grab some for local use. The others head to that hut to get fed and watered. From there they move wherever they're supposed to go. I don't ask."

"I expect I know, now that I know the hut's here. Redi-flow, where I work, is on the far side of those trees."

Joleo looked at Landis.

"We got a couple guys at the plant," Landis continued. "Drivers who haul the portable concrete plants. I've seen them drive a dirt path behind Olympia, come out a bit later and hit the road. Sometimes they return after just a couple days, still hauling the stuff, like all they were doing was taking the equipment for a ride."

"I know," Joleo said, pulling the rig into the dirt. "I

worked at Redi for a year. Best keep all that to yourself and let's git busy."

Landis grabbed the bolt cutters and jumped from the cab as Joleo climbed atop the rig. "Looks clear," he called. "Set 'em loose."

"What about that chopper over there?" Landis pointed to the west.

"Glades tours. They're too far to see anything, so we're fine."

"Glades tours?" Landis said. "What? They lookin' for 'gators up there?"

Joleo laughed.

I fixed the glasses on the Quonset hut as we approached. On the far side I was surprised to see a semi rig, even more surprised by what was atop the cab.

"That semi rig parked beside the Quonset hut – can you see it? There's a guy standing on the cab."

"Weird," the pilot said.

"Another guy's moving to the trailer, the rear. He's . . . at the door."

Even with the gyro I was getting a lot of bounce from the glasses. Add in heat distortion and it was like watching a jittering film. "Uh . . . the doors are swinging open and. . . . and . . . uh, one, four . . . uh, eight, ten, fourteen, fifteen, nineteen and twenty-one, two . . . twenty-three." I dropped the glasses for a moment's relief.

"Twenty-three what?" Gershwin asked.

"Twenty-three people leaving that trailer. They're

heading for the hut." I lifted the binocs again. "Well, looky here."

"What?" said the pilot, now as transfixed as Gershwin.

"A loaded semi moving from Redi-flow. Not north onto the highway, but south toward the Quonset hut."

"Are you seeing what it seems like you're seeing?" Gershwin said.

"Watching hell from the heavens," I said. "Wonder how that fits into Kazankis's theology?"

I grabbed the phone and dialed Roy. Perhaps it was adrenalin or maybe being loosed from the bonds of blindered earth, but as it rang I felt a moment of pure triumph, the sense of pulling victory from thin air, of fulfilling my heart's every desire in law enforcement.

It wouldn't last.

44

Without knocking, Orzibel entered Amili's office, crossed to her desk and stood beside her. Amili was making calculations with a pad and pencil. Orzibel plucked the pencil from her fingers.

"Forget Kazankis's numbers, Amili. Tonight we start making our own."

Amili closed the pad and set it atop the ever-present laptop. She gave Orzibel a questioning eyebrow. "This deal with Chalk, Orlando? I am truly to receive twenty-five thousand dollars?"

"Ah, the money has your interest now?"

"I have never lost interest in money. Otherwise, how should I find myself in this place?"

"You've been here one year now, correct? A very prosperous year for a girl from the Honduran country-side? But we shall prosper tenfold in this next year,

Amili Zelaya." He winked. "In the business and in the bed."

"Is Chalk coming here to the club, Orlando? Is there risk?"

Orzibel waved it away. "Risk is slight and to be shared. I am to pick up a Lincoln Town Car rented by Mr Chalk. Chaku will follow me to Marathon Key where Chaku will enter a certain bar. Mr Chalk will arrive by cab. When Chaku enters, Mr Chalk will exit, and check his merchandise. If satisfied, he will leave the blessed money and return to Key West in the Lincoln with a shiny new toy in the trunk."

Amili closed her eyes. "Toy."

Orzibel grinned. "Who knows, Amili Zelaya. Perhaps Leala Rosales will capture Chalk's heart, just as you captured the heart of El Jefé."

"Kazankis has no heart, Orlando. He has only desires. In his own way he is as sick as Chalk, just more sane."

"Sometimes you make no sense, little whore."

"I am to be your partner and you call me whore?"

"Amili . . . I make a joke. We can joke now, can we not? We have enjoyed one other to the fullest. And we will continue to do so, correct, my little . . . lady? Lovers and partners."

Amili nodded toward the hall where Guzman sat. "You have no trust in your partner? I continue to be guarded."

Orzibel moved behind Amili, his hands stroking her shoulders. "Only until little Leala has been delivered. You have not been yourself in matters of Leala Rosales.

338

Fighting my wishes to discipline the mother, wanting to send Leala home when she is worth much money." He lowered his head to whisper in her ear. "Did you recognize something in Leala, Amili . . . this girl delivered a year after you arrived? Do you see something I cannot?"

Amili sighed and shook her head. "Your mind is too busy, Orlando. You make me more than I am."

"So you have no feelings for the girl? No *similitud*?"

"I saw only a danger, that's all."

Orzibel's fingers slipped beneath Amili's chin and turned her face to his. "Prove it then, Amili Zelaya. Prepare Leala for her journey tonight. Can you do that?"

Amili shrugged as if asked to paint a door. "Of course. She is an investment."

Orzibel grinned. "Ah . . . here's our true Amili Zelaya again. Maker of contracts, seller of flesh. Bookkeeper of souls."

Taunts. All true. Amili spun away and stood. "Enough for now, Orlando. Do you have the clothing?"

"Let's go and decorate Leala Rosales. She has a big date awaiting."

The pair stopped at Orzibel's office where several pink dresses lay on his couch. "I keep several sizes for Mr Chalk. They will get used."

Amili picked the size she knew would fit Rosales and they went to the depths of the nightclub, through the sturdy gate and down the shadowed hall to a locked room. "Are you to follow my every step, Orlando? Or do you have more important tasks?"

"I will tell Chaku we are preparing to leave. Guzman!" He motioned the gangster to continue watching and strode away. Amili paused at Leala's door, pushed it open. The girl was sitting on the bed, her eyes lost. Amili knew the look: the girl had given up hope.

"I warned you to behave, Leala Rosales," Amili said. "This is not my fault."

"How do you do this thing that you do?" Leala said quietly. "How do you look at yourself?"

"Shut up! Put on these clothes. Now."

Amili threw the clothes in Leala's face. Pink dress and shoes, white panties. With Guzman at her back, she set the red scarf carefully on the bed. "Put the clothes on. The scarf must be last. Keep it nice."

Leala stepped into the clothes like a robot. Amili nodded at the ensemble. "Now give me your face."

Leala closed her eyes and Amili applied lipstick and eye shadow and brushed rose into her cheeks. "Don't touch it or Señor Orzibel will put it back on. You will not like his methods."

"We must go," Guzman said from the door. "I hear Señor Orzibel calling."

Amili looked into Leala's eyes. "Go to the bathroom and relieve yourself. I am sorry, it is all I can manage in the circumstances. But you have a sharp mind. Use it and let it take you away."

Leala stared. "What are you saying?"

"Bathroom," Amili pointed. "Now."

Leala shuffled to the dirty toilet. Amili went to the

door and stepped into the hall. Guzman started to push into the room but Amili stopped him with a hand on his chest.

"She is urinating," Amili told Guzman. "So she will not piss herself on the journey. She will be out in *dos minutos*."

Leala stepped to the toilet but was as empty in her body as in her heart. Something terrible was about to happen. She wanted to cry but her eyes had emptied as well. Everything was gone. She passed through the room for the door, but stopped. She had almost forgotten the headscarf. She plucked it from the bed and was surprised by its weight. Something was knotted into the fabric. She slipped loose the knot and a small black object fell to the bed.

A phone.

The yellow tab stuck to it said simply, *911 = Emergencia*.

Amili returned to her office with Orzibel's minions at her side. Guzman sat on the couch and ticked at the video game, the other gangster wandered the hall and sucked a soda pop. Music from below shivered the floor. Amili marked on a large pair of padded envelopes and snapped her fingers.

"The bank deposit is prepared. Can you be trusted?"

"Of course," Guzman said. "I am selected by Mr Orzibel."

Amili handed him an envelope. "The address is there,

the bank downtown. It is closed until Monday but there is an outside deposit window."

The man frowned in confusion. "I must watch you. Can Jorgé take the envelope?" He nodded toward the man in the hall.

Amili rolled her eyes. "Is he smart enough to read the bank address?"

"I will tell him where to find it."

Guzman passed along the package and instructions. Outside, the twilight beaconed toward Tomorrow. "Now I must go to the bathroom," Amili said. "Are you to watch me there as well?"

Guzman looked stricken: Orzibel was his boss, but Señorita Zelaya was also very powerful and rumored to be one of El Jefé's lovers.

"You have no phone?" Guzman said. "I am sorry to ask such an impertinent question."

"Search me."

"I-I will have to touch you."

"Then hurry, but do not let fingers linger."

Face averted, Guzman patted Amili down. She went to the bathroom and closed the door. Her hands moved beneath the sink and found the packet kept for long days at the office. She returned with fingers rubbing her temples.

"I do not feel well, the migraine. I must be alone to take a nap."

"I-I am sorry but I am not permitted to permit it."

Amili frowned in thought, nodded. "Aha! There is a

342

simple solution. I will go to the basement and take my rest there."

"Basement?"

"So you can be certain no communications will take place." She aimed an accusatory finger at Guzman. "Unless you people leave phones laying about down there."

"Never! Señor Orzibel strictly forbids—"

"Then put me in a room and lock the door. I assure you Mr Orzibel will approve. You have found a good solution, Guzman."

"Thank you, Señorita. Thank you."

They descended into the stink of mold and the rustle of rats. Amili chose a small bare room centered by a yellowed mattress and stained pillow. Concrete bricks formed the horizon and pipes the sky: It was the room where Amili had been imprisoned one year ago.

Guzman looked uncertain. "Are you sure that you wish to rest in—"

"I will be fine, Guzman. Do not disturb me until Mr Orzibel returns. Tell him to come wake me with a kiss."

45

"I bought four sleeping bags as you instructed, Orlando. And pillows."

"Line the trunk."

Leala heard tape stripping from a roll. Her ankles and wrists were crossed and bound.

"Careful of bruises, Chaku. I promised perfection."

"A towel between her and the tape?"

"Yes. But make sure the tape is tight."

Leala's crossed legs pressed the small phone tighter into the junction of her thighs. Her hands were bound at her waist and she could touch the phone through her clothes. She was lifted from the warehouse floor and set into the padded cushioning of the Lincoln's cavernous trunk.

"How is that, Orlando?"

"Like an egg in its nest, Chaku. A nest egg . . . how

perfect! A symbol of our new wealth. There are other Chalks out there, and an endless supply of Lealas. Close the trunk, my large friend. Time to vamos."

Leala's world turned dark. Her fingers began clawing the fabric of the short dress higher.

We hovered afar for twenty minutes before a line of vehicles roared to Redi-flow like a cavalry charge, sirens their bugle, the blue lights beating like volleys from Remington rifles. Within five minutes a dozen men were belly-down on the lot with hands behind their heads. I aimed the glasses toward the hut, another four men on their bellies as the former slaves-to-be huddled in fear and confusion. It was time to put our feet on the ground.

We landed in the lot and the pilot buzzed off, the chopper replaced by Roy at the wheel of his Yukon. "Come look at something interesting," Roy said, waving us inside. "You're gonna love it."

He roared across the lot to a semi rig carrying a bus-sized metal tank marked *Redi-flow Porta-Plant*. An opened hatch revealed a line of rickety benches bolted inside the tank. Gershwin and I stared in amazement.

"How's that for a slave-delivery system?" Roy asked. "Even if the rig gets stopped by a cop, who'd look inside mixing machinery?"

We saw a black SUV barreling in, the door bearing the insignia of Homeland Security. The driver stopped beside us and Rayles exited, the implacable and chin-led face now looking worn and too far from sleep. I waited for Pinker to exit, but Rayles seemed to have left the pet monkey at home.

"There's been a troubling discovery," Rayles said as his weary face nodded toward the office. "Let's go inside to talk."

I shot a look at Roy and we followed Rayles toward the empty office, all occupants outside and being readied for a trip downtown. Kazankis stood to the side with hands cuffed behind his back and doing his best to look distraught. He saw me and did several frantic come-hither nods.

I kept walking. I'd get to Kazankis soon enough. We entered the spare meeting room and Rayles closed the door. Roy gave Rayles a *what's happening?* look.

"It's Robert Pinker, my adjutant, assistant, whatever . . ." Rayles stopped and seemed lost for words.

"What is it, sir?" I asked.

"Pinker is . . . He's dirty, I suppose, as you people say."

"Come again?" Roy said, eyes wide.

Rayles sighed and leaned against the wall with arms crossed. "I've been bothered by Robert. It started that day at the crime scene when I passed the case back to the FCLE, reluctantly, I admit. Did you find Robert's behavior odd?"

"He almost went physical," I said. "It seemed unprofessional."

Rayles nodded at my assessment. "It wasn't the deferential Robert Pinker I knew, respectful of my decisions.

346

I asked him about it later, what had angered him so. His answers were plausible: lack of sleep, a lingering sinus infection, a touch of nerves."

"You didn't buy it?" I asked.

"His answers came with troubling microfacial shifts. It was like seeing a different face, another Robert Pinker breaking the surface."

I hid my surprise. "You're acquainted with microfacial analysis, Major?" Though the minute shifts in facial musculature were termed "lie-detector expressions" by some, they were not, though an experienced professional could glean such traits as evasion and stress.

Rayles nodded. "I spent ten years at Gitmo in interrogation and studied all the techniques and situational adaptations. I analyzed faces as the interrogators asked questions. Got pretty decent at it, actually. I became intrigued by Robert's insincerity and took a background interest in the cistern case, finding he chose an inexperienced team for a complex assignment. Then Robert handed the Paul Carosso investigation to the Miami-Dade department, which made little sense unless it was to keep HS out of the loop."

I looked at Rayles with fresh eyes. He was a lot sharper than I'd given him credit for.

"Three days ago I put Robert under surveillance by our best people," Rayles continued. "This morning he and two confederates on the Miami docks falsified records on an incoming shipment, essentially making it disappear. That cargo module is now on a truck by the

Quonset hut, where it seems our investigations have become one."

"Jeeeeezle," Roy said. "Pinker would be the perfect insider, access to shipment dates, cargo manifests, backgrounds of dock workers. You know how Kazankis got his claws into your man?"

"I figure Robert happened onto the trafficking operation and approached Kazankis or someone in his operation. The bane of our business, gentlemen, a weak employee near large amounts of money."

"Where's Pinker now?" Roy asked.

Rayles glanced at his watch. "Fifteen minutes ago Robert was arrested coming out of a downtown health club. He loves his workouts, but I hear most federal prisons have excellent gyms these days."

The requested jail transport was arriving, a faded blue bus with smoked windows. There was a lot of sorting out to be done. Kazankis was at the end of the line, side-whispering to a couple of men, heads bowed like a prayer session, but I figured they were getting stories straight.

The line shuffled toward the bus as a Miami-Dade sergeant wrote their info on a clipboard. When I walked to Kazankis he produced a convincing sigh of relief.

"Thank God you're here, sir. Surely you know I'm an innocent man."

"I'm uncertain of what I know, Mr Kazankis."

"I never suspected the terrible things those men were

doing. I'm sick at what I'm hearing happened. Those poor, poor people."

"Sure. Illegals traveling a thousand miles to be deposited a thousand yards away. A Redi-flow tank has its guts replaced with seating. Your employees driving the truck."

"They're ex-cons, Detective. I'm a victim of scoundrels. Men I thought I'd saved from sin, like poor Paul Carosso."

I nodded toward the false plant atop the semi-trailer. "One of the drivers of the truck built to hold illegals was Thomas Scaggs, who supposedly watched Paul Carosso get mysterious packages. Scaggs said he was able to see all this because he worked in the tower. Yet he was caught driving a truck with a tricked-out concrete plant."

A pause to re-calibrate. "I-I made Thomas a driver a few days ago, Detective. At his request. I missed what was happening. It sickens me to my soul."

I put my hands in my pockets and rocked on my heels. "You somehow missed a human-trafficking operation that brought in how many people annually, Mr Kazankis? One hundred? Five hundred?"

"I sit in the office and make schedules. I gave my men too much leeway and some fell into old ways. I trusted them to the fullest and they repaid me with deceit."

"The story ain't working for me, Mr Kazankis," I said. "Someone's gonna talk. You think maybe it'll be Pinker?"

I waited for him to freeze at the name, but he stayed cool, giving me rumpled-brow curiosity and a four-beat pause. "Pinker? Who's that? I have no idea who you're talking about, sir. Never met a man with that name."

After speaking to Rayles I figured we might use Pinker to directly incriminate Kazankis. But if Mr Redi-flow was telling the truth, that road was gone. It hit me that a schemer like Kazankis likely used a middleman to communicate with the HS turncoat. He could spout that *never met the guy* shit into a lie detector and the needle wouldn't flicker. Like everything I was learning about Kazankis, he was a brilliant strategist.

"How about Orlando Orzibel?" I asked. "He's your knife-kissing enforcer, right."

My shot in the dark drew the rumpled-brow again. "Orlando worked here a few years ago. As far as I know he's not been in any trouble since. But I haven't seen him in months."

"Which came first?" I asked, angry that Kazankis was finding an answer to everything. "The redemption project or the trafficking business? Hell, it doesn't really matter: You're a soulless piece of garbage whose only god is money, and you found a way to invest in human misery. Oh, and it brought you into contact with a lot of naïve young girls. You do the preacher act with them, or do you play Daddy?"

A twitch; I'd hit a nerve somewhere. Kazankis's eyes moved left and right, making sure we were the only two people within earshot. "You're a big Boy Scout, aren't you?" he whispered, his voice as cold as death. "My lawyers are gonna piss in your mouth, Ryder. I'll end up suing you for false arrest."

When I turned, he was staring straight ahead, as if he'd never uttered a sound. A cold wind began to blow across my spine: I imagined Kazankis on trial, his select hardcase employees taking the heat without ratting, part of an upended honor system. I saw Kazankis blubbering on the stand, invoking God and all the angels, not to mention personal testimony from men honestly claiming salvation through the ministry. All it took was one doubtful juror and the scumbucket was back in business with the FCLE hauled through the mud for terrorizing a modern-day Samaritan whose only crime was trusting those he tried to heal.

The probability was real and even a mid-level lawyer might pull it off.

I pushed Kazankis toward the bus, only barely avoiding wringing his neck. "Put this trash in the can," I told the sergeant as Gershwin sauntered up, hands in his pockets.

"Kazankis is nailed tight, Big Ryde," he smiled, clapping his hands. "We got him."

"No," I said, suddenly wishing I was back in the air and atop the world. "We probably don't. Plus Leala is out there. So is Orzibel. You found nothing on the guy?"

Gershwin hadn't expected my gloom, but he lacked experience with the Kazankises of the world: sociopaths who didn't expect to get caught, but planned for it.

"The address on Orzibel's driver's license doesn't exist. No tax records, he's off the grid. You look worried, Kahuna."

"I'm bad worried, Ziggy. Leala was a runner, Orzibel lives to punish people."

Roy rolled up and told us he'd left us a vehicle for the ride back, and roared to Miami to coordinate the arrests. I told Gershwin I was heading home and did he need a ride?

He shrugged. I'd deflated his victory balloon. "It's outta your way. I'll see who here's heading downtown."

"Or," I said, "you could come home with me. We'll catch a few hours' sleep and start tomorrow hot on the trail of Leala."

46

The phone Leala had hidden in her panties felt the same as the phone of her aunt in Tegucigalpa. Her aunt had let her use the phone to call cousins in the city.

"Marica, guess who this is? And how I am calling you?"

Did the US phones work the same? She pressed where the On button had been on her aunt's phone. A sparkly sound and . . .

Light! Coming from the box and behind the *numeros*! Praying, Leala dialed the three digits. Ringing. But not too loud.

"911 Emergency services. What is the nature of your call? Hello?"

Leala tried to speak at the phone but not enough sound came through the soft cloth taped over her mouth.

"What? Is anyone there? Hello?"

353

Ten seconds later the phone clicked dead. Leala felt like bursting into tears. Every call would end the same. Did the phone have the text? Her aunt's phone did not because the text cost too much. Leala had no idea how the text worked or if this phone had it.

In anger and frustration Leala slammed the phone against her thighs.

thump

Gershwin and I were sitting on the deck in the light of a single citronella candle, watching a cloud-shrouded moon float above the water. We'd gotten to my place and found neither of us ready for sleep. The freshening breeze generated enough wave action to create a rhythmic hiss in the dark and keep mosquitos at bay. I'd explained the way Kazankis could slip through our fingers and we weren't celebrating.

"The weather service says a thin band of rain's gonna slip in from the west," Gershwin said, sipping at his light rum and tonic.

"Maybe it'll wash the stink from Redi-flow."

"It's just a couple showers, not a monsoon."

My cell phone rang. I checked the screen: *Unknown Caller*. "Ryder," I said.

Nothing.

"Hello?" I said again. I looked at Ziggy and shrugged, clicking the call off. The phone rang again. And again, nothing.

"What is it?" Gershwin asked.

"Empty air," I said, pushing the phone to my ear. "The line's active, but no one's talking."

"I sometimes get ghost calls on my cell," Gershwin said. "Glitches in the system."

I clicked the call off. Ten seconds passed and it rang again.

"An insistent ghost," Gershwin said. I cranked the volume to max and held it up so we both could hear. Nothing but a buzz, a hissing sound. Then, a muffled *thump*. Followed by two more thumps. Then three more. Gershwin gave me a quizzical look as it started again: one thump, pause, two, pause, three. The thumps were erratic, not electronic. A human was on the other end.

"It's her," I said. "Leala."

"How do you know?"

"It's the only thing that makes sense. She has my number."

It began again: *Thump. Thump-thump. Thump-thump-thump.* Like a heartbeat. My mind ran the possibilities. "I think she has a phone but can't talk."

"Gagged, maybe," Gershwin said. "She's hitting the phone on something. Can she hear us?"

"Leala," I said, "Make one thump if it's you."

thump

"Is there something over your mouth?"

thump

I turned to Gershwin. "I can barely hear. Call tech services. Explain the situation. See what they can do."

He ran inside while I tried to figure out the best way

355

to communicate, given the limitations. "Here's the code, Leala: one thump, yes, two is no, three is you don't know. Do you understand?"

thump

Gershwin returned. "The techies are on it. What's happening?"

"I'm trying to figure out what to ask."

Gershwin put his ear to the phone. "The background sound. Tires? A vehicle, maybe?"

"Nice." I leaned to the microphone. "Leala? Are you in a vehicle?"

thump

"Trunk?"

thump

"Do you know your destination?"

thump thump

"Were you in Miami?" Gershwin asked. Another good question.

thump

"That's my partner, Leala," I said. "Ziggy. When you meet him you can ask how he got such a weird name. He knows Spanish. Do you need him to talk to you?"

thump thump

I thought a moment, though my heart knew the answer before I asked the question. "Leala, is the driver a man named Orlando Orzibel? Do you know?"

thump

I blew out a long breath and shook my head, then asked Leala to relax and let us listen. Gershwin and I put our heads together and listened intently for long minutes. The tire sound would slow and stop, then pick up again, traffic lights, we assumed. Or stopping at intersections. The vehicle wasn't on an interstate or deserted highway. We also heard traffic in the opposite direction or passing, and the occasional growl of a motorcycle or horn honk.

Gershwin looked at his watch. "Twenty-five minutes. If she started in Miami . . ." He let it hang and I knew where he was going.

"Do you know how long you've been . . ." I asked. "No, wait. Have you been in the car longer than a half-hour, Leala?"

thump

"She's outside the city by now," Gershwin said. "But which direction?"

It started raining. We retreated to the kitchen and I plugged my phone into the charger and set it on the counter.

"Check this out, Big Ryde."

Gershwin had turned on the TV and was pointing to the regional Doppler radar. A slender circle of showers was crossing swiftly from northeast to southwest, the lower band now crossing over Upper Matecumbe. The northern edge was swinging into central Miami. Brilliant.

"Leala," I said. "Can you tell if it's raining?"

thump

Rain meant she'd headed south from Miami. There wasn't much land south, everything turning to water save for the Keys.

357

"*Hello?*" an electronic voice said. The gate. "*Hello in there?*"

I opened the gate and seconds later saw a cop cruiser whip down the drive and slide to a halt. An older guy jumped from the cruiser with a brown duffel in hand, said, "Should just take a few." He crouched under rain, a short, pudgy man with twinkling eyes behind silver glasses. "I'm Frank Craig, a ham from Islamorada, ten minutes away. I got a call you might need some help."

Ham was shorthand for an amateur radio operator, folks whose hobby was communicating around the world on special radio frequencies. I'd never met a ham who wasn't a default electronics geek.

"You're not with the FCLE?"

"No way your people could make it here fast enough. I brought a couple things. That the phone?"

I nodded. Craig produced what seemed a shoebox-sized tackle box with electronic gizmos inside and a couple small speakers facing outward. "A reception booster for the signal and output amp to enhance volume and fidelity, especially in the voice spectrum. I build these things for hearing-impaired folks."

He duct-taped the phone to the box and attached some wires. It looked like a makeshift bomb. "You can charge everything by plugging it into a wall socket," Craig said, which he did. "If you need to move, this is the plug for the car socket."

"Any way to block our voices from going out unless we want them to?" Gershwin asked.

"Not without getting inside the phone, dicey. Best thing is this." Craig handed Gershwin a small square of soft putty. "Put it over the mic when you need muting, lift to speak."

Craig flipped a switch and sound filled the room, the hiss of wet tires now so distinct I heard seams in the roadbed. We could hear the moan of a powerful engine, the shifting of the transmission.

"Damn," Gershwin said. "It's like being there."

"Leala," I said. "You still OK?"

thump

The sound filled the room like a bass drum. Craig picked up his duffle and boogied away to our complete admiration. We turned back to the phone and startled to a furious scratching sound that seemed to echo from my walls.

Then, utter silence.

"What the hell?" Gershwin said, eyes wide.

"They've stopped," I said, leaning close to the speaker. "I can't hear an engine."

"Leala," I whispered to the phone. "What is it?"

No response. I thought I could hear a faraway drumming of rain on metal. Or maybe it was a terrified heart.

"Jesus," Gershwin said, a shade whiter. "What was that sound?"

"I'm hoping it was Leala hiding the phone," I said.

359

47

Orzibel parked to the side of the roadhouse, the wipers beating against slackening rain. Seconds later Morales splashed into the lot in the Escalade and strode into the bar. A minute later Orzibel saw a man leave the roadhouse. He wore a creamy white suit, a briefcase in his left hand, umbrella in the right. Orzibel flashed his headlamps and exited the car as the suited man approached.

They went to the rear of the Lincoln and Orzibel opened the trunk. The light inside had a yellow cast, like buttery candlelight.

"Is everything to your liking, señor?" Orzibel said.

Chalk stood spellbound, his mouth drooping open. A shaking hand passed the briefcase to Orzibel. "Yes," he finally said. "Everything is beyond perfect."

Chalk started away, looking like a child lost in a dream.

He paused and turned to Orzibel. "Have you finalized instructions for when she is . . . when I am done?"

"Ah, that has been made easy," Orzibel said. "Folded in the back seat is a large and reinforced cardboard box marked with the name of a local charity. It is used to donate books and clothes and other discards. Put the object in the box and call me. I will give you a time to put the box on your porch. Minutes later the box will be removed. Everything will appear perfectly normal to neighbors' eyes."

"You have thought of everything," Chalk said, retreating to the driver's seat. Orzibel's lips twisted into a malicious sneer as he leaned into the trunk and stared into the eyes of Leala Rosales.

"Do you love your mother?" he asked. "And she you?"

Leala's eyes were wide with terror, but she nodded yes.

"I was going to tear out one of her eyes. But now I will tear out her heart. They say such is the pain when a child disappears." Orzibel's hand reached to the trunk lid. "Farewell, little Leala. My friends will gather your remains next week."

He closed the trunk.

I heard the trunk shut and pulled the putty from the phone mic, keeping my voice calm, though my heart rang in my throat and my palms were cold. The meaning of the words was clear: Leala was doomed.

"Leala? Are you there?"

thump

"Did you see anything when the trunk was open? Anything that suggested where you are?"

thump thump

"Is Orzibel still driving?"

A pause. Then in quick succession: *thump thump thump* brief pause *thump thump*

"Five?" Gershwin frowned.

I sat perplexed until her math made sense. I turned to Gershwin. "An *I don't know* added to a *no* gives you an *I don't think so.*"

"*Oy caramba.* We can't let anything happen to this girl, Big Ryde. The world needs her."

"The rain is lessening," I said, canting my head. "Or maybe stopped completely."

Gershwin ran to the TV and looked at the Doppler radar picture. "The north edge of the band is in Fort Pierce or thereabouts. South edge is moving east from the Saddlebunch or Sugarloaf Keys area."

Stay calm, my head told my heart. Calm is control. I pulled the phone assembly closer. "Hey there, Leala, I need a weather report. Is it still raining?"

thump thump

"Did it just recently stop?"

thump

Gershwin pointed to the screen. "She's minutes from Key West. It's the only answer. Either that or she's way up north. Everywhere else is rain."

I stared at the television. Leala was heading toward Key West.

"Get Orzibel's pic on a BOLO to the Key cops. If he's seen, notify us ASAP, but do not approach, right?"

"On it. Then what?"

I was picking up the board wired together by Frank Craig. "See you in the Rover."

We hit the highway and turned west with lights flashing and siren howling, racing toward the end of America.

48

Leala squinted toward the phone at her waist, the only light left in her life. In the upper corner was a box that showed how much talking was left. The box was mostly empty which in her aunt's phone meant it would soon stop working. She thought a moment and tapped the phone on her leg, first fast, then slowing down.

"Leala?" the man named Ziggy said. It sounded like they were in a car as well. "What is it?"

She repeated the pattern. *thumpthumpthump* . . . *thumpthump-thump-thump* . . . *thump* . . . *thump* Trying to make the sounds fainter as they progressed.

"We don't understand."

Leala again performed the tattoo. She heard the men talking between them. "Slowing then stopping," Detective

Ryder yelled. "Do you mean your phone charge is getting low?"

thump

"Can you turn the phone off and turn it back on when you need to?"

thump

The phone box went as silent as death. I kept my foot deep in the accelerator as cars pulled to the side of the road. The radio crackled as we crossed Big Coppit Key, minutes from Key West. "Got it," Gershwin said, putting the mic on speaker. Roy McDermott's voice filled the Rover, hissing and popping with interference from the storm between us and Miami.

"Pinker's spilling his guts," Roy said through the static. "He's sure Kazankis is behind it, but never had any direct contact. Communications went through a guy named Chaku Morales. They'd meet at a health club downtown, but main operations are centered in a titty bar called the Paraíso. Ownership is buried under a bunch of dummy corporations, but Orlando Orzibel is listed as the manager. We just put surveillance on the place."

"Down the block from where Perlman got a couple tickets," Gershwin said. "Friday mornings."

I recalled the joint, a ghastly three-story building with silhouettes of naked female forms painted on the walls. "Probably picking up his paycheck," I mumbled.

"Any input?" Roy asked.

"Just watch the joint for now," I yelled toward the mic. "If Orzibel shows up, take it all down. Careful around Orzibel, he's a cutter."

"Bang," Roy said. "What a happy sound."

The Escalade slipped down the side street and pulled into the back entrance of the warehouse. The rain was still pouring and if they parked in the club's lot Orzibel would have to splash through rain and puke from the Saturday-night conventioneers. He planned to hand Amili her cut, have a quick celebration fuck, then a late dinner at a fancy restaurant. To enter with a woman as beautiful as Amili Zelaya would pull every eye to Orzibel. She would be his whore queen. In a year, with planning and stored money, they could take over the operation. Kazankis would have to die, of course.

Orzibel's heart was dancing as he started up the stairs, but Guzman waved him to stop. "Señor Orzibel . . . I have a message from Señorita Zelaya."

"What has she said?"

Guzman nodded to a closed door. "She is behind here. Sleeping. She had the migraine."

Orzibel frowned as he approached, boots echoing from the concrete floor. "Why here?"

"Her idea. A place to rest where I would be sure she had no way to communicate. She said sleep would restore her."

"And what was this message she had for me?"

"When you returned you were to enter. And awaken her with a kiss."

Orzibel beamed and pointed to the stairs. "Go upstairs, Guzman. Tell the barman you have earned a bottle of Dom Pérignon. In fact, I wish all the men to drink Dom tonight. A gift from me."

The man grinned and started away. "*Gracias, señor*. You are *muy generoso*."

"Close the door at the top of the stairs, *por favor*," Orzibel winked. "I don't wish the club's music to be overwhelmed by the sounds of passion."

The man disappeared up the stairs. Orzibel inserted his key in the lock. "Here comes your king, *mi puta*," he said, pushing open the door. "Prepare for the night of your life."

Amili Zelaya waited for him on the mattress, her arms outstretched and her long legs spread wide, the vomited froth of her overdose now dried on her chin and neck, the syringe still hanging from her cold arm.

Tomorrow had passed.

49

"It's him," Lonnie Canseco said to Roy McDermott, the phone clutched to his cheek. "The Orzibel guy." Canseco was crouching beneath a soaked poncho on a rooftop across from the Paraíso and watching through binoculars. "I dunno how the fuck he got inside. Must be a hidden entrance."

McDermott was smoking a cigar in a command vehicle parked in an alley a block away, Degan at the wheel, Valdez and Tatum in the rear. Canseco had drawn the short straw and was leading the reconnaissance team.

"How do you know it's Orzi-doodle?" McDermott asked Canseco. "If he's inside."

"Because he just kicked open the front door and ran outside, Roy."

"In the rain?"

"Hang on a sec, Roy, he's uh . . . holy shit."

"What?"

"Orzibel's shaking his fist at the sky and screaming curses. Not a happy man, Roy. Wait a minute, I uh . . . this keeps getting weirder."

"What now?"

"Some huge bald muthafuck just ran out. He picked up Orzibel like a baby and is carrying him back inside the club. What should we do?"

"Take the place down, Lonnie. That's per instructions from our very own Detective Ryder."

A pause. "You mean the asshole who stole all my money, Roy?" Canseco said.

Back in the command vehicle, Roy McDermott smiled and blew a smoke ring.

Minard Chalk turned down his foliage-shrouded drive and parked in the grass behind the looming white house. The rain had blown northeast to leave a full moon hung above his house like a beacon. Through the trees and over the sea wall Chalk saw the dark sea, its surface sparkling under the moonlight as if sleeping beneath a blanket of stars.

He walked softly to the trunk and put an ear to the metal. Not a sound. She would be immobile in fear, terrified. Thinking of her fear, Chalk's hand drifted to his crotch.

Whoops. He hadn't dressed for the meeting.

It would only take a few seconds to strap in place.

Midnight was nearing and we'd parked in the lot of a shopping mall in the center of Key West. Being Saturday, the major streets were a traffic blitzkrieg. Horns honked, lights flashed, music blared from bars.

"The locals are on standby?" I asked Gershwin.

"That's the third time you've asked."

"Sorry."

He pointed to the far end of the lot. I saw two KW cruisers. "If we need an escort somewhere, that's our entourage. I've got it all set up, Big Ryde."

I started to lean back when Roy came over the radio. "We took down the Paraíso, Carson."

"Orzibel showed up?"

"Canseco was surveilling from across the street. Orzibel ran out front screaming when a monster now known as Chaku Morales followed and carried Orzibel inside. That's when we went in."

"You get Orzibel to talk?" I mentally crossed my fingers.

"The scumbucket didn't say a word. He just handed over a card with the name of a local criminal lawyer, an Armani-wrapped turd, but the absolute best in Miami at springing these bastards."

I figured Kazankis had the same representation. And also figured there'd be nothing in the club to implicate Mr Redi-flow. He'd probably never been within a mile of the joint.

"What's the place like, Roy?"

"Gets interesting here. The first floor has the standard strip-joint ambience that makes you wanna put on a hazmat suit. Upstairs are two offices, one quite fashionable. The other looks like Elvis's finest wet dream. Then there's the club's basement, Carson, a hellhole of rabbit-warren rooms, cells. Fifteen in all. They're currently empty, at least of living people."

I heard Roy take a puff on a cigar, blow it out.

"Living? Why the distinction?"

A pause. "We found a dead woman sprawled naked on a mattress, a needle sticking from her arm. Healthy-looking carriage, classy make-up, expensive-smelling cologne. There was a reeking, shit-stained commode in the room. You'll never guess what was in the bowl, Carson."

"What?"

"A diamond-studded Piaget watch. Can you freakin' believe that?"

The car had been stopped for several minutes. Then, the slam of a door like on a house, then footsteps. Leala had furiously pressed the On button as the feet drew close.

Please do not open the trunk while the sparkly sound happens.

The light flashed on the phone. The sound. As Leala tapped the numbers she heard the latch click on the trunk. She jammed the phone back into her panties and went still.

The trunk opened. A head leaned in. Far above it the sky was filled with stars.

The head said, "*Buenas noches*, Xaviera. Good to see you again."

50

Roy was telling me about the Paraíso bust when my phone rang: Leala.

"Gotta go, Roy." I bent close to the phone and heard rustling, bumping: Leala moving. We weren't going to attempt communication without a signal from Leala, the putty over the mic. Then, the sound of a trunk latch. We held our breath as a male voice filled the Rover.

"... *next, Xaviera, I need to put this collar around your lovely neck, then clip this to it. Think of it as a ... an elegant necklace. Sit up, Xavie. DO IT!*"

I looked at Gershwin; like me, he was barely breathing. More rustling. Another click. "*Sit up, that's it. Give me your hand. HAND! Welcome to Key West, Xavie. Doesn't the evening smell beautiful?*"

"Come on, pervert," I whispered. "Introduce yourself."

If we got a name, Gershwin would relay it to the Key

West cops. They'd match it with an address. Even a non-resident who owned a vacation home would be named on tax records, but I figured we were dealing with a resident, given Orzibel's reference to the perp's porch and neighbors. Plus my experience suggested that if this monster had bought Leala for the purpose it seemed, he would create a special venue for the event, a place to sit and fantasize prior to the act. The concept was grim and grisly and something I'd learned from my brother years ago.

My mind was racing, trying to recall everything I knew about disturbed minds when we heard the crunching of feet on gravel or shell.

A door opening. Closing.

"*Come in here, Xavie. I should have a kiss. An innocent kiss.*"

A pause. "*There we go. Wasn't that nice? Come over here, Xavie. To the bed. Isn't it pretty? I know how you love pink. Talk to me, Xaviera.*"

"What's with the Xaviera?" Gershwin whispered.

"It's either the name she was sold under, or part of this lunatic's fantasy."

"*I told you to talk to me, Xavie,*" the perp said, a thin wire of anger in his voice.

Leala found her voice. "*I'm sorry . . . my throat is so dry. If I had . . .*"

The anger seemed to turn to contrition. "*Of course. I'm sorry Xavie, you've had nothing to drink for hours. I have some Pellegrino water. Is that all right?*"

"*Si.*"

The captor offering an apology? It suggested the guy wasn't in full master–slave mindset. There was something almost childlike in his response, a small clue to his mental make-up.

Footsteps moving away. A door closing. And then, Leala, to us: *"He has gone for the moment. I am in a pink room in a big white house. There is one man wearing a robe. I think his mind is broken. There is a chain from mi neck to the above. My hands are loose but I cannot move far. I am very scared. When he looks at me he sees something not here."*

I pulled the putty from the mic. "Get his name," I whispered. "We need his name to know where you are."

"I am not sure if he any more knows who he . . . He comes. Please help me."

We heard the door. The perp's voice.

"What were you saying?" Suspicion.

"I was praying, Señor . . . Señor. . . ." Hanging the word out, hoping he'd supply his name.

A laugh instead. *"Please, Xaviera. Remember how you and your amigas used to make fun of the church and the priests?"*

"I do not remember, señor. I am not Xaviera."

A slap and a yip of pain. I felt my fists clench.

"Do not lie to me, Xavie. Your days of lying are over and I will not stand for it. I grew up. Would you like to see where I grew the most?"

"What's with his voice?" Gershwin asked. "It's deeper."

"The fantasy's taking over." Something else I had

learned about madness from my brother. "He's shifting to an inner vision."

"*Do you want to open my robe, Xaviera? I have a surprise for you.*"

A pause. "*Not until I hear you speak your name.*"

"*What?*"

"*Can you not speak? Can you not say your name?*"

"*Don't you dare make demands of me.*"

"*Then slap me again,*" Leala said. "*Maybe like your daddy taught you to do. Did he have a name? Does no one in your family have names?*"

"Uh-oh," I said. "Easy, Leala."

"*Me llamo es Leala Rosales,*" she said. "*I am proud of my name. Does yours disgust you? Are you shamed by your name? Does it bring vomit to your lips?*"

The sound of a slap. "*SHUT THE FUCK UP, XAVIERA!*"

"Jesus," I whispered. "He's going off."

"*My name came from mi madre y papa!*" Leala said. "*Did you have no one to name you?*"

"*I SAID SHUT UP!*"

Another slap. I pictured Leala half-hanging by a chain from the ceiling as a robed monster battered her face.

"*When it was asked what name to put on the certificate,*" Leala continued, "*did your mama say, 'That thing is so insignificant . . . it deserves no name. Is that what she said?'*"

Three slaps. It was like hearing a whip crack. Then . . .

"*You know who I am, you stinking little tramp*

376

. . . MINARD CHALK! MY NAME IS MINARD SIMPSON CHALK!"

"On it," Gershwin said, relaying the information to Key West cops hunched over keyboards and waiting. A long and frightening pause before Gershwin looked up. "They've got an address. They can be there in five minutes. It's ten from here."

"Tell them to roll. I gotta stay and listen."

Gershwin relayed the decision. Twenty seconds later the pair of cruisers hit the lights but not sirens, blasting away as back-up.

A minute passed. I heard slow footfalls punctuated by pauses. I pictured the guy circling Leala and letting his imagination run wild, the savoring phase. Our on-board computer buzzed with incoming info. Gershwin read the screen. "The fucker's in the national sex-offender database: Minard S. Chalk, thirty-four years of age, four arrests for voyeurism, San Clemente and Seattle, most recently in Minneapolis . . ."

"A peeper," I said, staring at Gershwin in disbelief. "That's all?"

"Two arrests for exhibitionism, Minneapolis and Seattle. Both times he flashed teenaged girls with a fake dick."

I was taken aback, expecting more violence in his past. Peepers, creepers and waggers were almost never violent; many were timid, painfully shy, inept. This guy had jumped from the box, maybe let his fantasies bloom to a dark garden of needs. What did the pseudo penis mean? Impotence? Insecurity?

The footsteps stopped and I held my breath and listened.

"*Look what I have for you, Xavie,*" the voice crooned. "*Go ahead . . . untie my robe. OPEN THE GODDAMN ROBE, XAVIE! There . . . that's the way . . .*"

A gasp from Leala. She started screaming.

"*HELP ME! HELP ME!*"

The pleas were to us. Gershwin looked at me, helpless.

"*Lay back on the bed, Xavie. That's an order!*"

Leala screamed again. "*STOP. NO! HELP ME!*"

There was one chance left, a long shot. I tore the putty from the phone and brought it to my lips. "MINARD CHALK," I said, a voice in total command. "This is Carson Ryder of the Florida Center for Law Enforcement. WE—"

51

"—SEE YOU! *Step back from the girl.*"

The words echo between the hard walls. Chalk looks frantically from side to side. "WHAT IS GOING ON?" Chalk yells, frantically searching for the voice. "WHO ARE YOU?"

"CHALK," the voice repeats, stentorian. "*Your house is surrounded. If you touch the girl, you will be dead within seconds. DO YOU WANT TO DIE?*"

As if stuck in a nightmare, Chalk looks behind him, expecting to see laughing teenaged girls pour from the closet, but sees only a pink concrete wall.

"*Leala!*" the voice commands. "*Hand Mr Chalk the telephone. Are you able to do that?*"

"*Si.* Yes."

Leala reaches into her panties and removes the phone. She holds it out in a trembling palm.

"Take the phone, Mr Chalk," the voice says. It's angry.

Chalk stares, his mouth drooping open. Leala sees a man with the face of a confused child. The terrible thing on his belt waggles back and forth.

"Take the FUCKING PHONE, CHALK!"

Minnie Chalk's hand is shaking. He takes the phone and brings it to his red mouth. "Yes?" It's a whisper.

"Go outside and stand in the street. That's an order. If you take one step toward the girl, you will die."

Chalk carefully puts down the phone, takes a step backwards and walks away like a boy scolded by his mommy. He ascends the stairs without a backward glance.

Tears trickle down Leala's cheeks, then become a flood.

When a weeping Leala told us her captor had gone, I jammed the Rover in gear and sped toward the scene. Minutes later we arrived at a huge Victorian mansion surrounded by towering palms, the yard flowing with bougainvillea. Six units and two ambulances claimed the street. I saw a prisoner in the rear of a cruiser, head bowed.

"That him?" I asked the nearest uniform. "Chalk?"

A nod. "The guy was just standing at the curb in a bathrobe with his mouth open. I don't know what he's seeing, but it's not us. I think his wires are fried."

"The girl?"

"Being attended by the medics. Physically, I think she's fine. You know her?"

"We met once," I said. Gershwin and I started to the ambulance. "Uh, Detectives?" the cop asked.

We turned. The guy held up an evidence bag. "We found this in the bushes."

Gershwin and I looked at the object for a two-count, all it took. We resumed our walk to the ambulance. Leala was inside, a medic holding ice to a swelling eye and cheek. She looked up and saw us.

She leapt from the ambulance and we held one another, Leala, me and Gershwin. No one spoke a word, since we'd been talking all night.

52

We got to my place at six a.m. on Sunday, Gershwin heading back to Miami. The department was handling all the prisoners accumulated in the trio of busts: Rediflow, the Quonset hut and the Paraíso. Roy told us to take the day and sleep and come in at ten on Monday for a recap and a day of relentless paperwork.

We both arrived a few minutes early, Bobby Erickson pointing to the main conference room. "They're all in there. I dunno what's going on, but everyone's acting weird."

He padded away in the fluffy slips and Gershwin and I went to the room. The whole crew was in attendance at the table, Roy leaning against the wall. It reminded me of my first dismal day, Roy grinning, everyone else staring.

Roy was fanning himself with a padded mailing package. We sat and he pushed from the wall with his ass, holding the package high. "This was delivered to the

SunState Bank after hours on Saturday, didn't show up until this morning. And inside . . ."

He reached inside, pulled out an envelope. *IMPORTANT!* it blared in red marker. *PLEASE RUSH TO FLORIDA POLICE INVESTIGATORS.*

"The bank folks didn't know what to do, so it came to us at eight this morning. Inside, we found this . . ." Roy did a drum roll with his tongue and produced a small silver rectangle. "Look what I have," he said, the Jack O'Lantern face ablaze with delight.

"Seems to be a computer," I said.

"Not just any computer, Carson. A computer belonging to Amili Zelaya, the dead woman in the Paraíso and the operation's accountant, as it seems. We've been reading snatches of information. It seems the late Ms Zelaya was a detail fanatic."

"Is Kazankis named?" I said, holding my breath.

Degan spoke. "Named every time he receives a payment. He's cooked."

I stared at Degan, unsure how to respond, joy at knowing Kazankis was nailed, or amazement at hearing Degan speak more than four words at a sitting. And not a single grunt between them.

Tatum's turn. "It also appears, Detective Ryder, that Kazankis used a familiar business model for slavery: rental."

"What?"

"The trafficked humans, women mainly, weren't sold, but rented or leased like construction equipment, so much for a week or a month."

Roy spun the computer my way. "Here's a typical rental contract, bud. Eight women, all named, rented to the Taste of Heaven Massage Parlor for fifteen hundred dollars per woman per month. There are dozens of contracts with massage parlors, strip joints, whorehouses and pimps. Not to mention a few private homes and back-alley sweatshops."

"Contracts placing slaves as far away as Atlanta." Tatum again. "Naming the rentees and the renters."

I was having trouble keeping it all straight. "Wait . . . you're saying we know where every slave is at this moment?"

Roy mimed swinging a lasso. "I already started round-up time. We'll get these people back. I put Degan in charge of coordinating everything. Ceel's taking some of Tatum's casework next week so he can jump in as well. He's gonna partner with Lonnie."

Roy's grin had spread beyond his face, like it was a separate entity. He pointed both hands at me in a magician's *ta-da!* moment. "Look at my boy, people. Didn't I tell you he was amazing?"

Everyone on the crew turned to Gershwin and me. They *applauded*.

"Truth time, McDermott," Tatum said. "'Fess up, you white devil."

"We've been rooting for you, buddy," Roy said. "Every teensy step of the way. We love you to pieces, cupcake."

I stared, forcing my mouth to shape words. "What about the money, the salary increases?"

"Everybody got bumps last year."

"Wait . . . I didn't waylay anyone's raises?"

Roy did sheepish. "What happened was, well, a sort of initiation . . ."

"Initiation, shit," Tatum said. "It's a fucking hazing, Ryder. They made me think I'd fallen into Klan central. Plus that bullshit about keeping everyone from a raise."

Valdez grinned and popped the gum. "I thought it was 'cuz I was female."

"Sorta," Tatum said.

"Fuck you, Tatum. And, of course, that I'd pulled cash from wallets."

"You want to punch McDermott, Ryder?" Canseco said. "We'll all be glad to hold him."

I don't think I could have lifted an arm. It had all been a stunt, a Roy McDermott artificial drama. But seeing the admiration in the eyes of my colleagues and knowing I'd run the same ridiculous gantlet these folks had run . . . I actually felt good.

"We even kept an eye on you, Ryder," Degan said. "Just to make sure you stayed safe in the big city. A now-and-then tail."

"I was sure I saw Canseco. You and Valdez, too, I think." I hadn't been losing my mind.

"I even did you a favor," Tatum said. "Sent you a gift. Actually I sent it to Delmara."

I thought a few seconds. "Blaine Mullard?"

"He's my snitch. He heard Delmara was looking for a knife man, but came to me after he got busted. I sent him to Vince, instead."

I shook my head. Not synchronicity but an invisible helping hand. Though if you looked at it just right . . .

Degan reached to the floor and produced a bag, sliding it down the table into Gershwin's lap. "Open it up, you fucking hotdog."

Gershwin pulled out a shiny new Glock. "It ain't a real gun, a wheel gun," Degan said. "But it's prettier than that beater piece you're carrying."

"Here you go, kid," Roy said, flipping Gershwin a badge wallet. Zigs studied the ID with a grin.

"Not 'Provisional'?"

"I've had my eye on you, Zigzag. Why I suggested to Señor Grocery-store magnate that he send you my way. A lot quicker than going through channels."

More laughter. Degan went to the coffee cart to find a cup to torment.

"Are you ever planning on growing up, Roy?" I asked.

"When it works for me. So far it hasn't." He walked to the front of the room, pivoted on his heels like a dancer, spun back to face us, clapping the hands. "So how about we go pull some folks out of hellholes? There are warrants to be obtained, local departments to be contacted. Time for you kiddies to earn your exorbitant incomes."

We filed out in unison, Roy McDermott's crime crew, the crème de la crime.

Three days passed. Kazankis was dragged off to jail screaming about being a martyr for Christ and I figured some prison psychiatrist was going to have a field day.

The crew, my crew, Ziggy's crew, told us to take a couple days off while they handled the legwork.

There was much good to study, and a tiny bit of bad to deal with. On the good side: My first-ever case in Florida was closing on a soprano arpeggio. Leala Rosales was being assisted by Victoree Johnson. I had high hopes, her resiliency was amazing, her fortitude uncanny. A survivor.

And the bad? I was getting booted from the coolest digs I'd ever known: a nifty house with my own private jungle. It seemed the parcel was zoned for multi-occupancy dwelling and had been bought over the weekend by C & A Enterprises to remake as a condo complex. I'd not had time to search out another place yet, so today's challenge was seeing if the new owners would give me a few days to find a cheap apartment where I could hole up and look for a house.

I was taking one of my final looks at the quiet little cove when the knock came to the door, a death knell. Roy entered, followed by one of the department's legal types, T. Raymond Bellington, a compact and overdressed guy with too much cologne and seeming a bit too happy at selling my transient digs from beneath me.

I tapped Bellington's fingers in the approximation of a handshake. "So you got a new place I hope, Detective?" he said. "Ready to vacate today?"

"Working on it."

Roy wanted coffee, which I had, Bellington asking did I have a non-caffeinated herbal tea? When I said I did not, but go outside and pick leaves from something and I'd boil them for him, he gave me a look and said water would be fine. I fetched beverages and we went out to the deck. I wanted to spend as much time as possible in my vanishing kingdom.

"Seems kinda sad to turn this into condos," Roy said.

Bellington disagreed. "Better land usage," he noted. "Higher occupant density."

We heard tires moving down the lane. I seemed unable to rise and Roy went inside to answer the door, stepping to the deck a minute later and leading a tall and square-jawed man in his early forties and his assistant, a squat and dark-eyed woman reminiscent of Gertrude Stein. His name was Alan Winquist, hers Francine Bashore. They wore conservative business attire, Winquist opting for a gray palette, Miz Bashore going for a subdued purple, though offset with a sunny orange scarf.

"You work for C & A Enterprises?" I asked, pulling out a chair for Bashore and trying to appear upbeat.

"On a retainer basis," Bashore said, nodding and sitting. "C & A has a finger in several pots, as they say. Development is a new endeavor."

"You're from a Memphis law firm?" Roy asked. He'd spent a few early years in Memphis where, I assumed, they were still recovering.

"Barlett, Duncan, and Ives."

"Haven't they all been dead since the Civil War?" Roy said.

"I believe Mr Duncan lived until the late fifties,"

Bashore said. "The rumor that he studied under Oliver Cromwell is incorrect, but he did clerk for Oliver Wendell Holmes."

The firm of BD&I was old line white-shoe. Not the type to grant exceptions. Dropping to my knees and begging was out.

"Our employer was considering sitting in," Bashore said, glancing at her watch. "But we're to go ahead if he couldn't make it." She pulled a sheaf of papers from her briefcase. "Any questions before we make it official?"

"Uh, Carson," Roy said. "Didn't you have a small request?"

I cleared my throat. "I've been, uh, intending to find another place, but it seems I've not quite located a suitable, uh . . ."

A frown from Bashore. "If you're asking if you can remain here, we're only here to transfer the property. I'm afraid you'll have to—"

A knock at the door. Roy jumped up to answer it, good, since my legs felt dead.

There was a motel down the road I could move to this evening. Or rent storage space and bunk with Gershwin for a few days. Or I could ask Dubois to store my stuff in his garage and . . .

"Our new arrival," Roy said, stepping back out to the deck. "To those who don't know him I'll introduce Doctor August Charpentier. Have a seat with the group, Doctor."

My heart stopped. It was my brother, Jeremy, in his false identity. He sat and crossed his long legs, a picture

389

of elegance in his sky-blue seersucker suit, open white shirt and blue-banded straw Panama. I concentrated on not keeling over as the head of FCLE's investigative division handed coffee to my fugitive brother.

"Sorry to be tardy," Jeremy said in a Frenchified accent. "I've been on the phone with my long-winded accountants. How are the proceedings going?"

"We're making the transfer, sir," Winquist said. "A wonderful site for multiple units, I'd say."

Jeremy nodded. "Excellent, though my accountants just advised me to delay actual site development until several new tax issues are resolved. I'll simply hold the property for a bit."

"Accountants know best," Bashore said.

"It does, however, leave me with a bit of a problem."

"Which is, Doctor Charpentier?"

Jeremy cleared his throat as if preparing to ask a great favor, and turned to me. "I guess my question is, Mr Ryder, if you haven't already made other plans . . . could you possibly remain here as a tenant? Keep the place safe and all?"

I tried to speak, couldn't. I cleared my throat and tried again. "I, uh, guess that might work, Doctor," I managed. "For a bit, at least."

Jeremy clapped his hands. "Splendid. My cab awaits so I'll leave you folks to work out the details. Rent of say, four hundred dollars a month?"

Winquist raised an eyebrow. "That seems exceedingly low, sir."

"Then I'll consider it an investment in law enforcement, an occupation that has always fascinated me."

"Are you heading back to Kentucky, Doctor?" Bashore asked as Jeremy turned for the deck door.

"No, I'm staying a few days to check out local properties."

I stood and walked him through the house as the lawyers scratched on papers. Roy followed to refill his coffee cup, too close for Jeremy and I to drop our façades.

"Local properties, sir?" I said, barely able to squeak out words.

Jeremy nodded as we reached the threshold, his hand on the knob. "I'm becoming attracted to sunnier climes, Mr Ryder. New worlds to conquer and all that."

"Uh, where are you looking, sir?"

"I'm considering Key West. It has such a romantic history. I hear a lot of pasts have been buried out there."

My mouth dropped open, and my brother's grin went as wide as the horizon. He whispered, "See you soon, neighbor."

And walked into the sunlight.